"One should not simply read *Super in the City*; one should gobble it up like candy. This is particularly intelligent candy, mind you—but don't let that stop you from indulging in a big old sack of fun."

—Elizabeth Gilbert, author of *Eat, Pray, Love*

"Fun . . . sassy!"
—*People*

"Witty and piquant."
—*The Wall Street Journal*

"Debut novelist Uviller borrows from her own life for this lively, smart chick-lit mystery. The characters are likable—especially Zephyr's overachieving, yet unassuming coterie of prep-school friends. Readers will also appreciate the many literary references and Uviller's insider's view of New York City."
—*Booklist*

"Part mystery, part screwball comedy, part sexcapade . . . and all entertaining."
—*Contra Costa Times*

"Gleefully unpretentious . . . gallops at full speed from the very first line . . . undoubtedly smarter and funnier than most other girls-in-the-city novels."
—*Publishers Weekly*

"[Uviller has] . . . a polished lead character, an ear for snappy dialogue and a propulsive storytelling style. . . . Funny, enjoyable caper about a dirty job and the unlikely young woman who takes it on."
—*Kirkus Reviews*

"Uviller's prose style throughout is confident, funny, often sexy and wonderfully insightful. . . . An impressive delight." —Bookgasm.com

"Daphne Uviller's new novel is not so much chick lit as lite fiction for the feminist-minded reader. . . . This is fun fiction. It flies. And it's really funny. Best of all, Uviller has an amazing imagination that's reflected in Zephyr's frequent flights of fantasy throughout the novel. . . . Feminist and fast-moving." —Feministing.com

BY DAPHNE UVILLER

Hotel No Tell

Super in the City

*Only Child: Writers on the Singular Joys and
    Solitary Sorrows of Growing Up Solo*
    (with Deborah Siegel)

MYSTERY

HOTEL
NO
TELL

a novel

Daphne Uviller

BANTAM BOOKS TRADE PAPERBACKS
NEW YORK

2011 Bantam Books Trade Paperback Original

Published in the United States by Bantam Books Trade Paperbacks, an imprint of The Random House Publishing Group, a division of Random House, Inc., New York.

BANTAM BOOKS and the rooster colophon are registered trademarks of Random House, Inc.

Grateful acknowledgment is given to Richard O'Brien and Rocky Horror Company Limited for permission to reprint lines from Richard O'Brien's *The Rocky Horror Show*.

Library of Congress Cataloging-in-Publication Data
Uviller, Daphne.
Hotel no tell : a novel / Daphne Uviller.
p. cm.
ISBN 978-0-385-34270-4
eBook ISBN 978-0-553-90819-0
1. Hotels—Fiction. 2. Greenwich Village (New York, N.Y.)—Fiction.
I. Title.
PS3621.V55H68 2011
813'.6—dc22   2010052232

Printed in the United States of America

9 8 7 6 5 4 3 2 1

Book design by Caroline Cunningham

For Talia and for Gabriel

"... When love comes to me and says

What do you know, I say This girl, this boy."

—"Looking at Them Asleep," Sharon Olds

Hotel
No
Tell

Expiration Date

I definitely should have lied. Until that moment, it had never occurred to me that I'd have to lie about my age for anything other than the kiddie rides at Coney Island. Tucked into an overstuffed armchair inside the sterile offices of Ova Easy, my feet straining to reach the floor, I faced a girl who resembled her metal desk: angular, sterile, unyielding.

"We only accept eggs from donors under twenty-five. And *you*. Are thirty-one." She glanced distastefully at the application I'd hastily filled out at the Formica counter at Groovy Smoothie, a block south on lower Broadway. From where I sat, I could see a pale-orange citrus stain dampening the corner of the paper.

"Thirty," I corrected tersely, adjusting the black rectangular frames I'd opted for instead of contacts with the express purpose of conveying youthful studiousness. Black miniskirt, black tights, black knee-high boots, black turtleneck. Perhaps I'd gone a bit too far on the artsy, intellectual university look. Perhaps I'd missed my stop and gone all the way to Paris in the sixties: The only items missing were a Gauloises and some pinot noir—not exactly the look you want to convey when posing as a candidate for egg donation at a fertility clinic recently featured on a Best Of list in *New York* magazine.

"Thirty-one next month," she countered. She put the application on her desk and pushed it toward me with her index finger, one of the most hostile acts I've ever witnessed by someone who displayed a framed picture of a Labradoodle on her desk.

I would have loved to pull back my houndstooth coat and flash her the Glock automatic I had been both legally permitted and officially obligated to carry for exactly two hours. But if I'd learned nothing else in my three enlightening years as a junior detective with the New York City Special Investigations Commission, it was that badges and weapons were not meant to be flashed just because a fellow citizen answered his cellphone in a movie theater, stepped into a subway car and parked herself in the doorway, or rudely reminded me that Mother Nature considered me to be past my prime.

I licked my lips roughly and recrossed my legs, an awkward maneuver given that I couldn't brace either foot against the floor. Did Ova Easy purposely furnish their offices with these chairs to keep their donors feeling as small and needy as possible? The women who usually occupied this spot, I imagined, were likely desperate for money, willing to pump themselves full of drugs and release their genes to unknown guardians in order to pay for college or rent or an ailing granny's hospital bill, maybe even cover the occasional funeral. But did some do it just for kicks? A couple of St. John's sophomores treating themselves to a South Seas vacation or a down payment on a Mini Cooper? What would I do with a windfall of eight grand mined from my ovaries? Given that I had no other plans for my eggs, perhaps it was something to consider. My opponent cleared her throat, and I steered myself back on track.

"But I'm healthy," I persisted. "I don't do drugs, smoke, or drink. No under-sixty cancer in my family. I could write my name by the time I was three. Really, I come from great stock." I put my palm flat on the application to slow its journey. Never mind that my great-grandfather had been jailed in Belarus for trying to smuggle dry goods in and out of his shtetl. That was actually a point of pride for my family.

"I'm sorry, Miss . . . ?"

This impertinent St. Peter of egg donation had already forgotten my name! Then again, so had I. I glanced at the application.

"Samson. It's Ms. Samson." What self-respecting detective uses her ex-boyfriend's surname as an alias?

"Ms. Samson," she said in a voice embattled by adenoids, "it's simply company policy. There are more than enough qualified and willing donors under twenty-five that we don't need to make exceptions. If you'd read our website, you could have saved yourself a trip. And your time." By which she meant *her* time.

I *had* read the website. Well, I'd skimmed it. Okay, I'd mostly scrolled through the photos of wholesome young women who looked to be just a yodel shy of Tyrolean citizenship, captured mid-laugh, their arms draped around one another as though Ova Easy was the ultimate sorority.

Fortunately, it didn't matter that I was bombing out. I was using Ova Easy only to get a feel for basic procedure in the egg-donation business, insofar as there was anything basic about what struck me as an exercise in science fiction. But I had hoped to get a little farther than this gatekeeper's office in my research process.

I spread my palms in a gesture of surrender. "Well, look, when I told my sister—my *younger* sister—what I was doing today, she expressed an interest in doing this for herself.

Could you tell me a little about the process in case she decides to apply?" I briefly wondered what a sister of mine might have looked like.

St. Peter mashed her thin lips.

"You know, to save *you* time?" I cajoled.

This case was in a stratosphere high above my usual docket of Board of Ed pension swindlers, falsely advertised going-out-of-business announcements, and the small-time licensing fraud ring I'd uncovered, if you could call some back-dated paperwork involving three nail salons in Rego Park a ring. One grim-faced junior paper-pusher with an inflated sense of her own importance was not going to stand in my way.

Chapter 1

Commissioner Pippa Flatland was now the newest and most unlikely addition to a growing club whose members thought that my disinclination toward motherhood was a personal taunt, a façade I was maintaining for the sole purpose of driving them insane. My parents, Ollie and Bella Zuckerman, were the original founders and most active members, though the award for angriest protester went to Gregory Samson, the gangly, moody, wisecracking, nerdy–sexy, perfect-for-me ex-boyfriend whose departure from our relationship and apartment on West 12th Street had been the only quantifiable casualty of my new life policy.

The air-conditioning throughout the downtown Beaux Arts building on Pearl Street in which the Special Investigations Commission's offices were housed had broken down for the second time that week. It was the sweltering Friday before Labor Day weekend, and Pippa—a six-foot-tall, sinewy, laconic British ex-pat in her late forties with a pageboy haircut, a penchant for polka-dotted linen dresses, and a heart that had never fully taken leave of the cool breezes of the Lake District—had stopped by my cubicle.

She brandished two sweating Nalgene bottles fresh from the mini-fridge beneath her desk and, with a curt tilt of her head, gestured for me to follow her. Pippa's favorite office alternative, the Staten Island Ferry, was a five-minute walk from the SIC, a free ride both ways, and she had double-checked that there were no conflicts of interest in holding the occasional meeting on the windy decks of the hulking orange vessels. We all knew that when she left the office for hours at a time to "get some proper work done," she was riding back and forth, MacBook on lap, editing a report for the mayor or a press release for a news conference, freed from the temptations of the Internet and landlines.

I had been subjected to ferry meetings only twice. No one had warned me that Pippa did not begin talking until she reached the ferry; had I known that before my first meeting, I could have saved both of us five minutes of flailing and ultimately futile attempts at small talk, an item not featured on Pippa's menu. The second time, I had been with a group of senior detectives, all of whom remained uncharacteristically silent. I got the picture.

"You can't possibly be serious, Zephyr," she finally said as we waited for the glass doors of the terminal's boarding area to slide open.

I tried to guess what conversation, in her multitasking mind, we had already begun. I looked at her helplessly.

"Gregory," she said curtly.

Oh no. No, no, no. In a moment of weakness, I had allowed Pippa to eke out some personal information. Specifically, I had, some months ago, let it come to her attention that Gregory was threatening to pack up and move back to a state he loathed to live with parents he loathed. I didn't mind her knowing, but I dreaded being the object of one of her famously awkward attempts to prove she cared about her staff beyond the office perimeter. Pippa herself had risen into existence on the half shell or been dropped by a stork or simply burst into being out of cosmic debris. The woman had us all believing she possessed no past. As a result, her take on personal relationships had about as much value as an expired MetroCard.

"Oh, I'm serious," I said firmly. "Gregory left. In June." I held myself taut so that I wouldn't graze the extremely appealing shoulder of the tall, clean-shaven collection of muscles in the hard hat to my right. Apparently, I had also been unable to keep my return to single status a secret from my libido.

The doors opened and Pippa and I moved with the rest of the crowd up the gangway, an experience that never failed to make me feel simultaneously like a herded cow and also like an Astor or Vanderbilt boarding a dazzling ocean liner of yesteryear, trunks and servants in tow. Other times, I imagined I was an emigrant leaving home for the last time, terrified of what lay ahead but even more frightened of remaining behind.

Once we had deftly threaded our way through the less decisive passengers to secure outdoor seats on the starboard deck, I figured we were safely past the personal. But, like a seagull with a scrap of garbage, Pippa wouldn't let go.

"No," she said, handing me one of the Nalgenes. "I mean, I don't believe you told him you wouldn't ever have children. You can't be certain." It occurred to me that her holding meetings at sea was not unlike a floating wedding—a power play. You will do things your host's way and you will not leave until you have screeched along to Gloria Gaynor's "I Will Survive" with twenty other women.

I raised my eyebrows slightly as we sat down on a plastic bench shined to a smooth finish by hundreds of thousands of commuting butts. I assumed this self-declared spinster was putting me on, but, despite nearly three years of an easy working relationship, we were not on jokey terms. Pippa was many things—a shrewd detective, an ardent cyclist, a just boss, and, somewhat bewilderingly, a collector of Lucite handbags (specifically, sea-green Lucite handbags)—but she did not have a jokey bone in her body. The guys in the office referred to her behind her back as Poker Pippa, for her discomfitingly unreadable face.

"Pippa," I said, unsure whether to delve into my boss's personal life. Hell, she'd started it. "*You've* made it abundantly clear that marriage and kids aren't for you." I wiped the perspiration from the crooks of my arms and tried to tuck some damp, unruly strands of hair back into my improvised chignon. In hot weather, we were allowed to dress down, and I steadily rotated through my modest collection of thrift-shop sundresses. That morning I'd chosen a red-and-white-checked number that caused no end of "lost your sheep?" and "how many cows you gotta milk to getta gallon?" comments from my colleagues, whose first instincts were rarely to put someone at ease. As professional interrogators, it came in handy.

"Well, yes, but that's *my* decision about marriage and children." She sniffed and squinted out at the water. "I don't think you've thought it through for yourself."

It was such an outrageously condescending pronouncement—of the kind favored by my mother—that I was struck speechless. I opened my mouth to issue forth an inchoate protest, but at that moment the boat's horn blasted; I'm sure it looked and I know it felt like I was the one letting out the enormous honking roar. I closed my mouth, feeling as though the ship had expressed itself on my behalf. We began our glide to the far side of New York Harbor.

"Just give it a bit more thought. Yes?"

I nodded, like a child promising to do better on the next spelling test.

"Right, then, your new case," Pippa said, and I exhaled.

She glanced distastefully at a small woman who had sat down too close beside her. The woman's hair was pulled into a painfully tight knot on top of her head, and she was studying the pages of a Crate and Barrel catalog as though she would be tested on the contents.

"I'm not done with my current case," I reminded her.

She fixed me with a cool stare and I sheepishly sipped from my bottle. Pippa knew exactly where each of her two hundred detectives was at every moment of the workday, where each stood in his or her caseload, who was best at surveillance, whose strengths lay in handling witnesses, who needed smoke breaks, and who preferred glazed to powdered.

"Tommy O. can finish the streetlight case. I'd like to get you in on something new involving the Greenwich Village Hotel."

I tried to look interested instead of crushed by disappointment. The streetlight vendor I was investigating had been giving cash kickbacks to a purchaser at the DOT. It was the first case for which I was going to get to wire someone with one of the sleek, 007-worthy gadgets designed by the guys in our tech office, Tommy T. and Tommy R. I had my eye on a nifty little necktie camera and had even gotten as far as arguing with our flipped informant, Eustace, about what pattern tie he wanted to wear for the handoff, which was scheduled to take place in just five days. In my opinion, paisley would ensure that the camera remained undetected, but Eustace maintained he was known for always wearing a navy-blue tie and that to stray from that habit would call attention to himself. I reminded myself that he was nervous—he was going to be the one alone in the car giving money to a mean, suspicious guy from the DOT—but I couldn't help feeling he should try to man up and set aside his sartorial concerns.

"Are you . . . unhappy with the way I'm handling streetlights?" I asked tentatively.

"Don't be absurd. Your work is always flawless." She ran her hands briskly over the black polka dots that danced across her lap.

In fact, this was the first direct compliment Pippa had ever paid me and thus the first time the rollicking parade of professional self-doubt that was forever marching through my psyche had whistled to a stop. I immediately imagined myself reporting this news to Gregory and just as quickly remembered that that was no longer an option. My stomach did its increasingly familiar aerial show, where it rose at the thought of him, then dropped when I remembered he was gone, and then dipped even farther as I recalled how uncertain I was that I had done the right thing by halting a trip to the altar.

"Thank you," I eventually remembered to murmur.

"Right, then," Pippa said, holding her hand to her brow to shield her eyes from the sun. "Shall I fill you in?"

As if "no" was a viable answer. I nodded.

"Old hotel, southeast corner of Waverly and Sixth. Owned by the same family for three generations. Ballard McKenzie, sixty-two, is the patriarch, and his only child, Hutchinson, twenty-nine, is poised to take over. The mother, Clarissa McKenzie, sixty, hand-painted the murals and whatnot on the walls of the foyer"—Pippa pronounced this *foyé*—"the grandfather laid by hand the mosaic in the floor, the grandmother wallpapered each room herself. Odd-looking place, to tell you the truth."

Pippa paused, distracted, as was I, by the woman with the Crate and Barrel catalog. She was now openly weeping over its pages, though whether it was from joy, longing, or some other reason entirely was not apparent. Pippa cleared her throat and shifted so that her back was fully turned on the spectacle.

"Right. There's never been so much as a picked pocket reported at the hotel, not in forty years. Not even an INS dustup with the staff. It's all very homegrown, lovey-dovey, family pride and all that. Until last spring."

I felt a delicious current of anticipation spread through my limbs and an alertness crackle across my brain. This was why I loved my job, or maybe this was how I knew I loved my job. I felt this way whenever Pippa assigned me a new case, no matter how dull it might have sounded to someone else. The truth was, I didn't mind paging through blurry Xeroxes in my cubicle, trying to cobble together evidence against the nail salons, or riding to interviews in the outer boroughs with the smoke-saturated senior detectives while they mocked me and my sheltered background. My dad's definition of professional happiness was finding something you love and getting paid for it. I was getting paid to be nosy.

"Last week," Pippa continued, "the father finally called intake to tell them he thought something was wrong with the books." She raised one eyebrow at me. This was her barebones version of mentoring. I jumped in, as I knew I was expected to do.

"I'm guessing there's a reason he didn't ask the rest of the family to take a look?"

"Ballard McKenzie is worried that it's his son, Hutchinson, who's cooking them, and he's devastated. Noticed something nearly a year ago, but it took him this long to admit it might actually be intentional thievery by one of his own." Pippa fluttered her eyelids to indicate her opinion of family loyalties.

"Why is this an S.I.C. case?" Our jurisdiction was city employees and contractors dealing with (read: cheating) the city. As far as I knew, the city wasn't in the hotel business.

"The Greenwich Village Hotel is one of a handful that agrees to accept a discounted rate for guests visiting the city on official municipal business," Pippa said. "Guests brought here on the city's dime, that is."

"The city puts up VIPs at boutique hotels?" I asked doubtfully.

"They're not necessarily VIPs and this isn't really a boutique hotel. It's just small. Say the Board of Ed is toting in a keynote speaker for a principals' conference. They don't always want to stick someone in dreary midtown. They want to show off the city's color. Downtown."

"Okay, so how much are we talking?" I looked out over the water as we passed Lady Liberty, feeling a renewed sense of connection to the amber waves of grain that lay beyond her, a surge in my chest that had been dead from Election Day 2000 to Election Day 2008.

"A hundred grand."

I actually choked on my water and turned to stare at my boss.

"Exactly." Pippa nodded, satisfied with my reaction. "He tried to convince himself that it was acceptable not to be able to reconcile a hundred thousand dollars."

"Any leads at all?" I asked incredulously.

"Not a one."

"Great," I muttered, trying to sound annoyed, when, in fact, I could have soared the rest of the way to Staten Island on my own excitement. I was getting in on the ground floor of a completely untouched case! No one else's notes and musings and misleading hypotheses to politely consider. Virgin soil.

"You know you love it," Pippa commented drily. "Don't try to be like your world-weary colleagues. Those blokes love it, too, you know."

I blushed. Someday I'd be like Pippa—an enigma, a closed book—but for now I had to make peace with being as understated as a carousel. The construction worker with the beautiful shoulders strolled past, and it became apparent to all that his shoulders were not even close to being his best feature. I inhaled the salty air and tried to regain focus.

"Why did you want to discuss this on the boat?" I asked suddenly. This assignment could easily have taken sixty seconds in her office. "Not that I'm complaining," I added hastily.

"Two reasons," Pippa said immediately. She glanced to her left and seemed startled to discover that the catalog cryer had left. She looked around quickly, and I could tell she was disturbed that she'd lost track of someone, as if she'd failed a surveillance exercise. "First, most important, this case will not be tracked through our central system." She paused to let this sink in.

"You mean, this is"—I tried to sound nonchalant—"confidential?"

She studied me, a wry smile playing on her lips. Clearly, I was failing at cool. "Yes. You are not to discuss this with your colleagues. Can you manage that, Zephyr?"

I blushed. The detectives had once tacked a sign to my cubicle that read *Morning Zoo with Zephyr Z*. But that would end *now*, I vowed to myself. This was the chance I'd been looking for, an opportunity to make a name for myself, to finish out my three years of training and finally get my private-investigator license, allowing me to work pretty much anywhere I wanted. I'd arrive at my state licensing exam in a hail of fireworks. Or at least not be teased so much by the senior detectives.

"You are most especially not to discuss this with family or friends."

I swallowed and tried not to think of my parents: Ollie, the assistant district attorney, and Bella, the founder of a financial-seminar franchise, who lived upstairs from me and who were once again my repository for daily musings now that Gregory was gone. I tried to block out thoughts of my coterie of four high school friends—we referred to ourselves as the Sterling Girls, in honor of the Upper East Side prep school we'd narrowly survived—who probably knew how much I'd weighed at birth. I ignored thoughts of my current confidante, a fabulously neurotic woman named Macy St. John with whom I consumed vast quantities of Roasting Plant coffee at the Leroy Street dog run, even though neither of us owned a dog. And I pushed aside the image of my auteur brother, who seemed to think my career served no better purpose than as a lode of material for his screenplays.

"Of course," I said.

She studied me for a moment. "Good."

"What was the other reason?" I asked, eager to get past the subject of my capacity for keeping my mouth shut.

Pippa looked uncomfortable, which was such a rare occurrence that I did a double take. She wrinkled her nose as if she smelled something peculiar.

"Right. Well. I wanted to make sure you were . . . all right. You know. After . . ."

I didn't want to make it hard for her, but I had no idea what she was getting at. After holding too many one-woman gelato-sampling events along Bleecker Street? After staying up too late with Sterling Girl Mercedes Kim and her movie-star husband, watching an early cut of his latest film in their multimillion-dollar loft? After accidentally dropping hummus into the cage of Hitchens, my post-breakup Holland Lop bunny?

"After Gregory."

I tried to hide my shock. This made two attempts to delve into my personal life during a single conversation, and it unnerved me.

"Oh, I'm fine," I said lightly, waving my hand, hoping to locate an escape hatch from the conversation. In fact, I had not been fine, but talking about it with Pippa Flatland was not my idea of a useful step on the road to recovery.

She touched her hair and straightened her shoulders. "As I suggested earlier, I really don't believe you should chuck the whole notion of motherhood. Of family and all that. Perhaps Gregory just wasn't the right fit for you. I assigned you to the hotel because the scion, Hutchinson . . . that is, he's, well . . ." She cleared her throat uncomfortably. "He's a bit of all right. You know. Rather handsome."

I blinked at her in astonishment. "You're setting me up with a suspect?" Only my own mother was that desperate to see me reproduce—so desperate that, for the first time in my adult life, our relationship was truly suffering. Not the adolescence-era kind of suffering caused by an unauthorized borrowing of a leather jacket, but a gut-wrenching, I-don't-feel-like-I-know-you-anymore kind of suffering.

She scowled at me, giving me hope that we would, once again, depart the realm of the personal. "Don't be absurd. Eye candy, merely. And I wasn't finished. I also think that, working in a hotel, you'll have an opportunity to meet a variety of new people and it may help you move on."

"Really?" I said incredulously.

"Oh, never mind, Zephyr," she snapped. "I give a damn about all my employees, and I give two damns about the young ones. Three damns about the young women, who are notoriously few and far between. I think being around a good-looking man—who may or may not be a criminal, I remind you—and whatever interesting guests might pass through the hotel will help get your mind off that chump and move you along. Let me remind you, though, lest there be any doubt, that I am giving you this case primarily because I believe you are ready for it. But never mind," she repeated petulantly.

I felt like I was gaining a window onto Pippa's skewed and

impoverished perception of the human heart. To her, A plus B equaled forty-seven: Her equations didn't match up with any noetic format I'd encountered. Still, I was pretty sure she was attempting a generous gesture, and I was touched.

"Thank you," I said, as the boat bumped up against the banks of Richmond County. We stood and prepared to make a U-turn inside St. George Terminal, then board the same boat for the return voyage. Our feet would barely skim the surface of Staten Island. One day, I promised myself as we hustled down the ramp, I would explore this mysterious and occasionally seditious borough.

"One more thing," she said, clutching her oversize Harrods's tote bag tight against her chest as the crowd pressed in around her. "You're not permitted to interview witnesses or suspects. You start Tuesday morning as Greenwich Village Hotel's new concierge. Ballard McKenzie is the only one—and I mean the only one, Zephyr—who will know your true identity. You, me, him. There are simply too many unknowns to make the circle bigger just yet."

"I'm going undercover?" I suddenly had a little trouble catching my breath.

"Can you handle this?" she said, turning a steady gaze on me. "If not, tell me now and I'll put someone else on the case. It's embezzlement, likely forgery, and probably mail fraud, which means a federal indictment, if we're lucky."

I nodded vigorously, never imagining that embezzlement, forgery, and mail fraud indictments would be the least of the McKenzie family's problems and merely the beginning of mine.

Chapter 2

The night Jeremy Wedge was rushed to St. Vincent's Hospital was not a night I was supposed to be working the speckled Corian front desk of the Greenwich Village Hotel. I was supposed to be on my way to Orchard Street with my brother Gideon for a night of obligation art: two hours of tedious and under-costumed performance by a friend of a friend of Gid's in a poorly ventilated basement generously referred to as a black-box theater.

I'd finished my shift a half hour earlier, after a typically Rubik's Cubish day, one that included cadging backstage passes to BAM's Next Wave Festival for the puppeteers staying in room 203 and helping the Kiwis in 506 locate a restaurant in the Bronx that they'd heard served authentic Thanksgiving dinners all year long. But I was covering for my friend Asa Binsky and hoping Hutchinson McKenzie, Ballard's son, wouldn't notice the time.

Asa was late for the third time that week and lurching ever closer to unemployment. He insisted that his sessions with the Wiccan acupuncturist in Fort Greene were healing the chronic pain in his ankle, the result of an election-night-joy injury. He'd been at a Gay Deadheads for Obama party in the East Village the year before, and when Ohio was called, Asa and all his two hundred twenty pounds jumped off the baby grand. He'd been paying for it ever since but maintained that "Rosie Two"—Asa's sweetheart term for the man he considered Roosevelt II—was worth every twinge. It didn't help his case that when he *was* at the hotel, Asa had trouble curbing his 800-number habit. He regularly phoned a wide variety of companies to offer comments, suggestions, questions, and critiques about their products on the proven theory that most conversations resulted in free stuff being sent to him.

I was savoring a brief lull in front-desk activity, surreptitiously browsing Facebook—while maintaining a slight frown to give the illusion of work—when the voice that belonged to the love child of Katharine Hepburn and William Buckley pounded through my respite like a dropped anvil.

"Where's your friend?" drawled Hutchinson McKenzie. He had slithered around the corner of the desk and settled his square chin onto his white-knuckled fist. Hutchinson was a constant lesson to me that a foul temper and unchecked arrogance were not automatic grounds for becoming a suspect.

"I have many friends," I muttered, casually tabbing back to the EZ-CheckIn screen.

"And with how many are you currently playing Word Scramble?"

Bite me, you overbred, J. Press–dressed ass. Was there a camera I didn't yet know about trained on the desk? I shuddered at the thought of Hutchinson McKenzie watching me on the closed-circuit TV in his office, the office he didn't know I had a key to. I adjusted the collar of my crimson mandarin jacket and met his gaze.

"Hutchinson," I said lightly, pretending not to ignite a firestorm, "is there anything that needs doing that isn't being done?"

His porcine nostrils flared. Hutchinson and I had gotten off on the wrong foot three weeks earlier, the day I began work at his family's hotel, and we'd continued our angry waltz without pause. He, for reasons I assumed had roots in some high-school-era insecurity, wanted to be called by his last name—McKenzie—but in my field reports I had to refer to the McKenzie men by their first names for clarity. It was too hard to switch gears in person and so I didn't. In any case, the man's first name sounded like a last name, so I couldn't understand why he even bothered trying to switch.

Hutchinson had what some people might have called preppy good looks—tall, with a chiseled face, aforementioned square chin, broad forehead, hair the blond that only a decade of Clairol can bring—but I thought there was a coldness to his slate-blue eyes that hinted at ugly secrets. After some of our sharper exchanges, I conjured up scenarios involving the hotel basement and unwilling, undocumented female workers, even though I knew this wasn't fair, not even for someone with a sphincter as constricted as Hutchinson's. Mostly I hated him because he hated me, and he hated me because, twelve years earlier, he had not gotten into Harvard, whereas the bogus résumé that Pippa and I had whipped up indicated that I had. We had assumed that the more white glove my pedigree, the more likely it would be that my hiring would pass muster with Junior. We had assumed wrong.

"I'm not paying Asa for you to do his job," he said through his perpetually clenched teeth.

"So it's on principle only that you don't want me covering for him?" I tried to make it sound like an earnest question.

"Yes, principles. You've heard of them."

Professional. I silently intoned my sporadically functional mantra. *I'm a professional. I don't actually work for this depauperate Ken doll.* I just needed him to keep believing that I did.

"My apologies." I eked out a grimace, the closest I could come to smiling at Hutchinson. McKenzie. Hutchinson. Maybe I should call him Chuck and see what happened. "Would you prefer that I leave?"

Before he could answer, the front doors slid open, letting in a cloud of humid, leftover summer air and a pile of drunken New Zealanders.

"Oy!" they cried cheerfully.

"Oy!" Hutchinson and I replied in unison. We threw each other startled glances, embarrassed as much by how stupid we sounded trying to echo our antipodal guests as we were by the undesired bond briefly forged by the shared stupid response.

"Whoa." I hurried out from behind the desk in time to catch the escaped contents of the handbag belonging to an inebriated twentysomething. She was being inadequately supported by two unsteady mates: one a stooped, blotchy-faced bloke with a diamond cross dangling from one ear, the other a rotund fellow sporting ringlets that belonged to another century. Right behind them was Asa, looking sheepish—more sheepish than usual. He made a beeline for the desk, avoided Hutchinson's eyes, and stood in front of the computer I'd vacated, apparently ready to act as though he'd been there all along.

"Did you find your Thanksgiving dinner in the Bronx?" I asked the woman, holding my breath so I wouldn't breathe hers.

"Yih, yih, we found a curry in Queens!" she slurred enthusiastically.

I glanced over at Hutchinson and watched him effortlessly maintain his welcoming-host face, ready to cater to his guests, no matter how fat-witted or bibulous they might be. In that respect, he was good at his job. What permitted me to loathe him was that it was all an act. He looked down on these people even as he hosted them.

"Zephyr," he said smoothly, "since you're still here, would you be so kind as to help our guests settle in to their room?" Translation: Go upstairs and make sure these unintelligible assholes don't puke on my furniture, and if they do, take pictures, write up a detailed report, and have reimbursement invoices tucked under their doors by dawn.

I should have been on the F train ten minutes ago. I glanced at my watch. Hutchinson caught me.

"I know how much you care about your job here, filling in for Asa and all, so I'm sure whatever plans you have for tonight can wait."

It was funny, really, his undertone of threat, his strutting like a castrated peacock, acting as though he could fire me. I could have talked my way out of nursemaid duty, but the truth was that I really didn't want to spend two hours suffocating underground on the Lower East Side watching *The Perilous Apple: One Man's Interpretation* and evading my brother's blatant attempts to trick me into telling him confidential details about SIC cases, his fingers itching for his notebook. Even though I'd been at the hotel since nine o'clock that morning, I preferred to hang around a little longer on the off off *off* chance that something—anything—would happen that would give me the tiniest lead in this case, which seemed determined to be the complete downfall of my fledgling career.

I had reviewed footage from the security cameras stationed over the safe, the owner's office, and at the hotel bar, but had spotted no one tucking stacks of bills under their arms. I had pored over bank statements on my days "off" from the hotel and agreed with an increasingly pallid Ballard McKenzie that, yes, his balance was off by a hundred grand but could not identify just how that had happened. In three weeks, I had (reluctantly) scratched Hutchinson off my suspect list: That was the full extent of my progress.

Pippa had been encouraging and patient, but I was getting frustrated, not least because the guys at the office were starting to get curious about my blatant absence from my cubicle. When I was first taken off the streetlight case, I'd gotten a few silent, sympathetic punches in the shoulder and even an anonymous package of condolence Twinkies deposited on my desk. But these guys were veterans, and they knew what the comings and goings of someone on an undercover assignment looked like. Weird hours, less face time at the office. Showing up at six P.M. to deal with desk work. Nothing to offer in the way of water-cooler conversation. I had the feeling they were going to start taking turns tailing me in their spare time.

My friends, on the other hand, had turned out to be more or less oblivious to my new schedule. I should have been grateful not to have to fend off queries on multiple fronts, but I couldn't help observing that only a few years ago, before I'd borne bouquets along aisles for three of my Sterling Girls, they would have been unrelenting in the pursuit of their suspicions—interrogating me about my odd hours and teasing me about the effort it took to keep a secret from them.

While the SGs had certainly not forsaken me post-wedlock—we had our guard up against the dangerous fiction that you need only one other person in this world—I was a touch nostalgic for the days of constant communication and group debriefings on even the most trivial incidents, for traveling en masse and crashing parties around the city in order to secure free food and drink. I knew, as Gregory and I parted ways, that I would not be able to return to the comfort of the group dynamic, but I was determined to adapt to this new climate. When Lucy, who was being consumed alive by her twins, needed me, I was ready with my size-ten shoulders and untested wisdom. When Mercedes wanted to vent about the vestigial vanities of her Hollywood-steeped husband, I was the flying buttress to their union.

Even as a willing and loyal third wheel, I found myself with plenty of time to catch free Alvin Ailey at SummerStage with my new friend, Macy St. John, to take a stained-glass class in Greenpoint, and to browse the New York Is Book Country festival, all with a steady stream of self-commendation silently broadcasting in my head the whole time: *Look at what a successful singleton I am!* I had none of the distractions that come with a relationship but, even so, even with the extra time and head space, I still couldn't crack this case, and that made me scared for my professional future.

I ignored Hutchinson McKenzie's idle threat and trailed the now-singing New Zealanders up the narrow, plushly carpeted stairs, reminding myself how convenient it was not to have someone waiting for me at home, demanding to know why I was late and where I'd been. Of course, Gregory, being an undercover NYPD detective himself, probably wouldn't have grilled me, but tinting him with a bit of 1950s TV husband made my current situation a little easier to contemplate.

"'The river was deep but I swam it, Janet!'" the stooped, blotchy Kiwi bellowed as he swayed unsteadily. I remembered too late that they were staying on the fifth floor. To make them turn around and use the elevator seemed more trouble than forging our way up the steps.

"'The future is ours so let's plan it, Janet,'" continued Ringlets. He lost his balance and I put both hands in the middle of his back to steady him. His sweat had soaked through his shirt, and I choked back a wave of disgust. He turned to me and crooned, "'So please don't tell me to can it, Janet.'"

"Okay, I won't," I assured him, pushing them down the

hall and through the door to room 506. "But you need to quiet down—"

"'I've one thing to say and that's . . .'"

All three of them shrieked, "'DAMMIT, JANET, I LOVE YOU!'"

"Shut UP," I hollered at them, and then immediately questioned my abilities to pass as a concierge. "Please shut up," I amended. I closed the door.

"Tha's from *The Rocky Horror Show*!" the woman informed her reflection in the vanity mirror.

"Great," I said, as the men collapsed onto the beds.

"Iz a Kiwi wrote that, yih?" said Blotchy. "You noy that? Richard O'Brien, you noy him?"

"Not personally," I said, unsure what to do next. Pull off their shoes? Make them brush their teeth? I surveyed the room, thrilled to get a glimpse into their privacy. As pretend concierge, I didn't often make it into the rooms while they were occupied. Like the others, this one was an eclectic—bordering on visually distressing—amalgam of art deco and Amish, with black-and-white portraits of 1930s movie stars gazing out at hand-carved furniture. The New Zealanders were a disorganized bunch, their backpacks and clothing strewn about. The air smelled a little like patchouli, but the room wasn't trashed and was no worse than you might expect from three pseudo-adults nearing the end of a round-the-world trip.

"*Rocky Horror* belongs to New Zealand," slurred the woman, growing serious. She swayed forward until her mouth was almost touching the mirror. She repeated herself slowly, entranced by her own lips. "It *belongs* to us."

"But not the platy," Ringlets chirped, wiping his damp forehead against a wall. "That's all Ozzie. You evah seen a platypus?"

I shook my head apologetically.

"No . . ." That one word had about four syllables: *na-ah-oh-oy*. "Me, neithah." His affect quickly grew morose. "Twinty-siven yee-ahs awld and nivah seen a platy. God's spare pahts, you know."

"Okay!" I clapped my hands like a camp counselor. "Shoes off! Right now."

To my amazement, they all obeyed. My goal, I decided, was to see our guests through to a safe state of unconsciousness and meet my brother as the play was letting out, just in time for a glass of wine at 'inoteca.

"Who needs to use the bathroom? Who wants Alka-Seltzer? Who's sleeping where?" There were two beds and three people. The thought of this woman coupling with either of these objectionable representatives of the species was not pleasant. At the foot of one of the beds was a magenta nightie, neatly folded.

"Is that yours?" I asked the woman. Dreamily, she glanced at it.

"Na-ah-oh-oy. 'S Marty's."

Smack in the heart of Greenwich Village and I assume the negligee belongs to the woman. No wonder this case was still open.

There was a faint knock at the door. I took quick stock of my charges, confirmed there were no signs of imminent up-chuck, then pulled it open.

I had to lower my gaze substantially to see the top of Samantha Kimiko Hodges's head. Mrs. Hodges was a bantam version of a grown woman without actually being a midget. Everything about her, except her attitude, was miniature. Her husband had died earlier in the year: She had sold their apartment on Gay Street and was now trying to figure out what to do with whatever was left of her eighty-one-year-old life. This, Ballard McKenzie told me as we reviewed regular guests on their roster, was how she had phrased it to him while working out a reduced rate for her extended stay. When I began working at the hotel, she'd been living there for a month.

Mrs. Hodges kept to herself, leaving at eight every morning, returning at six, dining in the restaurant adjacent to the lobby, and retiring upstairs by seven. She appeared to own exactly seven dresses, which she wore in the same sequence every week. Monday was the blue paisley, Tuesday was the red kimono-looking silk, Wednesday was the green stripes, and so on. She wore stockings with seams up the back, even in ninety-degree weather, and her silver hair formed a shiny cap around her walnut-wrinkled face.

I had exchanged words with her only a few times. Despite her unmistakable Japanese provenance, she seemed to have learned her English from a kasha-cooking, free-advice-for-all bubbe.

"So, what's the ruckus?" she demanded.

"My apologies, Mrs. Hodges—" I began.

"I've told you, it's Mrs. *Kimiko* Hodges. Like Rodham Clinton."

"Sorry, Mrs. Kimiko Hodges," I continued, not bothering to point out that while our secretary of state did indeed use three names, she used only one of them in conjunction with "Mrs." "I'll have this under control in a moment."

"Dammit, Janet, the fuckin' platy," moaned someone behind me, and I heard a retching sound. I whipped around in time to see Ringlets lurching for the bathroom.

"Some Pepto they should take," Mrs. Hodges proclaimed, wrinkling her nose. "Before they drink. You oughta line your stomach in preparation if you're gonna drink."

"I'll suggest that," I told her anxiously. "I'm really sorry to have disturbed you. How about breakfast on us tomorrow?" I loved offering compensatory meals without prior approval. Hutchinson would be apoplectic.

"I should hope so," she said, crossing her arms and trying to peer around me into the chaos. The young woman who had been admiring her oratory skills in the mirror groaned as she took Ringlets's spot on the bed. I felt a flutter of panic in my belly and began to wish I was elbow-to-elbow with my brother in a subterranean theater.

"Again, Mrs. Hodges, so sorry." I began to close the door on her.

"Wait!"

"Mrs. Hodges," I pleaded, "I really have to deal with this now!"

"No, I hear something else. You hear it?" She pointed down the hall. "Sounds like an emu."

I blinked at her. How was I supposed to know what an emu sounded like? How would she know?

"There's somebody yelling, you hear that? You got another one of these drunk foreigners down the hall?" I spent a quarter of a second observing the irony of a Japanese woman with a Yiddish accent calling someone else foreign, but then, a foreigner in New York was anyone who arrived on the boat after one's own.

I was about to ignore her when I heard it. A horrible, guttural moan. A long, sickly summons for help. A whole other class of moaning from the garden variety on display here in room 506. I bolted down the hall and stood still, heart pounding, waiting for another one.

There it was. I spun around. Room 502. I pounded on the door, aware of Samantha Kimiko Hodges's tiny form trailing close behind.

"Hello? Hello? Open the door! Are you okay in there?" I pounded again, feeling guilty for loving a good adrenaline rush while truly hoping nobody inside was mortally wounded.

"No," came the raspy voice. "Help me."

"Jesus Christ," I whispered in alarm, digging out the master key only Ballard knew I carried. "Mrs. Hodges, please go call 911, then tell the front desk I need help," I said, knowing that, even in a crisis, the old woman was not going to take kindly to being ordered around.

I turned to look at her. Pale and scared. Great. All I needed was for our octogenarian widow to collapse from heart failure.

"Never mind." There was only Asa at the desk, anyway. I let myself in and heard Mrs. Hodges gasp behind me.

Hanging upside down off the foot of one of the unmade beds was a khaki-clad man who was well under six feet tall and probably only a hundred seventy pounds, but who looked enormous given his dramatic presentation. His face was puffy and pink, his eyes bulging. His red hair stuck straight down, making his head look like a stuffed animal. He was clutching a fistful of paper scraps.

"Zephyr, help me," he gurgled, right before he surrendered to unconsciousness. Mrs. Hodges scurried out of the room.

This inverted, florid bear of a man was Jeremy Wedge, whom I'd come to know in the previous three weeks as a slightly aggressive, slightly hypochondriac genetics researcher who was first cousin and best friend to Hutchinson McKenzie. The two of them often hung out in the hotel bar, sipping sherry and saying things like "physiocrats," "distortionary costs," and "fucking Adam Smith," loud enough to be overheard by whatever attractive young woman was within earshot. I didn't know why they had settled on a general bashing of eighteenth-century economic theory as a mating call (especially since they were both obvious beneficiaries of laissez-faire in more ways than one), but I had begun to notice that Jeremy loitered around the hotel only when there was a gaze-worthy beauty staying upstairs. Clearly, his thoughtful cousin was looking out for him.

I quickly scanned the messy room for signs of whatever

guest he had managed to seduce, but there was no concrete evidence of a woman. No suitcases on the folding stand, no clothes anywhere, no shoes, no hairbrush, no earrings on the sustainably harvested mango-wood mission-style dresser. But the room looked post-checkout: bedspreads balled up (Mrs. McKenzie would be incensed—she had personally selected every quilt in the building, a detail proudly touted in the hotel brochure), damp towels over the backs of the chairs, smudged water glasses on the bedside table.

Apparently, Jeremy had been used and left behind by one of his conquests. That gave me a certain amount of satisfaction insofar as I maintained a low-frequency desire for ill to befall him, merely by dint of his familial connections. But *this*? I did not want this to happen to him. Or to me. I didn't want anyone dying on my watch, but I specifically didn't want a McKenzie relative dying on my watch.

I bent over him and put my ear to his mouth. Breath, check. I put my fingers to his carotid, marveling at the chances of having unwillingly touched two sweaty men in the space of five minutes. Pulse, check.

Fortunately, everyone at the SIC was required to become certified in first aid and CPR training during their orientation weeks. Unfortunately, everything I'd learned promptly flew out of my head and so I resorted to slapping Jeremy's mottled cheeks and screaming his name.

My fourth heroic shriek was interrupted by three firefighters storming into the room. Until that moment, I had never indulged in rescue fantasies. Sure, there had been a few dark years when I had wished that anyone—man, woman, goat— would help me figure out what to do with my life, but I didn't actually dream that they would pick up the various pieces and bond me into a coherent whole. I hoped that maybe they would take me to the art-supply store and show me where the glue aisle was.

However. I was now an instant convert to rescue fantasies. These men tromped in with their boots and their oversize gear; these men disregarded civilized niceties like wiping their feet or making sure the doorknob didn't gouge the wall when it swung open; these men embodied aptitude and control, and I'd never seen anything sexier. They were sexy in their utter domination of the situation, and they were sexy because confidence-verging-on-cockiness radiated from the yellow stripes of their open jackets to their clean-shaven faces. Why the paramedics right behind them—one with a thin ponytail, the other with a tattoo of a bull that ran down his neck—were not sexy, even though they, too, had the power of rescue, was an intriguing mystery I'd devote some time to later.

"Outta the way!" the shortest of the firefighters bellowed. I jumped away from the bed. In fact, all he did was make way for the paramedics to move in with their defibrillator, stretcher, and bags of tubes, needles, and vials. I was handed off from one firefighter to another until I was back in the corridor, straining to see over their bulk and equipment.

"Do you know what happened? How long have you been with him?" asked a baby-faced fighter with absurdly long lashes. Surely those lashes were a fire hazard. Could firefighters be required to trim lashes, the way they were required to shave off beards? (A tidbit I'd picked up from one of the Tommys at work: Chin whiskers interfered with the seal of oxygen masks.) I spent a distracted moment watching him blink, then found my voice.

"I have no idea. I was working the desk downstairs, then came up with some other guests who needed help. We heard Jeremy and came running—"

"You know him? And who's 'we'?" he interrupted.

I ask the questions! I wanted to snap. I was dying to flash my badge and let him know he could talk to me as a fellow professional. Though, truth be told, a member of New York's

Bravest was not likely to be impressed by an employee of New York's Awfully Capable, as my colleagues—most of them former Finest—sometimes glumly labeled themselves. We were a law-enforcement agency that worked mostly undercover, or at least behind the scenes, and as a result found ourselves having to offer lengthy introductions to people even as we were arresting them.

"He's the nephew of the hotel's owner. 'We' is me and a guest." I pointed down the hall toward Samantha Kimiko Hodges's room. "The woman in 505 heard him and, no, I don't know who was in the room with him," I added as he opened his mouth to ask. The mouth went nicely with the lashes.

"What did you hear?" Lashes cocked his head at me, unsmiling. Clearly he was not distracted by anything on my face.

"A groan, a few groans, and then I went in. He was already upside down. He said my name and then passed out. I haven't been downstairs to see who the room is—or was—registered to." As I spoke, I realized that something was bothering me. "We only heard him two minutes ago. I don't understand how you guys could have gotten here this quickly."

The hero frowned. "You don't really mean two minutes. We got the call about ten minutes ago."

"That's impossible," I said flatly. "Unless . . ." Unless Jeremy had a heart attack and grabbed the phone himself before he yelled out to us. Unless the unidentified companion called—and then left. Where was she? *Who* was she?

"I need to get back in that room," I told Lashes, emerging from the spell of his well-placed features.

"Why?" He crossed his arms comfortably, letting me know that I was not going back in anytime soon.

I glanced over my shoulder, dug out my badge, and flashed

it. To my utter humiliation, he leaned forward to study the crest, as if it potentially was a fake ID.

"Undercover," I murmured, knowing Pippa would kill me, possibly even fire me. "Please don't blow it."

"Is that a pigeon?"

"It's an eagle. May I?" I asked haughtily.

He stepped back and made a grand gesture toward the door. "Be my guest."

I strode past him, daring to make eye contact. He held my gaze . . . and then winked. He actually winked. Oh man. Minor blows to the ego aside, I did love my job.

Jeremy was already on the stretcher, an IV bag resting on his chest, syringe packaging littering the floor. Next to the paramedics' discarded cellophane were the scraps of paper Jeremy had been clutching. I bent down and swiftly pocketed them. As I did, I noticed something else on the floor, peeking out from under the nightstand. An orange prescription vial. I grabbed it and took a quick look at the label. Black lines had been drawn across it, obscuring the patient information.

"Is this yours?" I demanded of the paramedics. The tattooed one, who reeked of cigarette smoke, looked at me impatiently, then did a double take.

"Presumed OD!" he called to his colleague. "Ambien party." He turned to me. "You know how much was in here?"

I shook my head.

"Okay, move it out!" he yelled, and off rolled Jeremy Wedge. I really hoped, if only for his kind uncle's sake, that it wasn't the last time I'd see him.

* * *

I hurried back along the corridor to 506, home away from home for my sloppy friends from Down Under. I prayed they were all sound asleep so I could get a call in to Pippa.

Something, or someone, was blocking the door. I threw my shoulder against it and peeked inside. Blotchy was crumpled in a heap on the floor, his arms encircling a puddle of vomit. The woman was flat out on one of the beds, and Ringlets was nowhere to be seen.

"Hey, wait!" I yelled down the hall to the last of the rescue circus piling into the tiny hotel elevator.

Lashes said something to his buddy and they both jogged toward me, their clonking gear making them look like giants overtaking a miniature village. I pushed the door open a little wider and directed them inside. Ten minutes later, two more teams of paramedics had filled the corridor to capacity and hotel history was made as all three guests were ferried off to the hospital to be treated for alcohol poisoning.

At nine-twenty, barely an hour after I first followed the *Rocky Horror Show* enthusiasts up the stairs, the last ambulance pulled away. Hutchinson McKenzie, wan beneath his perpetual tan and glistening with sweat, had waited for his father to arrive, then jumped in a cab bound for the hospital. The fear in his eyes was genuine, and for once I felt sorry for him.

I sank down on the stone ledge outside the entrance, watching Asa and Ballard through the frosted-glass entrance as they made nice with concerned guests in the lobby. The air was cooling off and there was a handful of stars defiantly outshining the city lights. A couple with matching spiky gray haircuts slipped into Babbo for a late seating. Joggers picked their way through an ever-shifting obstacle course of dog leashes. The air was noticeably crisper than it had been three weeks earlier and the city seemed to be breathing a collective sigh of relief after a particularly wet summer.

I leaned back and felt exhaustion flow in like a tide. I flipped open my battered cellphone and left a message for my brother, trying to find words that apologized for my absence without piquing his interest and eliciting a barrage of questions later. Then I pulled out the scraps of paper I'd grabbed off the floor of room 502 and smoothed them out. A coffee-stained taxi receipt, a credit-card receipt from Ansonia Pharmacy for deodorant and hair gel, and a crumpled piece of hotel stationery with a phone number on it, which I promptly dialed.

"You've reached Large Tomato Walking Tours. Our offices are now closed. . . ."

I hung up and dialed Pippa.

"Zuckerman," she answered curtly. "Should you really be calling me?"

"Absolutely," I said confidently, one moment before spotting Lashes rounding MacDougal Street and heading straight toward me on Waverly. "Actually, no." I casually flipped my phone closed, hanging up on my boss, and shoved the receipts back into my pocket.

A rush of unfounded excitement, the kind I figured I'd been required to check at the door of thirty, washed over me, and I braced myself. He probably forgot something inside. A hose, maybe. Or perhaps he had to use the bathroom. Or was curious about our room rates. Maybe he—

"Hi," he said, coming to a stop in front of me. He delivered a lopsided grin, apparently not in the least concerned about a wayward hose. "I'm Lieutenant Fisk. Call me Delta."

"Call me Ishmael," I replied instantly, then clamped my mouth shut. Three years in a relationship had, it appeared, severely hobbled my flirting skills.

He looked confused. "Is your name Ishmael?"

I resigned myself to explaining, but he broke into a big smile.

"I'm messing with you. I've read *Moby Dick* three times. Firefighters have a lot of time on their hands. So are you off work from your pretend job now?"

"Yes, but . . . " I tried to clear my head and catch up.

"Are you single?"

I gaped at him. Cheeky. Pippa would have called him cheeky.

"It's a fair question. We're both adults. I'm about to ask you out. But I won't if you're not single." He crossed his arms.

"You're very . . ." I sputtered, looking for the right words.

"Practical. I'm almost forty and I'm practical."

"You're *forty*?" I said before I could stop myself.

"Do you edit yourself at all?" He grinned.

"Do you?"

"Actually, yes. Do you want to go rock climbing with me?"

"You've concluded I'm single?"

"Yes."

"I've never been rock climbing."

"No time like the present."

"You want to go rock climbing *now*?" I laughed. I was on the verge of growing rather practical myself, about to point to my watch and shake my head reprovingly, like a schoolmarm, when I remembered that in the belief system of the Sterling Girls, it was sinful to decline an opportunity for urban adventure, which carried with it myriad benefits: no woods to get lost in, no chance of avalanche, no need to engage in risky hitchhiking.

"Yes. Now. At Aviator Sports. Less crowded than Chelsea Piers."

And so, two hours after Jeremy, Blotchy, Ringlets, and The Girl moved their party to St. Vincent's, I was not ten feet below Orchard Street but rather thirty feet above Flatbush Avenue, proving to myself that I was game for trying new things, even if they occurred after ten-thirty, the hour at which I regularly turned into an exceptionally grumpy pumpkin.

"To your right, your right, grab that red foothold to your

right!" Delta shouted up, regarding me from an angle I'd never imagined permissible on a first date. "You're doing great, Zephyr, really great! Almost there!"

"Thank you," I mumbled to the wall.

I couldn't tell whether I was having fun. Reaching the top of a cliff, even a fake cliff in a former airplane hangar, using only my hands and feet, was thrilling. It was an endorphin high unmatched by biking, Rollerblading, or even sitting with friends drinking coffee. It was a high intensified by the fact that I was loopy with exhaustion. But the stress of doing something new, something that required a harness around my butt in the presence of a man whom I'd known so briefly that I'd not yet had the chance to see him in daylight, was dampening the thrill.

"Okay, now the blue! Reach your right hand out for the blue hold!"

I grasped the highest handhold on the wall and heard cheers rise up from Delta and the paid-to-be-enthusiastic employees on belay, into whose unfamiliar hands I had casually placed my life. I peered down at them and attempted a smile. Delta grabbed a hold and nimbly maneuvered up the path next to mine, reaching me in about ten seconds. It had taken me a good five minutes to summit the gray plastic-derived compound mountain.

"You've done this before," I observed.

"I have."

"I think you do this to show off your quads."

"And my biceps, too, don't forget," he said.

"And your biceps," I agreed.

We looked at each other with matching stupid smiles.

"Can I kiss you?" he asked.

"Well, you haven't taught me how to get down, so I don't have much of a choice." I wasn't surprised by his question, but I had to stall. I really wanted to kiss this guy, right here, right now, but I needed to gird myself. This would be The First Kiss Since Gregory. I needed to open a new page in my mental album, and I wasn't a hundred percent sure I was ready.

I leaned back and studied him. Ninety percent would do.

Three stories above southern Brooklyn, we kissed. And, oh, I'd forgotten how a first kiss is a species unto itself. With first kisses, it hardly matters whether they're good; they're inherently exciting even if they're wet or limp or tentative. But Delta's lips weren't sloppy. They were firm, gentle, obviously experienced. Due to circumstances, it was a hands-off kiss, which made it all the more gentlemanly and at the same time all the more exciting. I fought off the sensation that I was cheating on Gregory.

Hoots and cheers floated up from our two protectors below. We pulled away.

Delta grinned at me.

"So is this your MO?" I asked. "Firefighter impresses first dates by taking them climbing and smooching at the top?" I wasn't complaining.

"Zephyr, I swear I've never done anything like this. I mean I've rock-climbed before. Obviously."

"Obviously," I teased him, and he had the good grace to blush.

"But you just seemed game."

"Swear on the fireman's code of honor?"

He laughed through his nose. "I swear." He kissed me again. And right there, under the fluorescent lights, a whole world of kissing and groping and sleeping around reopened itself to me. Freedom.

"Do you want kids?" I suddenly blurted out.

He looked startled. "You *don't* edit yourself."

"No," I agreed, feeling my face grow hot. "I guess I don't. I think I used to. Maybe."

"Do we have to sort out the kid thing now?" he asked with mock seriousness. "I try not to visit that subject until I've known someone at least twenty-four hours and/or have slept with them. Otherwise, it's really a moot point, you know what I mean?"

I rolled my eyes, more at myself than at him. "Yes, I know. Forget I said anything. It's an issue of mine at the moment." I wanted to wave my hand at him, but it was still glued to the blue hold and beginning to cramp. "So how *do* we get down from here?" I eyed the floor warily. It was farther away than I'd realized.

"Although," he said lightly, ignoring my question, "if I'm gonna be hanging out with an undercover, we can't talk about work, so maybe we *should* talk kids."

I clenched what few parts of my body remained un-clenched. "If you ever say 'undercover' to me again, I'm leaving," I snapped. And although it was an absurd threat given the circumstances—me hanging on for dear life somewhere above Flatbush Avenue—the panic in my eyes must have been evident. He looked contrite immediately.

"Hey, I'm sorry. I'm kidding. I promise I won't jeopardize your job, even if I never see you again."

Was that a threat? My God, what had I done? A moment of hubris in the fifth-floor hallway because of some long lashes and strong shoulders and I'd blown my cover with a complete stranger. When would I learn how to control myself?

"But," he added quietly, "I hope we do. See each other again."

My fingers were aching and now my left calf was also cramping. "Me, too," I said, although what I wanted was the kissing, not the talking. I nodded toward the floor. "Can we go down now?" I practically whispered.

He nodded reluctantly, as if he'd blown it, and showed me

how to rappel. We bounced down the wall and finally reached terra firma. At the bottom, we avoided looking at each other as we unclipped and joined the line of nocturnal climbers waiting to return their gear.

A heavy-breathing blond woman with runny makeup was in front of us, waiting to hand in her harness. She reached into a fanny pack and extracted an orange vial, unscrewed the top with her palm, and popped a pill into her mouth.

She turned to us and held out the vial. "Percocet?" she offered pleasantly.

We declined, and she tapped the couple in front of her, eager to share her bounty with others who might be in need of some hospital-grade pain relief.

"Gives you the warm fuzzies, doesn't it?" Delta quipped, but I was distracted, thinking again of the vial I'd picked up in room 502. I had accepted the paramedic's immediate assessment that Jeremy had attempted suicide. It explained—sort of, in a hurried, sloppy calculation kind of way—why the room he'd been in had not belonged to a young beauty but rather to Mr. and Mrs. Whitcomb of Akron, Ohio. He had merely wanted to find a place to die.

But that assessment did not explain why the label on the vial had been redacted to the point where it resembled an FOIA file. The names and numbers had been crossed out, leaving only the drug information legible. And it didn't explain the scraps of paper in Jeremy's hand; why would he have gone through the Whitcombs' garbage before trying to kill himself in their room?

I thrust my harness at Delta. "Would you mind returning this for me? I have to call my boss."

"At eleven-thirty on a Saturday night?" He looked hurt. "If the kiss sucked, just say so."

I was startled. I'd forgotten how carefully one had to tread immediately after starting up with a new person. Were we starting up? I had no idea. I only knew that we had kissed. Couldn't we keep it simple? I felt a wave of longing, not so much for Gregory himself but for our hard-won familiarity. I wouldn't have had to explain Pippa to him, or my need to check in with her at impossible hours.

"No, no, I swear, you're great, the kiss was great." In fact, I had no idea if he was great. Why was this so complicated? Could I simply come out and tell him I'd like a bit of no-strings fun until I found someone who shared my vision of the future? Was that actually what I wanted? "It's just that I have to call my boss with anything—" I stopped short.

"I know, you can't talk about your work." Delta cocked his head, and I fought the urge to run my fingers along the taut tendons of his neck. "Go. If you're there when I come out, great." His voice was flat.

I'd screwed up. The call to Pippa could have waited another few minutes. But at that moment, as interested as I was in smooching Lieutenant Fisk, he of the beautiful black hair and superior musculature, I was even more interested in the Greenwich Village Hotel. Maybe, I thought as I threw him an apologetic glance and headed for the front door, if he'd still been wearing his yellow-striped firefighting garb, I wouldn't have been thinking about Jeremy Wedge, the garbage in room 502, and a bowdlerized prescription label.

Chapter 3

The second time I met Macy St. John was in August 2007. She was supine on my friend Lucy Toklas's couch, holding an upside-down can of whipped cream to her lips while training her glassy-eyed gaze upon the pages of *Valley of the Dolls*. Every few seconds—*pfft*—she'd inject another dollop into her mouth, never taking her eyes off the book. When it came time to turn a page, she'd use the hand holding the whipped cream to do the job, then put the nozzle back in position. *Pfft.* Pause. *Pfft.* Pause. *Pfft.*

Macy was thoroughly ensconced in a nervous breakdown. It wasn't Lucy's fault and it wasn't Macy's first breakdown. An alabaster-skinned, flame-haired, blue-eyed sprite who all but glowed in the dark, Macy was a former book editor, and one of some renown. She'd steadily worked her way up from editorial assistant, acquiring increasingly successful books. Then she published John Douglas's memoir, *Praying with the Mamas*, an insider's story about growing up in a fundamentalist polygamist enclave in Texas. The book topped the bestseller list, and Douglas made the media rounds from Lopate to Oprah. It was a heady time for Macy—lunches in Bonanza

Books' executive dining room, drinks at Elaine's, an enormous budget at the Frankfurt Book Fair—until The Smoking Gun posted a piece questioning whether Douglas's memoir was truthful. It turned out John Douglas was really Isaac Fishstein and the book had begun as a dare by a friend at the Iowa Writers' Workshop and had gotten a tad out of hand.

Macy apologized to her bosses, made some statements to the press, doubled up on her Guided-Mindfulness Stress-Reduction classes, and returned to work. Unfortunately, first one and then the next and then the third of her ensuing acquisitions all met the same or a similar fate. One writer after another came forward with a riveting and often prurient story of putting herself through Harvard on her prostitution fees or of overseeing his synagogue's marijuana-production facility or of camping by the side of the Palisades Parkway and evading state troopers for an entire year. There seemed to be an epidemic of writers who felt that coming from middle-class intact families would undermine their worth as artists. Publishing fiction was not enough for them; they needed to believe they *were* their main characters. I sometimes wondered whether there was a stall in the bathroom at The Writers Room that had Macy's direct phone line scribbled across the door: "For certain publication, call Macy St. John—memoir sucker."

Even her closest friends and colleagues couldn't understand how Macy could have fallen for the fabrications the third and fourth times. By the last book, *Escaping Englewood Cliffs,* Macy, now afflicted by acne, insomnia, and TMJ jaw pain, had enlisted the help of every fact-checker and intern available to her at Bonanza, plus a freelance researcher she paid out of her own pocket. But these crafty authors seemed to have made faux memoir a sport, and no one could find holes in their stories until after the books were on the shelves. When the final author appeared on *The View* to gleefully and insincerely expiate his sins, few people felt compelled to comfort Macy and so no one really tried.

Macy spent the following three months developing an intimate knowledge of her parents' couch in Durham, New Hampshire, until one day her father handed her a NOLS brochure and gently suggested she venture beyond the Stop & Shop. She suited up at EMS and headed to Wyoming for four weeks. She learned to use a compass, outsmart bears, eat rattlesnake (just once, for bragging rights), and navigate whitewater rapids. When she narrowly missed dying in a flash flood, the fog lifted, clarity set in, and perspective reigned. She grew, by all accounts, impossibly cheerful and determined to begin anew.

Macy returned to Brooklyn and began her own business, which she swore up and down was what she'd always wanted to do anyway. She became the sole proprietor of No Divas, a wedding-planning service for women who were *not* petty, narcissistic bridezillas but who were too busy to plan a modest wedding day without some assistance.

No Divas boiled nuptial celebrations down to eight elements: dress, guests, location, music, flowers, food, ceremony, invitations. Macy told her customers they could prioritize two of those and for the rest she would be unforgiving in the name of thriftiness and moderation. If you cared about the dress and the music, then your only choices for flowers were "formal" or "wild," and she would decide the rest. If you cared about flowers and food, then she gave you three bridal shops to pick from and urged you to go with a white bridesmaid dress. To the bride who wanted to schedule a two-hour meeting about her cake, Macy said, "It'll be white and it'll taste good." The client nearly wept with relief. To the betrothed who expressed concern that her dress was ivory and the invitations white, Macy offered to dunk all the invitations in a bathtub full of tea. The bride scampered off with her tulle between her legs.

No Divas was an immediate success. And even though nearly half of Macy's clients were actually picky, petulant people who wanted their shoes to match their cake, they wanted even more to be known as people who weren't. Macy had hit on marketing magic: Women who were in denial about being high-maintenance hellions could wave No Divas around as though it refuted all their distasteful qualities. They seemed to relish being disciplined by Macy, the way some CEOs and governors like being tied up, ordered around, or systematically belittled.

For nearly two years, Macy St. John could do no wrong in the correctly prioritized, morally upstanding, urban wedding-planning department. Word of mouth spread rapidly, and she hauled in cash at the speed of falling rice (an environmental no-no replaced by bubbles, of course). Then, six days after one of her couples exchanged vows, the bride was disemboweled by a nearly extinct, monstrous bird called a cassowary while on her honeymoon in eastern Australia. Macy was beside herself, especially as the woman, a lion tamer with a Ph.D. in animal psychology, had been one of her favorite clients and a true non-diva. But Macy went to the funeral, dried her eyes, and returned to work.

Her next clients were Lucy and her fiancé, Leonard. Their wedding went off without a hitch, but soon after, Macy staged the nuptials of a woman named Elsa Barges, a petite, giggling park ranger posted to Governors Island. She and her husband chose Rome for their honeymoon, and it was there, while waiting in line for hazelnut gelato, that she was fatally mowed down by a blue Vespa belonging to the prime minister's alternate-weekend mistress.

When Macy got the news, the insomnia and the jaw pain

returned, but her parents and her extant clients begged her not to quit. With great trepidation, she tended to the details of a dog runner's wedding: The bride supported herself by jogging with other people's canines to give them the exercise of which their office-bound owners were so dismally deprived.

There was one awkward moment during the planning stages, when Macy paused during a discussion of music (options: live band or DJ) and begged the bride to consider postponing her honeymoon. The bride confronted Macy with her suspicion that Macy, who had become inordinately clingy, was in love with her. Macy had to come clean and admit the fates of two of her three previous clients. The bride laughed, threw her arm around Macy, and promised not to die on her honeymoon.

When Macy received word that the dog runner had been impaled by a stalactite during a spelunking accident in New Mexico, she returned to couch territory, only this time she chose Lucy's brand-new sage-green sofa, fresh off the truck from Bloomingdale's. She became obsessed with protecting Lucy, since, to Macy's mind, she had been the only client to escape the grim reaper since the death streak began, and Macy felt compelled to keep watch over her.

Which is exactly what I found her doing that August afternoon two years ago, while overdosing on aerated dairy and Jacqueline Susann.

I had come directly to Lucy's sun-soaked apartment after work to assess the situation. Lucy, a tiny, bony, excitable social worker whose metabolism was kept elevated by an excessive need to organize, had come to my rescue countless times before. That she now needed me was a turn of events I found bracing. Macy had been installed on the couch for a couple of weeks, and Lucy had careered from sympathetic to frustrated to anxious, fearing that she might soon be claiming Macy as a dependent on her income taxes or at least requiring the services of an upholsterer years sooner than anticipated. The challenge of Macy-St.-John-on-the-couch riled Lucy, who was accustomed to successfully giving succor to the downtrodden. Macy turned out to be more difficult to fix than the meth addicts and alimony dodgers Lucy normally tended to, whose problems had obvious if not easily attainable solutions.

"What about a real estate broker?" Lucy was pleading over her shoulder as she let me in to her quiet glass palace in the sky, where the sweat on my skin instantly evaporated in the centrally cooled air. She was in shorts and a tank top, her blond hair pulled into a high ponytail, and she looked like she was about seven years old. In each hand she was clutching a bunched-up skirt.

I dropped my backpack on the floor and followed her into the living room, an echoey space with floor-to-ceiling windows that practically dumped you into the Hudson River. When she was a child, Lucy's parents had owned a Tibetan import boutique, and their frequent donations to that beleaguered nation sometimes meant they struggled to make the stabilized rent on their Riverside Drive classic six. In marrying Leonard Livingston—the awkward genius who had designed Speed-X, a program that made all other programs run eight times faster—Lucy had found true love and enough money to guarantee an instant identity crisis shot through with a heavy dose of guilt.

As a result, this sprawling loft, which she'd reluctantly agreed to purchase after their wedding, was sparsely furnished with grungy items left over from college days. The Poggenpohl stainless-steel countertops were a playing ground for mismatched plates, jelly glasses, and an assortment of chipped public-radio mugs. The gallery lighting showed off Ansel Adams reprints in plastic frames acquired at Target. There were two couches in the living room, one a gruesome brown plaid covered with an Indian print that was forever slipping to the floor to reveal a historical collection of burns, stains, and rips. The other couch was the recent arrival from Bloomie's, the solitary new item Leonard had insisted on buying amid the uxorial asceticism he was patiently waiting out.

Macy removed the nozzle from her lips long enough to mutter a response to Lucy's suggestion. "If I became a real estate broker, all the houses I sold would burn down."

Lucy took a deep breath through her nose. "I know," she said. "An unemployment-benefits administrator. People would have already lost their jobs."

Macy didn't even look up. "They'd leave the unemployment office and get run over by the M14."

Lucy gripped the skirts even tighter in her fists. "Then something with inanimate objects," she said through her teeth.

"Computers would freeze, produce would carry E. coli, books would turn out to have poisonous ink and kill everyone in the bookstore."

"How about an undertaker?" I suggested, leaning against a white column in the middle of the room. "Your clients would already be dead."

To my great satisfaction, Macy put down her book and glared at me.

"Who are you?"

"Zephyr Zuckerman," I said, and braced myself. Over the last three decades, I had suffered a variety of reactions to my name. "We met at Lucy's wedding in June."

But Macy was in no condition to judge anyone else. She merely looked at the ceiling. Lucy widened her eyes at me, imploring me to fix the situation. She and Leonard were headed to a Hudson Valley bed-and-breakfast for a weekend of Lovemaking with Intent to Conceive.

I nodded toward the bedroom. "Finish packing," I told Lucy.

"Packing?" Macy sat up and fixed her eyes on Lucy like a lion spotting its kill. "Where do you think you're going?"

"Uh-uh." I shook my head at Lucy, whose knuckles were white. "Go. And bring an iron," I added, nodding at the balled-up skirts. Lucy fled.

"I'm going with them," Macy said, slamming her book closed.

"Actually, you're not." I hooked one ankle over the other, as if I were a 1930s gumshoe leaning against a streetlamp.

"You can't stop me." Her blue eyes glowed with indignation.

"Of course I can. You don't even know where they're going. Macy—"

"How do you know my name?"

"What do you mean? You're ruining my friend's life. We all know your name."

"Who's we?"

"Lucy's friends."

"I'm Lucy's friend."

"No, you're her tormentor."

"*No,* I'm making sure she doesn't die like everyone else I've worked for."

I paused for a moment, then tilted my head at her. "By lying on her couch?"

Macy sank back down on the sofa and covered her face with her hands. "It's working so far," she muttered.

"But don't you think Lucy's already safe? I mean, the other women all died within a week of their weddings. She's two months out." It was fun pretending this was a rational conversation.

"That's almost a good point."

"Why almost?"

"Because what if it's just untested? What if the second I leave her, bam, she's gone?"

"You let her go to work, don't you?"

Macy sniffed.

"Don't you?"

"Usually I follow her."

I tried not to show my alarm. "You *follow* her?" Technically, Lucy could take out a restraining order. But any judge confronted with this pathetic creature, with her red-rimmed eyes and a smear of whipped cream across her freckles, would laugh at the request.

"You do *not* understand the bad luck I attract. You should leave now before a meteorite crashes through these windows and takes you to your maker." She stood up, made her way around the enormous island separating the living room from the kitchen, and returned the whipped cream to the gleaming fridge.

"My maker?" I laughed, then stopped when I saw the look of genuine anguish on Macy's face. "It's just that I . . . never mind." This was not the moment to expound on my theological views. "Look, when was the last time you had a drink? Or ate food that doesn't spray? Or went home to your apartment?"

She shook her head stubbornly.

Even I recognized these as inadequate calls to action. Surely, standing here twelve stories up in the air, gazing out at a behemoth cruise liner bellowing its way south from 53rd Street, I could do better.

"Wanna go fishing?" I tried.

"Where?"

"Off the back of Pier 40."

"What do you mean the back?"

"The part that faces New Jersey."

"You mean . . . the *west* side?" She looked at me as if I were a simpleton.

I returned the look. "Yeah, the *Jersey* side."

She headed toward the couch. I blocked her path. I had to keep her ass from hitting that cushion again.

"Okay, you know Lucy's and my friend Mercedes Kim? The one who lives in that building?" I pointed to the glass tower across Perry Street, the fraternal twin to the one we were in.

Macy frowned for a moment, then raised her eyebrows in surprise. "The one who married Dover Carter?"

I nodded. "Dover has a premiere tonight at the Ziegfeld. Red carpet, Brangelina, free food. We could go to that. It might distract you."

Macy guffawed. "We can't just show up at a movie premiere. There's security, guest lists, rope lines. . . ." Macy trailed off as she exhausted her knowledge of Hollywood protocol.

"Yes, but if any Sterling Girl calls Dover's assistant before an event, we can go to whatever he's invited to that night."

"Just like that?"

"Just like that. When he married Mercedes, he got all of us."

"Is he invited to something every night?"

"Pretty much. But he'd usually rather watch Mercedes perform or stay at home."

"She's an actress, too?"

I shook my head. "Violist. Philharmonic. So which do you want to do?"

"You just call him Dover," Macy mused incredulously. "You just call Dover Carter . . . Dover."

"Last option," I said impatiently. "We could buy a couple of boxes of granola bars and hand them out to homeless people."

Macy's face grew stormy with betrayal and she pointed her finger at me. "Don't pull that Pollyanna bullshit with me."

That was the moment I knew I wanted to be friends with Macy St. John.

She waved her arms, looking like an angry bird. "This is not some exercise in wallowing and self-indulgence. I am *cursed*. Do you understand me? I am not fit to have contact with anyone besides Lucy, not until I figure out why she's still alive."

Ultimately, we neither fished nor gawked. Macy meekly agreed that she could use a shower and a change of clothes, and so I accompanied her back to Red Hook. On the subway, she began to tell me her woeful story of a cursed professional life, and we missed our stop and wound up near Prospect Park. We soon found ourselves among a group of happy, tipsy Park Slopers, cheering for the newly invented sport-as-avant-garde-performance called Circle Rules Football. It involved a huge exercise ball, orange pylons, and a healthy dose of self-conscious irony. For the life of us, we couldn't figure out the rules, but it didn't seem to matter, not even to the players.

I wish I could say I was the one who convinced Macy to stop being so superstitious, but ultimately it was good luck that ended her tenure on Lucy's couch. One of the couples on a nearby blanket, swilling Asti Spumante and shouting encouragement to the performers, happened to be former patrons of No Divas. Most significantly, theirs had been the wedding Macy worked on immediately before the disemboweled lion tamer's wedding. Seeing the bride alive and well—albeit in an unflattering baby-doll dress and a poor-quality roots job—did wonders for her outlook. Or, more likely, Macy had come to a point in her depression where she was yearning for just the smallest sign, some event in the outside world that her frazzled brain could grab a hold of and interpret as the end of her curse.

We stayed until it was too dark to see the game/performance. As we left the park, Macy promised to spend the next few days returning all the calls that had gone unanswered and trying to rescue No Divas from its state of near extinction. We parted ways at Grand Army Plaza.

"I feel like a guy," she said sheepishly, sidestepping the flow of suits returning home from Manhattan offices.

"What do you mean?"

"You've spent this entire evening listening to me go on and on and *on*. I didn't ask you one thing about you."

I waved my hand at her. "I'm just glad you're—" I started to say "off Lucy's couch" but caught myself. "Glad you're feeling better."

She scrunched her nose sheepishly. "How fast are you going to call Lucy and tell her you fixed everything?"

"If it were you, how long would you wait?" I felt like I was flirting.

She guffawed. "Please. Me? There'd be skywriting and a blog post before you could say 'Nevins Street.'"

*　*　*

Over the next two years, Macy became the first new confidante I'd made since college. It seemed I'd never know her as well as I knew the Sterling Girls, but I was learning to be comfortable with the fact that I couldn't catalog every scar, every boyfriend, know for certain whether she was more passionate about the Promenade or the High Line, or recount on her behalf an embarrassing incident involving jelly beans and underpants. For the first time in my adult life, I maintained a friendship based not solely on history but on an exhilarating brew of proximity, unmarried status, a love of the city, and a shared desire to remain childless.

And on the glorious blue-skied Monday morning following my rock-climbing debut with Lieutenant Fisk, I was thrilled not to have kids merely so that I could be right here, right now, sipping Sumatra, watching a Weimaraner and a vizsla romp in the plastic pool at the Leroy Street dog run, listening to Macy chatter on about her latest bridal victory. I wasn't worrying about whether a new nanny was slipping nonorganic contraband to my offspring. I wasn't wiped out from night feedings. I wasn't thinking about affording nursery school or saving for college. My day wasn't going to be circumscribed by an obligation to enforce someone's eight o'clock bedtime, with the promise of an hour or two to myself and another adult (with whom conversation would presumably revolve around the diminutive members of the family) before I collapsed into bed to begin the whole exhausting cycle again.

Instead, I was waiting for visiting hours to begin at the psych ward at Bellevue so that I could go have a chat with Jeremy Wedge, who had, apparently against his will, lived to see another day. After that I would go to the office to check in with Pippa and catch up on e-mail. Then I'd head home at around five and take a nap before going out again. I had a few options for the evening, including a free dinner cruise around Manhattan, given to Macy and one guest courtesy of a No Divas client. Macy had calculated for the bride that the wedding shoes she wanted would average out to a hundred dollars an hour and would never be seen beneath her floor-length gown unless she hiked up her dress and pointed. Macy had talked her down to a pair of comfortable white sandals from Payless for thirteen bucks. As thanks, the relieved woman, proprietor of a fleet of event boats around the city, had offered Macy the free ride. We could go or not go, and the decision could be made at the last minute.

Two dalmatians streaked by and I steadied my coffee cup against the force of their tails.

"Remind me, which train do we have to catch tomorrow

for dinner in Hellsville?" Macy stretched her pale, freckled legs and rested her head on the back of the bench. "I need time to wash and dry my straitjacket."

"Do you have an extra for me?"

"At the very least, I'm gonna wear old, dowdy clothes. I suggest you do the same," Macy added ominously.

"Yeah, and exactly how much of the night are you going to spend within spit-up distance of the babies?" I asked, nudging her foot with mine.

"It's not for the babies. It's because if we don't look even a fraction as exhausted and miserable as Lucy, she'll start crying."

If my life and Macy's were a series of various freedoms, Lucy's was a suit of chain mail. To be sure, at the beginning, her troubles were self-inflicted. Three years earlier, not long after she'd begun dating Leonard, Lucy called me in the throes of indecision over whether to keep her name or take his.

I sat up in bed. "You're engaged?"

Gregory groaned beside me, not because his slumber was being disturbed but because, regardless of which Sterling Girl was on the line, this news would disrupt his foreseeable future.

"No, not exactly." She sounded out of breath.

"What do you mean 'not exactly,' Luce? And are you *exercising*?" I accused her.

"I'm trying to find matching lids for the Tupperware and, no, we're not engaged. But we will be, and then what? I don't want to change my name!" she wailed, as a drawer slammed in the background. "I love that people ask whether I'm related to Alice B. I love that people don't always know how to pronounce it. It makes me feel unique. And, Zephyr, I love Leonard, I really do, but I just don't like his last name. Do you?"

This was a terrifically loaded question on two counts. First, I couldn't remember Leonard's last name, which made me a certifiably lousy friend. If I'd known that he was a matrimonial candidate, I would have dislodged some other bit of trivia from my brain and made room for it. Second, even if I did know what it was, in the name of future peacekeeping there was no way I was going to give anything other than a noncommittal response.

"His name is fine. Whichever you choose, you'll be fine," I said smoothly.

"Really?" Lucy asked hopefully. "You don't think Lucy Livingston is too much alliteration?"

Livingston, of course.

"Actually, I think it sounds pretty great," I told her truthfully. "A great stage name."

"Plus, I haven't met his mother yet—what if I don't want to be another Mrs. Livingston?"

A year later, with Macy firmly steering Lucy clear of her own proclivity for melodrama, Lucy was still Lucy Toklas, but the blinding bling on her left hand proclaimed to all the world that she was, now and forever, Mrs. Leonard. As it turned out, Lucy's name-keeping decision was studiously ignored by her mother-in-law, who gave the newlyweds household linens monogrammed with Lucy's would-have-been initials: "LL." It was a portentous gift, and if we'd all known what lay ahead, we might have advised Lucy to melt the ring and flee to another borough.

Not long after their wedding, Lucy and Leonard's conception project moved declivitously from romantic getaways in the Hudson Valley to an IVF clinic in a Manhattan office building. The moment it was confirmed that little Alan and Amanda were certain arrivals, Leonard summoned his thus-far-missing backbone and insisted to Lucy, a lifelong New Yorker, that they move out of the city. A few months later, on bed rest in her new four-bedroom colonial in an upstate town called Hillsville—five minutes' drive from his parents—Lucy wept and blamed the surfeit of hormones for her temporary but disastrous insanity.

The twins were now thirteen months old, and Macy and I, and occasionally Mercedes, hopped a Metro-North train whenever we could bear it. Sacks of Murray's bagels and City Bakery marshmallows hanging from our wrists, we vacillated over the best approach to comfort: Agree that car culture was soul-sapping and remind Lucy she could always move back or point out the benefits of life with a lawn? Agree that her mother-in-law, around whom Leonard shrank to half his size, really was the most oppressive human being we'd ever met outside of a Dickens novel or point out how helpful it was to have her take care of the twins, even if the first thing she did upon arrival was change them into outfits she preferred?

"Seriously," Macy said, drawing in her legs as the dalmatians made another frenzied circuit past our bench, their soaking-wet coats brushing against us. "I don't even know how to have a conversation with Lucy anymore."

"Don't say that. That's her worst fear!" I chastised, feeling sorrier than ever for my upstate friend. I wiped water from my legs with my hands and then tried to dry my hands on the bench.

"She *says* she doesn't want to bore us with talk about the kids or complain about Lenore, but she has nothing else to talk about, and then if you talk about your own life, she gets that hangdog look."

"So talk to her about weddings."

"Are you kidding?" Macy used a paper napkin to wipe away a wet streak on her skirt. "Then she gets nostalgic for the days when wedding planning was all she had to worry about."

I glanced at Macy to gauge the true extent of her exasperation with Lucy. Surely, this woman who tutored, ladled, baked, and phone-banked for no fewer than four different service agencies had a little extra room in her heart for a friend. It turned out that Macy's hostility to my early granola-bar-distribution proposal was atypical and that her own aversion to parenthood was driven by a desire to serve many rather than just a few. There were times when it was clear that Macy had an easier time caring about strangers than about her friends. Well, why not? It *was* easier to give someone all your energy and focus between three and five on a Monday afternoon than to give it all day every day.

I couldn't believe Macy's friendship fuse was this short. She had shown extraordinary patience with me as I navigated one failed volunteering attempt after another. Inspired by her insistence that refusing to burden ourselves with financial and emotional dependents did not make us socially irresponsible, morally deficient, or—that blackest of character stains—selfish, I eagerly followed her to The Door, a drop-in center for teens. During my second tutoring session, though, the heavy-lidded, multipierced dropout across the table did *not* suddenly look up—eyes shining with the beauty of the John Updike passage I'd assigned—and declare herself Eager to Learn. She left the program soon afterward, and I slunk away, in search of another, hopefully less boring means of giving back.

Macy gently prodded me toward food pantries, park spruce-ups, a school for the deaf, and even boatbuilding with shelter kids, but I was a poor fit for all of them. Finally I settled on accompanying her to the Hudson Street Nursing Home every few weeks to chat with residents. Some were angry with dementia, some were eager to treat me as family, and there was one who took enormous pleasure in pretending to me that she'd been the mistress of President Kennedy, Robert Kennedy, and Robert McNamara—simultaneously.

The time passed quickly there, but, unlike Macy, I couldn't pretend to myself that the reason I wanted to remain childless was so that I could help Mrs. Lefkowitz finish her scrambled eggs or try to instill political sensitivity into a half-blind, mostly deaf racist World War II vet named Mr. Frankenmuller.

"So how many party boats does this bride own?" I asked, deciding just to be grateful that Macy wasn't backing out of the upstate trip altogether.

"Four. Two of them she won in the divorce from her last husband." Macy slurped the dregs of her coffee.

"You don't think she's going for boats five and six with this husband, do you?"

Macy shuddered. She perceived a divorce by her clients as a personal failure on her part, an irrational attitude that confounded me.

A jogger unlatched the gate and let herself in to the dog run. We both sat straight up as she headed to the doggie pool, lifted the hose, and doused her head under the cold stream.

"Uh-oh," I said.

"Here he comes." Macy covered her face with her hands and peeked out between her fingers. "I can't watch."

The self-proclaimed mayor of this nine-hundred-square-foot patch of concrete stalked over as forcefully as a person can stalk while wearing bright-orange testicle-outlining Lycra biking shorts. His bald, freckled pate reflected sunlight, and a gold chain with a heavy crucifix swung against his bare gray-haired chest. He yelled as he approached the pool.

"Hey! HEY! That is for the doggies *only*." He put his hands on his naturally padded hips.

The jogger put down the hose and looked around.

"Do you mean me?" she asked, confused.

"Do you see any other bipeds taking advantage of the doggies' cooling system?"

The jogger's mouth fell open.

The mayor wagged a finger at her. "And where's your doggie? No people unaccompanied by canines allowed in here. New York City Parks Department *rules*."

The jogger wiped her dripping face with her arm and sized up her foe. We could see her making the do-I-or-don't-I-get-into-it? decision.

She shook her head at him and walked out, taking the high road, while he yelled at her all the way to the double gate. Actually, this tirade, which we'd heard before, was minor compared to the one he bestowed upon those who carelessly opened one gate before the other was shut.

It looked like the jogger was going to stay above the fray, but once she was safely outside the dog run and had resumed jogging, she tossed out a parting "Psychotic faggot asshole!"

"Frigid Republican bitch!" he parried without pause, then rolled his eyes at us, as though we were compatriots in his battle against the dogless. He headed back to his bench, his encased thighs swishing, and resumed his post.

We had no idea why he didn't oust us from this four-legged haven. We suspected he thought we were a gay couple and that he was wont to make exceptions as he saw fit. Or it could be that we'd been coming for so long that he'd forgotten we didn't have dogs.

Macy stood up and tossed her cup into the trash. "Ah, now I can start my day. Coffee and a hostile exchange that didn't involve me. Invigorating." She stretched her arms wide. "Headed to the office?" she asked casually.

If Macy had noticed my unusual new schedule, she'd refrained from asking me about it directly. I suspected she was trying to spare me my own blabbing tendencies, and I tossed her a grateful glance. In fact, her self-control only increased my urge to tell her about the Greenwich Village Hotel.

"I am," I said truthfully, slinging on my backpack and

following her past the garbage can to the gates. "But first I have to go do an interview over at Bellevue."

"Interesting case?" she asked, opening the gate.

I thought for a moment. Right now the only interesting thing about the hotel case was why I was still on it.

"Not really."

"Even though you met this rock-climbing firefighter?"

So I hadn't been *completely* tight-lipped about the investigation. But I had remained vague about the circumstances surrounding my meeting Lieutenant Fisk, an introduction I couldn't possibly be expected to keep to myself. Early on, when a courtship was not yet a relationship, a large percentage of the fun was had in the reporting and the analysis. Going rock climbing at ten-thirty on a first date with a firefighter was exciting, but dissecting it later with Macy made it much more so.

"Even though," I said.

"Are you going to call him?" she asked as we waited to cross the West Side Highway. Cars whizzed in front of us, cyclists behind us.

"Undecided. I'm having trouble remembering how I know whether I'm interested in someone."

"Excuse me?" She raised one eyebrow, a move she'd confessed to teaching herself to do when she was twenty-five by holding the stationary brow in place with her hand.

"You know what I mean. I'm all out of whack after Gregory."

"You make him sound like a car accident."

"No, but my sensors are dulled. No first date is going to pass muster if I compare it to a terrific three-year relationship. I don't remember how to assess a new guy."

"So don't compare, don't assess, just have fun. Go out with him, go out with other guys."

I glanced at her as we headed east on Morton. "When's the

last time you took your own advice?" Macy had fully recovered from feeling like she was the kiss of death in her professional life. But after two different men sprained their ankles immediately following dinner-at-Momofuku/dessert-at-Veniero's second dates with her, she had declared indefinite single status.

She wagged her finger at me warningly. "We're not talking about me."

"Macy, come on. You're not really going to stay celibate for the rest of your life." She picked up her pace, as though she was trying to ditch the conversation. I hurried to keep up with her. "Want me to see if the lieutenant has any firefighting buddies?"

"Don't you dare," she said, stopping short at the corner of Hudson Street.

I stood my ground. "It's actually an excellent idea."

"If you do say so yourself."

"You're small potatoes compared to burning buildings. A firefighter couldn't possibly be felled by you and your lousy mojo."

She exhaled through her nose. "I'll consider it."

"Have your girl call my girl," I said, shaking my head.

I started walking, but Macy pulled me back. "Zeph, why do you care whether I date? What does it have to do with you?"

The answer was simple—I cared about her—but that truth would be met with suspicion.

"Nothing, Mace. It has nothing to do with me. It's just that I assume this isn't really the end of the road for you and relationships. I don't believe that, at thirty, you're done with penises and are devoting your life to work. And since I don't believe it, I thought it would be *fun* to help you date again."

An older woman wearing a John Lennon T-shirt and peasant skirt halted, prompting the mangy dog she was pushing in a shopping cart to emit a feeble bark. She looked Macy up and down and said, "My son is a dermatologist. He's thirty-five and could stand to lose a few pounds, but he's a good boy. You want his number?"

Macy had been poised to give me her opinion about my meddling, but now she closed her mouth, startled. The woman dug under the dog's ratty pillow and held out a business card.

"Think about it," she said. "Redheads are prone to melanomas. He'd look out for you, so that's a bonus."

Chapter 4

As far as the hospital personnel were concerned, I was now Jeremy Wedge's sister. I squished myself against the back wall of a Bellevue Hospital elevator and closed my eyes against my own stupidity. Two nights earlier, I had seen fit to jeopardize my undercover status because of the length of a guy's eyelashes, but here, trying to gain entry to the most notorious psych ward in the city, I chose to keep my badge hidden and instead get upstairs on wits and artful deception.

Two young doctors stepped in, murmuring quietly to each other over a chart. I studied them surreptitiously, with their stethoscopes and high-heeled shoes and pagers, and, for the briefest of moments, I envied them. In another lifetime, I'd spent a year at med school and then quit, denying myself the chance to attain the cool sophistication that comes from earning your prescription pad. Their white coats broadcast years of hard work and an acquired knowledge that was universally recognized as useful to all of humankind. I—finally—had a real job, one that I loved, but it seemed I was destined to always be on the scrappy side of things.

The doors opened on the eighteenth floor and I squeezed

past the doctors, hoping they wouldn't wrinkle their noses at the stench of failure. I glanced back, but no one pointed and yelled, "Hey, that's a Johns Hopkins dropout!" I exhaled and hustled off in search of room 1805.

After passing through a second security checkpoint, where my backpack was checked for photographs—potentially disruptive—I headed down the hall. I dodged meal carts and mop buckets and a woman in a wheelchair reciting the Pledge of Allegiance and found Jeremy's to be the last room on the antiseptic corridor. The hand-scrawled sign on the door said, *Window: Wedge.* Good thing his last name wasn't Ledge.

Sun flooded the room, making it atonally cheerful. I flashed an apologetic smile at Jeremy's roommate, a shirtless man with a many-layered belly and Elton John glasses. I did a double take at the crisp white toque atop his head, but he kept his eyes glued to the television above him.

I peeked around the nausea-green curtain separating the two beds to find Jeremy Wedge fully dressed, shoes on, perched at the edge of his neatly made bed. His ankle was crossed at his knee as he peered through his glasses at *The New York Times.* He could have been riding the 6 train to work.

"Jeremy?"

"It's Mr. Wedge," he spat, not looking up. "Time for another interview with an incompetent resident? Or is the asshole phlebotomist who couldn't get a job at a mortuary gonna stick me again?"

"It's your sister," I told him.

"I don't have a—" He whipped around. His eyes looked hollow, and the orange glint of stubble on his face did not do for him what it does for Brad Pitt. "What the—what are you doing here?" I almost took a step back under the force of his angry glare.

What *was* I doing here? Good question, and one I was prepared for. I'd observed Jeremy and Hutchinson in the hotel bar enough times to learn the best route to a productive conversation with them, and it wasn't, in fact, the price of rice in China. Impossible to pull off with Hutchinson, and just barely manageable with his slightly less offensive relation: I put on my best bashful look, bit my lip, and even cast my gaze downward.

"I was worried about you, Jeremy. Really worried." I made my voice plaintive and shyly proffered the bag of red grapes I'd bought from the fruit cart on the corner of 27th Street.

He narrowed his eyes at me, suspicious but hopeful. "What do you mean?"

Oh, he wanted to believe I spent my nights yearning for his metrosexually manicured hands on my body. Or at least that I wanted to hear him drone on about the rare genetic mutation he'd written about in *Science* when he was a grad student at Columbia. It had actually been his adviser's discovery and Jeremy was third author, but that didn't stop him from trying to pass it off as an accomplishment on par with a solo voyage to the Arctic Circle. Vanity, thy name is man.

"Hutchinson wouldn't tell me anything." Technically, this was true, as I hadn't crossed paths with him since he'd followed Jeremy to the hospital on Saturday night. "I wanted to see if you were okay."

"I'm fine," he said huffily, shaking out the paper and resuming reading, or pretending to. "As you can see, I'm perfectly fine. Only furious to be kept in this place full of lunatics, against my will." It was an effort for him to keep his voice calm.

"But, Jeremy," I said, summoning a meekness I didn't even know I could feign. "There was—" I put the grapes on the windowsill and looked at him over the paper.

"What? There was what?" He looked at me defiantly.

"An empty bottle of Ambien."

"So I've been told."

"You didn't take it?"

"Why do you care? Why did you say you were here?"

Because I want to know why the label was crossed out and why you were going through the Whitcombs' garbage.

"Because," I said, pretending to gather my courage. "Because I care about you."

He rubbed at his face roughly. "Interesting timing to profess your undying love."

I say "care," he hears "undying love." Whatever other problems Jeremy Wedge had at this moment, low self-esteem was not one of them.

"Zephyr," he said wearily. "I did not try to kill myself. But they don't believe me. And so here I am, in this germ factory, perfectly healthy, doomed to contract something or be victimized by an insane inmate the longer I remain captive."

"You didn't take the Ambien?"

"I have never needed anything beyond a glass of sherry to relax," he said haughtily.

But Pippa had placed a few choice calls on Sunday, including one to the East Hampton residence of the chief of Bellevue's psych department, who happened to be a fellow Lucite enthusiast she had befriended over a decade of traveling the auction circuit. Dr. Gross had confirmed that Jeremy's blood had been filled to overflowing with the tranquilizer zolpidem, familiarly known to the rest of my socioeconomic circle as Ambien.

"But there was that empty bottle—"

"It wasn't mine!" he shouted at me. This was a sore topic that had, clearly, already been exhausted. "It wasn't mine. But they don't believe me." His voice wavered.

"So what do you think made you so sick?" I asked gently, crossing my arms.

A pink plastic water pitcher suddenly flew through the air

and hit the television, sending ice chips flying to our side of the curtain.

"That is NOT how you make a fucking reduction, you stupid bitch!" Jeremy's roommate screamed, and I held my breath, waiting to see if an army of hospital aides would rush to the scene. Nothing.

"Guy owns five restaurants," Jeremy whispered. "Apparently it's four too many. He's not allowed to watch cooking shows, but there was no room for him on the floor without televisions. The staff has better things to do than keep track of Rachael Ray's airtimes."

"What would happen if I offered him your leftover tuna salad?" I suggested quietly. "Cardiac arrest?"

Probably for the first time since he'd been admitted, Jeremy allowed himself a wan smile. Then he tossed the newspaper on the bed and ran his hands through his bed-greasy hair.

"Can you do *anything* to get me out?" He looked at me like a dog begging for scraps.

"I can try," I lied.

His eyes lit up. "Wait, did you say you told them you were my sister?"

I knew where he was going and cursed myself again for my stealth routine at the front desk.

"I did, but—"

"Zephyr," he said, looking deep into my eyes. I resisted the urge to shrink back. "Zephyr, if you really care about me, sign me out of here. Hutchinson signed me in for an extended stay, but *you*, you can undo it." He took one of my hands in his. It was such a corny gesture that I almost laughed but coughed it down. Absurdly, I was on the right track.

"Jeremy," I said, going along with his Oscar performance, "I will. But you have to tell me everything you know. So that I can help you."

"I know what made me sick." He dropped my hand. "It was—" He shook his head.

"You need to talk about it," I said, assuming the ingratiating tones of a late-night Lite FM talk-show host. "Tell me what was on your mind that evening."

"Oh, for God's sake, Zephyr, I did *not* try to kill myself. It was the herbs that stupid bitch gave me! They almost fucking killed me."

"A woman you picked—I mean *met* at the bar gave you herbs?"

"No," he said petulantly. "That lady who lives at the hotel. That old lady."

I thought for a moment. "Mrs. Hodges?" I said incredulously. "You think she did this to you?"

"I don't know her name. Asian," he muttered. He lay back on the bed and covered his face with his arms.

I gaped at him. The man really was in trouble—he was suicidal *and* delusional. A wave of sympathy washed over me and I reassessed my entire mission, which I now suspected I was handling a little too cavalierly.

"She gave me a special drink. In the bar on Saturday night."

I waited and he looked exasperated. I was exasperated right back.

"Jeremy, this isn't Mad Libs. I can't fill in the story for you."

"Oh, fuck, fine." He punched the pillow and turned on his side. "A couple of weeks ago, she saw me trying to . . . to start a conversation with a woman. I wasn't getting much of a response."

"You mean you hit on someone and she wasn't interested?" I clarified.

He glared at me, which I took as an affirmative.

"So she said she had a remedy." He rolled his eyes at me as though I was the one suggesting such a preposterous thing.

"A love potion," I said, trying to keep a straight face.

"USE MORELS, NOT CHANTERELLES, YOU STUPID CUNT!" bellowed the roommate.

"No, not a love potion," Jeremy snapped. "More like, you know, like . . ."

"A love potion," I repeated.

"Yeah," he conceded, humiliated. "A love potion. I'm a scientist, a geneticist who's been published in *Science*," he whispered with anguish, his disgust with himself penetrating every syllable. "And I fell for a *potion*."

"It happens," I said charitably, thinking, *God, that really is desperate and stupid.*

"So she gave me this drink Saturday night," he continued. "I had wanted to have . . . a conversation with that Australian woman on the fifth floor."

"You mean the one from New Zealand?"

He shrugged. "Whatever."

I wondered how he'd feel if someone said, *Yeah, that Texan, New Yorker, whatever, lives on that big continent between the two oceans.*

"And I drank it and now here I am."

Lacuna beach. Elision island. Stop playing games, you bullheaded redhead. I cleared my throat.

"Mrs. Hodges, Mrs. Kimiko Hodges, gave you a drink. What time did you drink it?"

"Around eight-thirty," he said sullenly. "Right after she gave it to me. It tasted like lemonade."

"You drank it there at the bar or up in the room?"

"Right there."

"But the woman you were interested in was out to dinner."

"You keep tabs on all the guests?" He looked at me oddly.

"They were memorable."

"Well, anyway," he continued, "I drank it right there at the bar."

"Because there was another woman there?"

"What are you, some fucking morality patrol?" he sneered. "It's not your business who I drank it for."

"Definitely not," I agreed. "I just want to get the whole story so I can talk to the attending and try to get you out," I reminded him. "You drank it and then what?"

He mashed his lips together and inhaled loudly through his nose.

"I went over and started talking to her."

"How'd it go?"

"Fine, thanks," he snapped.

"Then?"

"Then I didn't feel so well. So I excused myself and went to find a room to lie down in."

I nodded and tried to make my next question sound casual.

"Why room 502?"

He looked at me sharply. "What do you mean?"

"I mean," I had to tread carefully, "why choose a used room, a dirty room? Why not go somewhere nicer?"

I refrained from asking whether his cousin had been kind enough to let him in or whether Jeremy inexplicably had free access to all the rooms. Family status notwithstanding, I was pretty sure Ballard McKenzie was not in the habit of handing out master keys.

"It was open," he said coldly. Any nascent trust he had in me vanished at that moment.

"Can I ask you something else?"

"No."

"Why were you going through their garbage? The guests' garbage."

"None of your fucking business!" he roared. "Are you *accusing* me of something?!" He stood up and I moved toward the curtain. As if the gastronomically unhinged patient in the next bed could come to my rescue.

I remembered a diversion I'd learned from my friend Tag, the Sterling Girl who had turned a career of studying tapeworms into a tightrope of international adventure. She was the only person I knew who had required the protective services of a U.S. embassy on not one but two occasions. Whether she was in a standoff with poachers off the coast of Senegal or staring down the host of a party she had crashed because she'd forgotten to load up on local currency and couldn't buy dinner, Tag brazenly took the high and mighty road. Turn the tables and momentarily confuse your adversary.

"I saved your life, you asshole! I'm trying to help. Forget it." I put my hand on the curtain, hoping to distract him from his suspicion of my suspicion. "Good luck."

"No, wait, Zephyr. I'm sorry! Don't leave!"

But I'd asked too many questions and needed to get out before I blew my cover. Besides which, for now, I knew what I needed to know, including the fact that Jeremy Wedge was safer here in the psychiatric ward of Bellevue Hospital than he was roaming free in Greenwich Village.

* * *

Two hours later, I was at my office, contemplating the fine line between insanity and its perceived opposite. Three detectives were draped over the sides of my cubicle—which they had apparently mistaken for a break room—trading stories that could easily have kept a psych resident busy for days.

"So the whole place is goin' apeshit lookin' for this guy's freakin' BlackBerry." Tommy O. was gesticulating broadly, despite the hot cup of Dunkin' Donuts coffee in his hand. His face was freshly shaved and pink, growing pinker as he spun a tale of urban spectacle. "And he's got blood down the front of his shirt, not a dribble but soaked through like a fuckin' maxi pad—pardon my French, Zepha—only no one's askin' about the blood. They're turning over the sofa cushions, people are spillin' their hot joe, flippin' cartwheels. Hell, people don't look for missin' kids this hard. And all of a sudden the guy turns to this lady and says somethin' and SHE starts freakin' out. Screamin', 'You accusin' me? You accusin' me of taking your goddamn BlackBerry? How fuckin' dare you? See, I gotta Treo, whaddo I need your fuckin' BlackBerry for?!' and all that shit. And it's gettin' ugly, but what the fuck am I gonna do? Yell, 'S.I.C., everybody freeze?'"

Eric, a twenty-year veteran of the NYPD, and Alex, a probie in my class who had actually run away from home to join the circus as an acrobat, before winding up here—"the other greatest show on earth," he liked to call it—guffawed appreciatively. The SIC's low profile was a constant source of emasculation among many of the detectives, but our cases tended to be less dangerous and at least as interesting as the best ones over at the NYPD—and the pensions on par—so they regularly washed down their pride with caffeine and alcohol.

"So I tell the guy to calm down," Tommy continued, letting fly a drop of coffee-colored spit, "but, right, that just pisses him off even more, so I ask him his name and he goes, 'Christmas.' And I say, 'What?' And he goes, 'Christmas,' again. So I think he's being fresh and I says, 'Yuh name is Christmas? *Christmas?* Idonfuckinbelieveit, show me some ID.' And now he's really ticked off, so he whips out his driver's license and, oh shit, the guy's name is Chris Smith and he has a lisp badder'n my sister-in-law's! Can you believe that?"

Tommy slapped the side of my cubicle so hard a photo of Gregory and me slipped from behind a stack of tacked-up business cards and floated to the floor.

"Aw, that's sad, man, that's sad. Imagine goin' through life like that?" Eric shook his head and sipped at his own coffee, kept warm in a standard Greek cup sold by the guy at the newsstand in the lobby.

"What about the blood?" I asked, giving up on ignoring them in the hopes that they would disperse and allow me to get some work done. I eyed the photo beside my sandal and wondered if I could retrieve it without anyone noticing.

"Oh yeah, right." Tommy took a long swig of coffee and tossed it in my trash, where it slowly stained the contents of the bin. "So for a second I think about pretending I have a lisp, too, you know, so he won't feel so bad, but, whatever, this guy's got so many problems, it ain't gonna help. So some Puerto Rican babysitter finally finds his damn phone—now, don't go gettin' all PC on me, Zepha, she was Puerto Rican, all right. Don't go reportin' me to Poker Pippa for cultural insensitivity. . . ." Tommy's eyes lit up and he gave my chair a little jiggle with his foot.

I knew what was expected of me—to play the part of the lily-white overeducated Manhattan innocent to their seasoned blue-collar outer-borough street smarts.

"Wha—I didn't say anything!" I protested. "Calling a spade a spade isn't racist!"

"Oh shit, you callin' Puerto Ricans spades?!" Eric yelped, and they all cackled. I rolled my eyes at Alex, in particular, who had managed to obtain a master's in philosophy during his spare moments away from somersaulting onto the shoulders of squat, muscled men in sequined unitards.

"You mean 'spic,'" I said, a second before realizing it was a trap.

"Ohh, ohh, you said 'spic,'" they screeched. "I'm tellin' Pippa!"

I sighed and waited out the ribbing. They were cracking themselves up.

Finally I interrupted. "So, the blood. What about the blood?"

"Yeah, yeah, okay." Tommy wiped his eyes. "So after the Puerto Rican babysitter finds the guy's BlackBerry in the bathroom, he actually orders a cup of coffee and sits down! And then he starts talkin' to himself. And it wasn't a Bluetooth—I checked. He's just sittin' there talkin' to himself. And I'm feeling sorry for the guy, so I go over and say, 'Hey, you need any help?' I'm thinkin' the least I can do is buy the guy some Clorox or somethin', right? And what the fuck, he spills this whole goddamn confession to me. He just came from stabbing his girlfriend. Upstairs. Killed her, then came down for a fuckin' double espresso and has the whole goddamn place searchin' for his BlackBerry."

"That was this morning?" I asked, my mouth hanging open slightly.

"On the way to fuckin' work!" He grinned and looked at his hand and seemed surprised to find it empty. "Anyone wanna go get coffee?"

"What were you doing in a café, fancy pants?" Eric teased. "Thought you were a loyal Dunkin' man."

"Oh, man," Tommy gushed. "Cuz they got this soda bread in there, real homemade Irish soda bread. I think they dug up my grandma and she's back there makin' it."

"Wait!" I yelped incredulously. "What about the guy who killed his girlfriend?"

Tommy squinted at me and shrugged. "Him? I collared 'im. What else was I gonna do? I brought him downtown and handed him over to Central. He's their fuckin' problem now."

The point of the story was the lisp and "Christmas," not the apprehension of a freshly minted murderer. After nearly three years, I was still adjusting to the vastly different ways that punch lines were viewed around here.

"Gentlemen," I said, trying to clear my head, "it's been real. But I need you to take your coffee klatch somewhere else."

"Ain'tcha gonna pick up yuh picture of Romeo?" Tommy said slyly, nodding at the downed photo of Gregory.

"Didn'tcha hear? They're ovah. Oh. Va." Eric confirmed with a slicing motion of his hand.

I dropped my head to my keyboard. I knew what was coming.

"No way. No way!" Tommy exclaimed, rolling in a chair from Letitia Humphrey's empty cubicle, plunking down, and putting his face right up in mine. "He was an awesome guy. You givin' up an NYPD detective? You ain't gonna do better than that, Zepha."

"He's right," Alex agreed, nodding grimly.

"You think you're Pippa?" Tommy said, so close I could see the rough and shiny texture of his jowls. He lowered his voice. "Listen, you don't wanna end up like the commish. Smaht lady, great boss, but you don't want that. She's lonely, Zepha, I'm tellin' ya."

"What makes you think *she* ditched *him*?" Eric teased.

Tommy's face grew stormy. He picked up the photo and flicked it as though drying a Polaroid. "Did that bastard leave you? Did he break up with you? Because I'll go over theah—"

"No, no, I ended it." I took the picture from him, touched by the avuncular, if somewhat violent, sentiment.

"Why? Why would you do somethin' stupid like that?" Tommy chastised me. "You shoulda married him. And don't tell me you ain't ready. I'm sicka you kids in your twenties with your fancy college degrees shirking responsibility and refusin' to grow up. I had four kids by the time I was thirty." He leaned back and crossed his arms like a school principal awaiting an explanation for a playground transgression.

"You do nothing but complain about your kids, Tommy!" I protested. "This one's an idiot, that one's gonna get himself killed, that one you're gonna kill if she winds up pregnant—"

Tommy *tsk*ed and waved his hand at me, a gesture that summed up the sea of differences in our approaches to family relationships.

"Are these men bothering you, Zephyr?" Pippa materialized beside my colleagues, who immediately straightened up.

"Morning, Commissioner," Eric said politely. "Tommy was tellin' us about his collar at the coffee shop this morning."

"Mmm." Pippa raised her eyebrows. "Actually, the DA's office just rang. His majesty Millenhaus took time out of his busy day calling press conferences to acknowledge the S.I.C.'s help. Not publicly, of course—we wouldn't want to let on that agencies cooperate." She turned to Tommy. "Your man wasn't just anybody, O'Hara. You nabbed the Con Leche Lech. Thank goodness you just happened to be engaging in the rare act of purchasing coffee."

The four of us emitted a collective gasp. The "Con Leche Lech," as the *Post* had christened him, or the "moLESter"— the preferred moniker of the *Daily News*—had been terrorizing the Lower East Side and dominating tabloid headlines for six weeks. On five different occasions, the cops had been called to the apartments of murdered young actresses and artists, all of whom were making ends meet by working as baristas in various coffee bars around the neighborhood. At the site of each strangling, stabbing, or smothering was a full mug of coffee with the women's initials lacing the surface in spoiled milk.

"No shi—no kiddin'?" Tommy's usual cloak of swagger dropped away for a moment and an innocent awe peeked through, a genuine pleasure in having made the world a mi-

croscopically safer place. This was why these guys put up
with boredom, danger, red tape, insufficient recognition, and
an inscrutable polka-dotted boss. Nearly every one of the two
hundred men and women who roamed these flickering fluorescent halls with the standard-issue gray ceiling tiles genuinely wanted to make a difference in the city. The talented
ones understood that it wasn't as simple as good guys and
bad guys.

"Poor, sick schmuck," Eric murmured.

"Those girls. Their families," said Alex.

I had nothing to add, as I was suddenly awash in a dis-
honorable wave of frustrated envy. Dumb luck in the shape
of a baked good had brought credibility and kudos to my colleague, and yet here I was scrolling futilely through the DMV
database and coming up empty. I didn't even know what I
was looking for.

Everyone was looking at me.

"Good detective work, Tommy," I finally said. "Lucky for
Gotham you gotta have your soda bread," I tossed at him.

Tommy put me in a quick headlock and tousled my hair.
"That's what I'm tawwwwkin' about!" I'd won a few points.

"O'Hara," Pippa said sternly, and I held my breath, wondering if she was going to chastise him. "Nice work. I doubt
very much whether he would have confessed to just anybody."

Tommy waved her away, but I could see he was pleased.

"All right, off you all go. Zephyr might want to work." I
watched as Pippa and the three men dispersed through the
maze of cubicles, grateful that the secrecy of my case inhib-
ited Pippa from asking me for an update on my unremarkable
progress.

I turned back to the gray screen of the DMV database,
which had turned up exactly nothing on Samantha Kimiko

Hodges. (Interestingly, though, I discovered that three of the four men I'd dated before Gregory had lied to me about their real heights.) I wasn't surprised that Hodges didn't have a driver's license. She was in good company with the enormous population of nondriving New Yorkers who toted their passports to bars for identification.

Just as I was trying to remember the last time I'd been carded at a bar, my desk phone rang. Lucy. Guiltily, I hesitated before I picked it up. I didn't feel like listening to another depressed rant, but I wasn't getting much done anyway.

"Hi, Luce," I said, preemptively sympathetic, my standard tone with her since she and Leonard had headed for the hills.

"Do you know what she said to me?!" screeched a fruit bat. "Do you know what she actually fucking said to me!"

I nudged out the bottom drawer of my corpse-gray filing cabinet and rested my feet on it.

"Okay, so, mind you, this is after I've gone out of my way to find her this goddamn make-your-own-seltzer maker. She was complaining about how they go through so much in a week and they're so heavy to carry up from their garage and she hates all the plastic bottles—like this woman really gives a flying fuck about the environment. Okay, maybe she does, I don't know. . . ."

"Luce?"

"So I get her this really thoughtful gift, right?"

"Extremely thoughtful," I assured her.

"And do you know what she says? She goes, 'I went online and saw how much it cost. Is that really how you should be spending my son's money?'"

I let my feet drop to the floor and leaned forward in amazement. "No. No one really says things like that. Are you *sure*?"

"Positive," Lucy said triumphantly. "This is what I'm living with. Well, this plus two drooling, peeing, pooping, puking bundles of joy." She spat the words.

This was getting scary. It's not that we didn't take Lucy's rants seriously when she first moved upstate, but we took them with a grain of entertainment. Her stories of bad mommy-hood and miserable suburbanism seemed in line with the current zeitgeist of parenting one-downmanship and the ancient practice of equating cul-de-sac living with soullessness. But there was a hardness to her voice I'd never heard before, a desperation beneath the in-law outrage.

"Macy and I are still coming up tomorrow night. Hang in there," I cooed, unsure whether Macy was angry with me after this morning's tiff about her dating philosophy. Once the dermatologist's mother/advocate had trundled off along Hudson Street, Macy and I had exchanged flat goodbyes and headed in opposite directions.

"You are? You're still coming? You don't hate being with me in my boring house with my hyperactive babies? My God, you're the best." She sounded dangerously close to tears.

"We are," I said firmly. "We are coming." I warded off the uncomfortable knowledge that part of why I was able to tolerate an overnight in the Hillsville House of Misery was anthropological fascination. Plus, and this made me feel even worse, it was very easy to win points for being a great friend. Lucy was so desperate for any kind of help that if I trailed the twins for an hour while they turned their thirty-second attention spans to everything from licking the refrigerator to unrolling the toilet paper, she was obscenely grateful. In truth, Alan and Amanda were extremely cute in small doses.

"I do love them," she assured me, her voice wavering.

"I know."

"I mean, I think I love them. I can't tell. Zephyr, I can't tell!" The floodgates opened.

Tommy walked by my cubicle.

"Zepha, wanna go to the courthouse and see your street-light guy get sentenced?"

I pointed at the phone and looked at him like, *Does this not mean the same thing in your country?*

He grinned. "Ya just tawkin' to ya girlfriend. Get back to work!" He gave my cubicle wall a thump and left.

"I know, you have to go," Lucy whimpered.

"I kind of do," I said apologetically. I hated to hang up when she sounded so despondent. "Hey, Luce, I can cheer you up. Well, not cheer you up, but . . ." I searched for the right word.

"Just tell me. Anything."

"Okay, give me the name of a guy you dated before Leonard."

"Are you trying to make me feel worse?"

"C'mon, you know you love him. Just give me a name."

She sniffled. "Brian Peel."

"As in banana?" I rolled my chair up to my computer and started typing.

"Yeah, and that's exactly what he used to say when he spelled his name. 'Peel, like banana, not like a bell.' That might've been why we broke up." Her voice trailed off.

"Five foot ten, West Eighty-eighth Street."

Lucy snorted. "What are you *doing*?"

"DMV records."

"Cool! Is that even legal?"

I hadn't thought about that. "Let's not think about that. Another name?"

"Wait, five ten? He always said he was six feet! Okay, how about Lamar Bodansky?"

I typed and waited. "Five foot six—"

"I knew it!" Lucy crowed. "Five eight, my tushy." This

was more like Lucy, coming down off the hardcore cursing and veering back into cute territory.

"And, Luce, holy crap, he's forty-two. Did you know that?"

"NO! That makes him ten years older than me, not five! Biggest liar *ever*."

"He lives in Park Slope now."

"Must have gotten married. Bet he has kids." She said this with dark satisfaction.

"Feeling better?" I asked tentatively.

"You're the best, Zeph." I heard a series of wails in the background. Lucy groaned. "They're up. Now I must forge ahead through the wilds of three-thirty to five-thirty, until I jump on the dinner–bath–bed train to bliss."

"Indulge in some chemical assistance," I joked, and immediately wished I hadn't.

"Actually, I'd love to try cocaine," mused the social worker who'd once specialized in treating drug addicts.

We hung up, with me only half certain she wouldn't go in search of a dealer operating out of the garden aisle at Kohl's, and I resumed staring blankly at the gray screen. Only now I began to ponder drugs.

Illegal drugs. Legal drugs. Ambien.

A moment for some mental self-flagellation.

I picked up the phone and dialed Pippa's extension.

"Zepha," she said by way of answering her phone. I reflected, not for the first time, on how both the British accent and the outer-borough accent dropped the "r" at the end of my name. I wondered if anyone in the entire office could pronounce it correctly.

"Do we have access to the records of whatever agency monitors prescription-drug transactions in the state?"

"That would be the Department of Health, Bureau of

Narcotic Enforcement. And I don't know what you mean by access, but health information is highly confidential."

She waited for me to prove I'd learned anything in the past three years.

"So I would need a *subpoena duces tecum* to find out whether someone filled a particular prescription?" I tried to keep the pride out of my voice: *Look at me, Commish, Latin at my fingertips!*

"Absolutely."

My triumph vanished. A subpoena based only on what was still a whiff of a whim of a suspicion. Not likely to fly with my boss.

Pippa cleared her throat. "Zephyr, I'm all for tying up loose ends, and the cousin's drug overdose was indeed rather diverting, but are you still, in fact, working on the case I've assigned you?"

I broke out in an embarrassed sweat, sitting there alone in my cubicle. "Yes," I practically whispered. "I'm still on it. Never mind. Forget I called."

"Forget you called?" she said archly.

Not really the thing to say to a boss.

"I mean," I choked out, "thank you, I'm fine."

I hung up, and my eyes fell on the picture of Gregory and me. It had been taken more than a year ago, at Point Reyes in Northern California, at my friend Abigail's wedding. I remembered thinking that I had never been happier in my entire life. My dearest friends were all together and I had never known I could love someone I wasn't related to as much as I loved Gregory. I shoved the photo under my keyboard, grabbed my backpack, and hurtled out of the office and the building.

I had to make some progress. On something. With or without a subpoena.

Chapter 5

That evening, for perhaps the thousandth time in six years, I found myself sitting in my parents' whirlwind of a living room and wondering whether I should move. Not move spots on the sofa—the growing pile of mohair blankets my mother had taken to knitting during the rare seconds her hands were unoccupied prohibited that—but move apartments. I didn't live with Bella and Ollie Zuckerman, not technically, but I did live two floors below them, in the four-story building they owned in Greenwich Village. Usually, I loved it, loved them and their self-described zest for life, but there were times, like tonight, when I wondered how much more I might be accomplishing with my own life were I not diverting energy and attention to them and their sustained chaos.

The return of my lanky, floppy-haired brother to the mix three years earlier had only dialed up the disorder, arriving as he did in a cloud of cinematic success bestowed upon him by the gods of the Tribeca Film Festival. At around the same time, my mother decided to take on a sultry forty-five-year-old former madam as a business partner, a turn of events that also did nothing to tone down the daily proceedings at 287

West 12th Street. And now my brother appeared to be taking a romantic interest in the self-same former prostitute. All of this, combined with a low-level desire to leave the apartment I'd shared with Gregory, had me thumbing through real estate listings with more fervor than the average New Yorker's daily EIK, HWF, square-footage gawking.

I had come that evening in search of some parental fawning and reassurance in the wake of what had been a demoralizing and fruitless day. After getting off the phone with Pippa, I'd charged uptown to the hotel with blind determination and a false sense of imminent conquest, ready to confront an elderly woman with an outrageous and utterly unprovable accusation of attempted murder. I'd blown past Asa, who was on the phone with Hershey's, suggesting a new shape for the Kiss.

Fortunately for everyone, Mrs. Hodges had not been in her room, or the restaurant, or the bar, and so I'd snuck out as quickly as I'd arrived, before Hutchinson McKenzie could spot me and grill me about my appearance on what was supposed to be a day off from the hotel. With considerably less energy than had spurred my arrival, I trudged up Sixth Avenue, dodging the incense-burning booksellers hawking reading material ranging from ancient *Playboy*s to pristine copies of *Dianetics*. I turned left on 12th Street and began to relax as I imagined a quiet evening with my parents, ordering in Korean food from DoSirak or maybe going out to Café Asean while I basked in their abundant, undivided attention. Basically, I was looking for a quick visit back to the womb, a balm I'd been pursuing more and more since Gregory's departure.

Instead, here I was, lying on their worn couch, my feet shoved under a teetering pile of baby-sized blankets, listening to my mother and Roxana Boureau put the final touches on a presentation they were to give the following day to the senior buyers at Banana Republic. My father was loudly humming Mozart as he unpacked groceries in the kitchen, announcing each item as he stashed them, while my brother tried to incite a conversation about Gregory as a vehicle for showing off to Roxana, erstwhile whore.

"Zeph, it was a case of failed syncretism between you and Gregory. Different philosophies. It's nobody's fault," Gideon said soothingly, as though we'd been on the subject. He plopped down on the blankets, nearly breaking my foot in two. I shrieked, but he barely flinched. He was too busy glancing at Roxana to see whether she'd noticed his impressive vocabulary. I considered reminding him that the Frenchwoman had what could best be described as a creative grasp of our native language but decided it would be wasted breath. Let him have his stupid, unrequited, puerile crush.

"I mean, personally, if the woman I loved didn't want children, I would just go with her wishes," he continued, lying through his recently whitened teeth. "If I loved her, I would do whatever she wanted."

"A nonissue when you're in love with a senior citizen," I hissed.

He pinched me. I kicked him.

The last thing I needed was for this subject to arise in my parents' presence. I would not be a sacrificial lamb for my horny brother. Normally a funny, thoughtful guy whose company I mostly enjoyed, Gideon was intolerably adolescent when he set his sights on a woman.

"Avocados!" my father proclaimed from the kitchen.

"Ah, Bella," Roxana cooed to my mother, causing Gideon's head to swivel. "Zat ees breeliant! Truly, you haf heet zee screw on zee nose." There was a moment of polite, confused silence.

"Nail on the head," I said throwing my arms up over my eyes. "You mean hit the nail on the head, Roxana."

"Ah, yis, sank you, Zepheer," she trilled with an easy laugh.

"Tuna!" cheered my father.

"You're welcome," I mumbled, once again mildly disconcerted by how tightly the progression of Roxana's career was intertwined with the progression of my own. A few years earlier, as a med-school dropout and a law-school-deposit forfeiter, in dire need of a yellow brick road, I found myself working as the super of our building. When I wasn't tackling the leaky oil tank in the basement and scheduling the exterminator and removing spontaneously reproducing locksmith business cards from our stoop, I stumbled across the brothel Roxana was running out of her apartment on the third floor.

Roxana saved herself from a decade of involuntary handcuffing by helping the feds and the NYPD lure in the reigning members of the mob family that controlled her and the brothel. I saved myself from a lifetime of professional soul-searching by throwing my hat into the law-enforcement ring, at the urging of Gregory, whom I met during the course of the whole surreal episode.

The feds had barely untaped the mike from Roxana's teddy before my mother, who regularly passed off her outlandishness as optimism, had come up with the idea of tapping the prostitute procuress for her business acumen. As the newly minted vice president of MWP Financial Seminars for Women, Roxana earned a salary that allowed her to continue renting apartment 3B, though it took a few months for her to afford to give it a full makeover. The first item to go was the leather-clad bondage jungle gym, which was replaced by a moiré love seat from Shabby Chic. (The gym sold in four hours on Craigslist.)

"Bok choy!"

Roxana was thriving, glowing, her French genes a guarantee of sexiness in perpetuity, and it was no wonder that Gideon was panting. I, on the other hand, had reverted to kicking my sibling and sulking on my parents' couch. I glared up at the pebbled skylight and wondered why I couldn't manage to get both love and work to flourish simultaneously. Forget flourish—I'd settle for something shy of flatlining.

"Roxana!" Gideon said suddenly. She and my mother looked up from their PowerPoint presentation printouts. I peeked out from under my arm. "I've decided I want my next movie to be about . . ." He took a deep breath and smiled broadly, like a first-grader about to unveil his best finger painting. "You. I want to make a movie about *you*." He sat back and waited for his magic to take effect.

"Oh, for the fucking love of—" I spat, and burrowed deeper into the couch.

"Gideon!" Roxana gasped. "Really? A movie about me? Zat is so flattering! How eggzyting!" She turned to my mother. "Bella, can you belief it?"

"Oh, I can," my mother said drily. She tucked a lock of silver hair behind her ear and studied Gideon. I could see the opposing forces of liberal motherhood taking up arms within. On the one hand, my parents had an "Endless This War" bumper sticker pasted below the Darwin fish and beside the "Coexist" banner on their Ford Fusion Hybrid. On the other hand, no woman, attendance at Woodstock and Stonewall notwithstanding, can get one hundred percent behind the idea of her twenty-eight-year-old baby boy taking an obvious interest in an aging former madam.

I devoted a moment to imagining Gideon and Roxana's wedding. Would she dare to wear white? What if they did have kids? Would they tell them about her past? If they didn't, would they ask me to keep the secret? Would I? I wanted to be the fun aunt, the honest aunt, the outrageous aunt. Maybe I could plant some evidence and let them find out by themselves. Mostly I just wanted to be there to see the looks on the kids' faces when they did, inevitably, find out.

My father pushed through the kitchen door and grinned down at us from his unflappable NBA heights.

"One hundred fifty dollars' worth of groceries and we have absolutely nothing for dinner!" he announced cheerfully.

"Ollie," my mother said, in a falsely light voice, "Gid says he'd like to make a movie about Roxana."

My father threw his arms out wide and gazed at Gideon with the same marvel he genuinely felt whether one of us had potty-trained or graduated summa cum laude.

"Brilliant! An absolutely brilliant idea! It makes so much sense for so many reasons!"

"Oh, Ollie," my mother sighed.

I hauled myself off the couch and headed for the door.

"Darling daught!" my dad crooned. "I didn't know you were under there! Stay for dinner?"

I sighed and managed a smile for him. "You just said there's nothing here."

"Define 'here'!" boomed the prosecutor. "If 'here' means New York City, well, then, there most certainly is something 'here.' There are ten thousand restaurants 'here.' Surely one of them will be happy to deliver food to our fine family!"

I stood on tiptoe and kissed his cheek. "Rain check," I said tiredly.

His eyes lit up and I groaned inwardly, knowing immediately what was coming.

"Rain check! A baseball term! When did it enter the common lexicon? Does anyone know? Do you know?" He turned to me earnestly, then to Gideon, my mother, and Roxana. They all dutifully shook their heads. "This century? Last century?" He strode down the hall, and we all knew he was headed for the *O.E.D.*

"Bye, Daddy!" I put my hand on the front door.

"Aren't you dying to know . . . ?" he called from down the hall.

"Some other time."

"Everything okay, Zephy?" my mom asked, as though she didn't spend every spare moment worrying for me and my future.

"She misses Gregory." Gideon smirked.

I spun around. "What are you, ten? Leave me alone!"

"Oh, Zeph," my mom sighed. A look of pity crossed her face, a look that irritated me to my very core, tied me into knots, because I was desperate to wail in her arms about Gregory but couldn't. There was this new barrier between us. Her daughter had declared that she didn't want to have children, a decision she could not fathom, a decision that, despite what she claimed, she took as a reproach and a personal failing.

"I am *fine*," I snarled, and headed down to my apartment to feed my bunny and call any one of a number of people with whom I shared not a shred of DNA.

* * *

My evening grew radically more interesting, and not just because Hitchens had escaped from his cage, shattered a miniature rendering of the High Line (the only surviving evidence of my stained-glass class), and chewed up four months' worth of *New Yorker*s. Three messages had come in on my landline while I was upstairs finding zero solace in my family. The first was from Lieutenant Fisk, and even though I wasn't sure how I felt about him, it was exactly the right time to hear how he felt about me.

"Zephyr," came his deep and preposterously confident voice. "I'm on duty and it's my turn to cook. Come by the station, have dinner with me and the men." He hesitated. "Actually, if you're a vegetarian, don't bother. But I think you'll like what you taste. I use lots of butter," he drawled. His tone was so brazenly suggestive that he could as easily have been asking me to arrive in nothing but an overcoat and lipstick. An involuntary shiver of anticipation zapped through me as I pictured a gleaming engine, a pole, and me, supremely feminine amidst the testosterone-saturated air.

I dumped a dustpan full of shredded summer fiction into the trash and hustled to my bedroom, hoping that my never-fail Levi's and long-sleeved H&M shirt (just a tad to the tight of respectable) combo were clean and ready to see action.

"Zeph!" It was Macy's voice. I stopped in my tracks and gazed hopefully at the answering machine. There was a crash in the background. "Crap. I can suck venom out of my own calf and persuade women to forgo matching bridesmaid dresses, but I cannot make bookends reliably hold up books. And, hey, sorry I was huffy today, but it's been about eight hours and apparently I'm codependent, because I miss you and we never figured out which train we're taking to Hillsville tomorrow. Alcohol consumption is permitted on Metro-North, so . . . *that's a bonus.*" She cackled over the last words, and I recalled the old woman foisting her son's skin-protection services on Macy that morning. "Yes, I called the dermatologist and we're going out next weekend. Call me!" she sang, and I could picture the mischievous grin on her freckled face as she hung up. I added this to my mental dossier on Macy: *Does not stay angry for long.*

As I shed my work clothes and stepped into my jeans, I realized I was nervous. As much as I was titillated by the nerve-racking component of a budding courtship, it was . . . well, nerve-racking. Not for the first time I wondered how hard it would be to get to know another man as well as I'd known Gregory. How long would I have to be with someone before I knew at which hospital he'd been born? Before I could read in bed with my headlamp? Before I didn't have to worry that an unusual lilt in his voice one morning signaled the end of the relationship?

I sank down on the bed, caught in a confused state between excited and sapped. This did not need to be a relationship, I reminded myself. This could be a hookup. This could simply be the first step in life after Gregory. At the very least, I would do it for Lucy and give her a good story tomorrow night. She counted on us for vicarious singledom.

I located the shirt on my floor, and as I performed a quick sniff test—shirt and armpits both passed—another message began to play. The air left my lungs when I heard Gregory's voice, deep and hesitant. I zoomed back to the living room and planted myself in front of the answering machine, hoarding every syllable.

"Zephyr." His gravelly voice cracked. "Hey, Zeph, it's me. Gregory. Uh . . . I'm coming to town." I closed my eyes against the wave of longing that threatened to overpower me. "Okay, actually, I'm already—I'm already in town." A long pause, during which I tried to regain control over my breathing. "Stupidly, *stupidly,* I'm at Bar Six. Okay? I'm around the corner, sitting in Bar Six, just sort of hoping you'll walk by—"

I never heard the end of the message. I slipped on my shoes, grabbed my keys and wallet, and was out the door in ten seconds, where I was greeted with a concerned look by Zoltan, our new super—a short, fastidious poet who had dropped out of refrigeration school. My parents were building a dubious tradition of hiring dropouts of every ilk as superintendents.

"Hello . . . ," he said, his eyes wide in surprise.

I nodded and tore down the stairs from the landing we shared to the front door.

"Zephyr!" he called after me, Hungarian lilt beautifully coloring my name.

"What?" I said, irritated by the millisecond delay.

"Are you sure . . . do you mean to . . . ?"

"WHAT?"

"You have no shirt on."

* * *

Figuring in for vacations and leaving town for college and a year of med school, I'd probably covered this stretch of 12th Street between Seventh and Sixth Avenues well over three thousand times since the age of five. That night, though, charging toward Gregory, the block looked unfamiliar. Had there always been an awning over the hospital entrance? Had the James Beard Society really never had a stoop? When had the owners of 153 planted a pear tree in their front yard? Who knew pear trees could grow in the West Village? *A tree grows in Manhattan,* I thought wildly.

I declined the offer of a pamphlet from a man wearing a sandwich board advertising eyebrow threading and turned onto Sixth Avenue. Bar Six loomed in the near distance, its outdoor brass-topped tables pulsing with the promise of heightened, extravagant emotion. Not unlike the way the Magic Kingdom beckons to the under-twelve set.

I pulled open the door.

"Zephyr!" Gregory's voice rose above the din; the place was hot and crowded, even on a Monday night. I had hoped to see him first, but he wasn't even trying to hide the fact that he'd been watching the door as intently as a driver searching for a parking spot. Gregory often ignored social norms, a trait that had required regular deciphering and Sterling Girl analysis at the beginning of our relationship.

I started to throw my arms out and race to him but caught myself and instead wound up awkwardly lurching and pretending to scratch my neck. He was perched on a bar stool, and even in the dim light I could see tension radiating from every gangly limb. Would we hug? Could I push the mop of chestnut hair off his forehead, stroke his sharp cheekbones, entwine my fingers in his?

For the umpteenth time that day, that week, that month, I nearly buckled under the impossibility of our situation. Neither of us, as far as I knew, had fallen out of love. When we were together, I'd only grown happier with him, and it seemed the feeling was mutual. There was only that single, cosmically huge sticking point. Was he back because he'd changed his mind? Decided I was more important to him than some unknown child?

"Why are you here?" I wailed, three months of barely restrained longing bursting forth. Our faces were inches apart.

He looked stricken. "What—"

"I mean . . ." I half-whacked him on the arm in a bizarre, man-to-man gesture. "Hi."

He shook his head. "Hi," he said quietly, letting a slow smile spread across his face. It was the same smile with which I first fell in love, and it took more self-control than I knew I possessed to keep from crying at the sight of it.

I slid onto the stool beside his, surreptitiously glancing down to confirm that I was, after my hasty initial departure from my apartment, fully clothed and shod.

"I'm at a loss," I finally said. "This is . . . I don't know what this is. Why *are* you here?"

"Here in New York or here in the neighborhood?" He studied the wineglass in front of him, placing his palms on either side of the stem.

"Both."

"Are you sorry I'm here?" His voice cracked and so did my heart.

"You dummy," I said, watching him watch his drink. "What do you think?"

"What can I getcha?" The bartender hovered in front of

me, broadcasting a fair-weather friendliness that was conditional upon an expensive order and commensurate tip.

"A glass of merlot?" I asked timidly, even though all I wanted was juice. "And ice water."

"You got it!" he singsonged, and darted away.

"You caved." Gregory grinned shyly at me.

I nodded, not trusting my voice.

"It's really good to see you."

I nodded again.

"Really good."

"Gregory." I lingered over his name, warm and spicy in my mouth.

He took a deep breath and suddenly I realized he was here to tell me he'd met a belle in Alabama and was headed to a chuppah made of hickory. No, he was already married. And he'd called because he realized he'd made a grave mistake. Oh, it would be complicated, sticky, but I'd take him back. I'd help him get an annulment, suffer through court hearings and property disputes, prepare for a mint julep or two to be tossed in my face.

Or he was dying. He had only a few months to live and he'd come back to get treatment and be with me. An ugly thought arose that I tamped down before it was fully formed but not before it registered: Impending death would instantly wipe out our hurdles. We'd have a blissful few months or years together, unhampered by irreconcilable long-term differences. I shook my head, disgusted by what my brain could come up with unchecked.

"I'm moving back," he said.

"Are you sick?" I cried out.

He shook his head, familiar with my diesel trains of thought.

"I'm moving back because I hate my parents and I hate Alabama and I love New York and I miss my job and . . ."

I held my breath, hoping.

"Well, obviously, Zeph, I miss you and I love you, but . . . that wasn't our problem, was it?"

I exhaled shakily. This was most unsatisfying and inconclusive.

"You knew you hated your parents and Alabama when you left," I pointed out.

"Yeah, well." He took a sip of his wine. "You didn't leave me a lot of choice."

"Heeeere we go!" sang the waiter, setting down my drinks with a flourish before bustling away.

Without looking at me, Gregory tapped his wineglass to mine.

"Are we toasting something?" I asked, trying unsuccessfully to keep sarcasm out of my voice.

"I'm just. Happy to see you again," he said simply. "But I already said that."

I took a sip of wine to hide the irrational, useless pleasure that flooded out of my belly and warmed my fingers and toes.

"The chief said I could end my leave early and come back next week. I found a sublet in Boerum Hill. One of the guys, his niece eloped to Sicily and isn't coming back. He gave me a good deal."

He was coming back to New York. He was coming back and we wouldn't be living together. He was coming back and he'd committed an act of real estate without consulting me. It had been sinking in for months that our relationship was over, but this cemented it, even as I could detect whiffs of a potential if unwise resurrection.

"I had visions, fantasies, of coming home," he continued. "To New York, I mean. Other guys fantasize about . . ." He paused and frowned. He probably really didn't know what lighted the libidos of his brethren. "I don't know. Big boobs? Lap dances?" He shook off his mental detour. "Anyway, I . . .

I'd lie awake in that stupid narrow bed in that stupid chintz-infested room with my judgmental, hypocritical parents in the next room and think about, I don't know, sitting next to you at one of Mercedes's concerts or watching you and your dad cheat at cards on Wednesday nights or standing at the cheese counter of Fairway with you, comparing Gouda varieties." He shook his head, then drained his glass.

"Wow," I said, and burst out laughing, giddy with the knowledge that I was still the object of Gregory Samson's love. "That last one's hard-core."

He shrugged, embarrassed.

"And disloyal."

"What!" He looked anxious. "How?!"

"Fairway? You're totally cheating on the Village."

He snorted with relief. "Okay, maybe it was Murray's Cheese."

"So it's really the cheese that's integral to the fantasy," I bantered, stalling for time. I still didn't know where any of this was going. My elbow brushed his, and I tried to ignore the heat that jolted through me. "I don't think I knew your passion for Gouda ran this deep."

"You should talk," he said, shorthanding a reference to my unappealing habit of gnawing on blocks of cheddar at home. I knew the relationship was serious when he stopped slicing off the teeth marks.

Gregory reached over and took a sip of my water. I tried not to stare. He acted as if he didn't realize what an intensely personal act it was, a vestige of intimacy. It was agony to be this close to him and not touching. Unnatural.

He put down his glass—my glass, our glass—and leaned over and kissed me. Then he pulled back, waiting for any kind of reaction, and when I remained speechless, he put his hands on either side of my face and kissed me again. *Second Person Kissed Since Gregory,* I thought, *and it's Gregory.*

"What are we doing?" I murmured anxiously, his lips still on mine.

"Kissing."

"When you were in Alabama . . . Never mind, don't answer that."

"Zeph . . ." And then he shook his head.

"What? What were you going to say?" I broke away from the embrace but took each of his wrists in my hands—his strong, beautiful wrists that I'd kissed a hundred times.

Resolve dissolving, I thought, rubbing my fingers over the tendons. There it goes, carried off by the heat and the rumble of Bar Six. This was not the smart thing to do. This was not what an almost-thirty-one-year-old woman with any instinct for self-preservation should do. But how often in a lifetime did a person get to feel the kind of longing that I felt at this moment and have the instant means to satisfy it? Everything was going to get messy and, right then, even as a fire engine roared by, reminding me of the pole not slid, I didn't care. The only people who could get hurt were the two of us.

"I want you," he said urgently, plaintively. "Now."

Dammit, Janet.

Chapter 6

At seven A.M. the next morning, I was in position at the front desk of the hotel. My eyes were gritty, my legs hollow, and I sipped steadily at my second cup of coffee from Ciao for Now, willing it to transport me back to the land of the living. I pulled my bulky thigh-length sweater tighter around me to hide my wrinkled hotel uniform. The hardest part of going undercover was having to think two outfits ahead—a challenge, needless to say, for someone who could barely dress herself in one complete outfit. When it wasn't on me, my uniform was usually in a ball at the bottom of my backpack. I hoped we'd be too busy today for Hutchinson to remark on my need for an iron.

"I wish I could just give Rosie a big hug," Asa cooed, thumbing through the *Times*. "He's working so hard to make everything all better, the money stuff and the health stuff, and those nasty Southerners are just getting in the way."

"Not all Southerners are nasty," I felt compelled to croak.

"What's wrong with your voice? It's very hoarse. Want me to make you a little chamomile? I got three boxes yesterday from Good Earth, and all I did was ask them where they grow their leaves."

Asa neatly folded the paper and dug through his oversize striped beach bag, which he toted around in all seasons. Inside, it looked like he'd robbed a mini-mart.

"Voilà!" he sang, brandishing a tea bag. "I'll be right back." He grabbed a mug from the cabinet that held extra toothpaste and razors and waddled off in the direction of the hotel restaurant, leaving me to man the desk alone. I really hoped Hutchinson wouldn't come by and catch Asa AWOL again, but mostly I prayed to the gods of timing that Samantha Kimiko Hodges wouldn't leave the building while I was solo.

The glass doors slid open and a young woman who looked as tired as I felt trudged in, rolling a suitcase behind her.

I put on my best smile and straightened my collar, acutely aware of how much I enjoyed my phony job. All those wasted hours studying for the MCATs and LSATs could have been spent hanging out here with Asa, earning decent wages.

"Hi there! Welcome to New York!"

She tried to return the smile.

"Hi," she said quietly, scratching her head through a mound of honey-colored curls. Her voice sounded as rough as mine. "I have a reservation. Last name is Herman. Zelda Herman."

"The Z club," I observed, typing in her name. "My first name begins with 'Z,' too. Actually, so does my last name."

She nodded politely, and I decided to take the unforthcoming follow-up question to be a sign of exhaustion rather than rudeness.

"You'll be in room 232. Are you named for Zelda Fitzgerald?" I couldn't help asking, even though, according to the reservation notes, she was from Sonoma County and had just survived the red eye. She didn't need to be saddled with small talk.

Zelda gave another quick nod, determined to nip any conversation in the bud.

As I programmed a blank key card in the VingCard machine, I surreptitiously glanced at her. There was something familiar about her, something about the square of her chin, or her high forehead, or her long lashes and almond-shaped eyes. Either that or my attraction to long eyelashes was approaching affliction status. She caught me staring and shifted her weight slightly away from the counter.

"Sorry," I babbled, even as I knew I should shut up. "I was just noticing that your eye makeup is perfect, even after an overnight flight." It was, in fact, flawless.

"Tattoo."

"Excuse me?"

"My eyeliner. It's tattooed on. Permanent."

"Ouch."

She shrugged, as if she'd had this conversation before. "Saves time. And I can cry."

I cleared my expression, returning it to cheerful and objective. "Okay, well. I see you're staying with us for two nights. Will you be needing any restaurant or theater reservations?" I chirped, handing her the key card.

She managed a snort. "Definitely not."

I hid my surprise. "Do you want to leave your bag for us to bring up, or will you be—"

Out of the corner of my eye, I caught the small quick movements of Samantha Kimiko Hodges, a streak of red silk (this being Tuesday) bustling out of the elevator and heading through the lobby. Right behind her was Asa, carefully balancing a mug of tea on a square teak tray.

"Asa!" I called out. I turned suddenly on Zelda Herman. "Asa! Asa has brought you a cup of chamomile. We always do that for our early-morning arrivals. We're all about the service!"

I ducked under the counter to dig my wallet out of my backpack—if I was going to chase Samantha, I needed to be prepared to pay for any mode of transportation—and heard our guest comment with surprise, "That *is* good service!"

Followed immediately by the Drawl: "Puh-leeze. What did they pay you for *that*?"

Noooo, I thought, leaning my head against the wall of the counter. Why was Hutchinson forever materializing out of thin air? Did he do nothing but sit in his office watching the security monitor? The thought made me queasy, as did the knowledge that Samantha was almost at the front door.

I popped up, startling everyone at the counter.

"Jesus, Zephyr!" Hutchinson crabbed. With his blow-dried hair, salmon polo shirt, and pressed khakis, all that was missing were a martini, a yacht, and a *No Coloreds* sign.

"What did you say about *paying* me?" Zelda demanded coldly to Hutchinson. She looked pale, even paler than she'd been moments ago. Hutchinson, Asa, and I looked at her blankly.

Samantha turned left out of the hotel. I could only hope her short legs would slow her down.

"I'm sorry, I meant . . ." It was lovely to watch Hutchinson fumble. "About saying the service is good . . . ? I was joking."

Zelda blushed. "Of course. God, that's embarrassing. I'm just very tired."

I had no idea what was going on, but I took the opportunity to escape, mentally thanking Zelda for distracting Hutchinson. I popped around the desk and slipped through the doors while Hutchinson tripped over himself trying to make amends with the small-boned beauty. She was the type for whom he and Jeremy would have displayed their finest financial footsie at the hotel bar.

Jeremy.

I hustled out the door and peered down the block. Samantha hadn't made it far; she was headed into the park from the northwest entrance. I picked up my pace, dodged a line of cabs turning south on MacDougal, and fell into step beside her.

"Mrs. Kimiko Hodges!" I said, as though surprised and delighted to find a fellow early bird taking a morning constitutional.

She glanced over at me, not breaking her stride. The corners of her lips turned up for a moment, acknowledging that I was not a pickpocket or a drug dealer. Despite the park's face-lift, both thrived, the latter to the general benefit of the neighborhood. A well-known, if unspoken, symbiosis still existed: The dealers protected the NYU faculty kids who lived around the park and made sure no one sold to them. In return, the professors turned a deaf ear to the urban susurration, "Smoke, smoke?"

"You leave the fairy to run the desk?" she asked.

"Mrs. Hodges!" I said, laughing despite myself. It was so mean and so outdated.

"*Kimiko* Hodges. What, he's not a fairy?" She stopped abruptly and pulled a handkerchief out of her knock-off Gucci handbag. She dusted off a bench and sat down.

"No, no, he's a fairy." I watched her settle in. "Very nice guy, though." I waited until she was done adjusting her tiny rear end, then sat down beside her.

"Never said he wasn't."

A pack of three dogs zoomed across the lawn in pursuit of a traumatized squirrel. Samantha *tsk*ed and shook her head, presumably at the regulation that permitted dogs to be off leash before nine A.M.

"How's the guy?" she said.

At first I thought she meant Gregory, whom I'd left

sprawled diagonally in my bed about an hour earlier. Despite my exhaustion, I felt a bullet of adrenaline launch from somewhere behind my heart. It had been a long, active, imprudent night, one during which we'd blissfully managed not to address anything other than the business at hand. But had I ever mentioned Gregory to Samantha? Was she spying on me? Was everyone watching me on monitors, witnessing my monumental lapses in judgment?

"Who? What guy?" *Calm down, Zephyr.*

"The *dummkopf.*" She flipped the back of her hand at me. "The one who got sick."

Something lurched inside my belly. All plans for slowly broaching the subject had been a waste of precious brain power.

"Jeremy?" I said carefully.

She rummaged through her purse. "I don't know. Was he the upside-down copper top?"

"He's still in the hospital," I said, watching her take out a small comb and run it through her hair, which shone brilliantly in the morning sunlight. "Psych ward. He's going to be there awhile."

One of her shoulders twitched and I waited for her to say something. When she didn't, I took a deep breath and jumped in, all but squeezing my eyes shut.

"He mentioned you gave him some kind of love potion—doyouhaveanythingforme?"

She put her comb away, keeping her eyes on her purse. "You? What do you need a love potion for?"

She wasn't denying she'd given him a drink! *Slowly, Zephyr, slowly.* The thought crossed my mind that even though I was only a block from the hotel, I was a universe away from the case I'd been assigned.

"I do," I protested, surprised to realize it was true. I longed for a potion to make me want kids. Or to make Gregory not want them. I wondered if there was a formula to hasten reconciliation. "What was in it?"

She looked at me sharply. "Ancient Chinese secret," she said in a ridiculous imitation of a Manchurian accent.

"You're Japanese," I reminded her, then thought of her Yiddish locution and wondered if she would dispute this label.

"Schlemiel doesn't know the difference. It's all the same to him."

"Come on," I wheedled. "What was in it, Mrs. Hodges?"

"Kimiko—"

"Oh, cut it out," I snapped, and regretted it instantly. I sweetened my voice again. "Just tell me, what's your secret ingredient? Maybe it could work for my problems."

"What are you, some kind of a detective?" I froze for an instant, but she continued. "Look at you, you don't need a potion. You're . . ." She turned her head to give me a blatant once-over. "Well, you're not drop-dead beautiful, but you look like one the boys would like to squeeze."

I snorted with embarrassment, but then I considered her assessment.

"It's true," I admitted, watching the dog owners corral their charges. "I don't have trouble getting—" I couldn't say "laid" to this woman, could I? "Dates."

Samantha rolled her eyes. "Don't make it family-friendly on my account," she sniffed, snapping her purse closed, folding her arms, and turning her face up to the sun.

"I've still got my problems," I protested.

"Such as?"

"Such as, the man I love wants kids and I don't." This conversation was the stuff of the psychiatrist's couch (or a Sterling Girl couch), not standard investigative protocol, but I flattered myself by thinking it was an excellent and innovative use of my natural, overly personal conversational skills.

Perhaps I could codify it and trademark it and call it the Zephyr Technique. My mom and Roxana could use it—

"Kids are a pain in the tuchas," Samantha decreed.

"Do you have them?"

"It's complicated."

"Complicated like stepkids?"

"Complicated like dead kids."

I sucked in my breath. "I'm so sorry."

"Don't be."

A pack of testosterone swathed in NYU track jerseys and shorts jogged by, each pair of muscular legs a glistening testament to the triumphs of natural selection. With a start, I realized I was too old to respectably date them.

"So you think it's okay not to want kids?" I asked, wondering if I actually cared about her opinion or whether I was that desperate for a sounding board.

She shot me a look of irritation.

"Well, but I love this guy. And I don't want to be seen as stunted and irresponsible just because I don't want children."

"Is that what he thinks?"

"It's what my mother thinks."

"You're marrying your mother?"

I pulled my sweater around me defensively. How many of my choices were still influenced—clouded—by my mother's opinions?

"It's not even about what he thinks of me," I informed her. "It's that we're at an impasse." A jolt of anger shot through me. If Gregory *hadn't* changed his mind, then why had he started up with me last night? I remembered the feeling of freedom and excitement I'd felt while kissing Delta, even with a climbing harness digging into my crotch. Was Gregory going to appear anytime I had a shot at moving on?

"You have to end it," Samantha said.

"We already did."

The Japanese bubbe turned fully on the bench to stare at me. "So what are you bothering *me* for?"

"Because we could get back together." I wondered if that was true. "If there was a potion to—"

"Don't start again with the potion mishegas. You two shouldn't get back together. Children aren't something you negotiate. What, you say you'll pop 'em out, but he'll be the one to raise them? You do that, you better start saving for their therapy now." She closed her eyes again. "On the other hand, you might find you like 'em."

"Then you *do* think I should have them!" I felt betrayed.

"I didn't say that. Kids make everything harder. I'm just saying, my first husband got a cat and I thought I'd hate it, but I loved it. Loved it more than the husband. Which is why I moved on to the second husband."

Samantha stood up suddenly.

"Where are you going?" I demanded.

"It's not a free country?"

"Depends on who you ask," I quipped, buying time.

"I'm tired of talking to you. I'm not used to so much talk anymore."

"Mrs. Hod—Mrs. Kimiko Hodges," I said desperately as she began to walk away. I resisted the urge to grab her tiny wrist. "Why did you put Ambien in Jeremy Wedge's drink?"

I had just nudged a two-ton boulder over the crest of a hill; I could almost hear the villagers screaming as they ran from it. A light sweat broke out on the nape of my neck.

She froze mid-stride for a split second, then kept walking.

I jumped up and followed her.

"There were lethal amounts of Ambien in that drink!" I yelled at her rigid back.

A woman wearing Julius Caesar lace-up sandals and a leather jacket sporting an anti-fur button glanced up from her bench and openly watched the free spectacle.

Samantha stopped, and this time she whipped around. Her eyebrows furrowed until they merged, and she pressed her lips together so hard they turned white. She pointed at me, her hand shaking. I leaned back under the force of her fury.

"You," she whispered. "You get away from me. You stop bothering me with your idiot questions and you leave. Me. Alone." She took off again.

I started to follow, but an angry glance back from her stopped me. She stomped eastward as fast as her silk stockings and orthotics would carry her.

Julius Caesar leaned forward and scrunched her nose sympathetically. "Don't worry, honey. If she'd really wanted to kill you, she could have found something more reliable than Ambien. For example, rat poison."

"Thank you," I said absently, heading back to the hotel. I would need a pen and paper to tally how many parts of that interaction I'd grossly mishandled. And yet it would seem that I very likely had an attempted murder on my hands.

Chapter 7

B
ut if you so much as touch the box, the juice comes spurting out. The design is atrocious," Asa was pleading into the phone, holding aloft a juice box as evidence. "Hello? Hello? Did customer service hang up on me?" he asked incredulously, looking at the receiver.

I scurried behind the desk and dropped my wallet into the backpack at my feet. "Try drinking your juice out of a glass like a grown-up," I suggested.

"The woman at Apple and Eve said the same thing! This is very irregular. They're supposed to *fawn*." He turned his pudgy palms to the ceiling, looking like a bewildered balloon.

"Surely, Asa, you can find love elsewhere. Hey, where's Lockjaw?" I asked, trying to sound casual but beginning to perspire. The lobby seemed unusually warm. I shook off my sweater.

"I get plenty of love, Zephyr," Asa said huffily. "But I like free stuff. I didn't hear you complaining when I brought in the Oreos. Or the pantyliners."

"No, that was extremely thoughtful of you," I conceded.

"Or the dental floss or the cereal bars."

"The cereal bars were disgusting."

"The cereal bars *were* disgusting. But what did you think of the bath oils? Didn't you think the cucumber aloe was exceptionally smooth?" Asa asked earnestly, his face furrowed in concentration, the Plato of perks.

"Oh, good, we've resumed our blinding levels of focus and dedication. At least no one's running out the door fifteen minutes after they've come on shift." Hutchinson oozed into the lobby. I was now thoroughly convinced that he spent his days glued to the security monitor.

I was about to apologize, when I caught myself and invoked the Tag method.

"Actually," I said haughtily, addressing my computer screen, "Mrs. Hodges had asked me to find out whether Spa Belles or Bloomie Nails did a cheaper mani/pedi. I was following up on a *guest request*."

Hutchinson cleared his throat. "Guest request" was one of his father's favorite phrases, a clarion call to duty, a crystal-clear delineation of priorities.

"Right, well." He peered at a mosaic on the far wall of the lobby. "Just make sure checkouts are on time this morning. We have a dozen arrivals, a bridezilla is dropping off gift bags, and I'm going to be out the rest of the day, so I won't be here to put out your fires." He scowled at each of us in turn and then strutted toward the door, his arms swinging a little too forcefully.

"Oh, thank goodness," Asa breathed as soon as Hutchinson disappeared. He reached for the phone. "He makes my toxin levels go sky-high."

I turned to Asa. "Can you cover for just ten more minutes?"

"Zephyr," he whined. "You're going to get in trouble! You're going to get *me* in trouble! Where are you going, anyway?"

"Come on, Ace." I patted his soft shoulder as I left the counter. "It's like we're Janet and Michael Jackson. Before he died, I mean. Never in the same place at the same time. Could be the same person, right?"

His eyes lit up. "We do have very similar hair!"

"Maybe you should give Revlon a call," I suggested, heading for the elevator. "If we both used the same conditioner, we could be twins."

"Oh, Revlon blocked my number ages ago." The elevator dinged. "But don't worry, Zeph," he said resolutely as I stepped in. "I've got Clinique on speed dial."

* * *

The fifth-floor hallway was silent, with no evidence of Saturday evening's medical drama. Three of the six rooms up here were vacant, including the one previously occupied by the New Zealanders, which had required the services of a professional carpet cleaner. A fourth was being used by a German couple who designed playgrounds from recycled materials; that pair had been up and out cruising the city's jungle gyms by seven every morning. Two women who came every month to carry on their extramarital affair were in a fifth room. They made a point of loudly discussing their husbands whenever they passed through the lobby; I don't know whom they thought they were fooling, but they often slept late, so I wasn't concerned about them, either.

I lingered outside Samantha's room, willing myself to go in. My plan called for quick and deft maneuvering, not loitering. And yet I stood there, examining the ceiling, formulating excuses. If I encountered a chambermaid, I could say I was checking the placement of smoke alarms. Or making sure no paint was peeling. Or confirming that the spacing of the ceiling tiles was—

The elevator dinged, announcing the imminent opening of

doors. I thrust my key into the lock and leapt inside room 505. I waited for a moment in the dark, heart threatening to pound itself up and out of its assigned location, then dared to look out the peephole. Maria Lopez, the oil painter who worked as head chambermaid to pay the rent, was beginning her rounds. She was starting with the Germans' room. I took a shaky breath, reminded myself that I was within my legal rights to look but not touch, and flipped on the light.

My first thought was that I liked what Samantha had done with the place. Even though the room was the mirror image of the others on this floor, hers looked like a home. She'd put down a thick Turkish rug and brought in two of her own lamps. There were thriving plants, one of which sat on a wooden chest that replaced the hotel's standard boomerang-shaped glass coffee table. There was a coat rack, a small bookcase filled with paperbacks and framed photographs, and a mauve shelving unit that held a small collection of ceramic dishes—two plates, two mugs, two bowls. On a lower shelf were a box of cornflakes, a container of Metamucil, a basket of single-serving nondairy creamers—like the kind you might pocket at a diner if you were so inclined—a bottle of vanilla extract, and a bottle of Tums. She'd even replaced the McKenzies' movie-star photos on the walls with prints by de Kooning and Picasso.

Her bathroom, surprisingly, held few personal effects. My recent experience at the Hudson Street Nursing Home had indicated that the need for bathroom shelf space increased with age. Here, there were only a toothbrush and toothpaste, a travel-sized bottle of lotion (interestingly, from the Larchmont Hotel, a competitor on 11th Street), and a single bottle of generic aspirin.

What had I expected to find? Annoyed with myself and increasingly anxious, I sidestepped a potted ficus tree, noticing that the tin watering can beside it sat in a saucer filched from the hotel bar. So far, that was the most incriminating item I'd found.

I started to pick up a dead leaf that had fallen onto the polished desk, then thought better of it. The desk was covered in tidy piles of papers, and along the back stood more framed photographs. I bent over to study them, keeping my hands behind me. Most of the photos were of Samantha and an unassuming bald man I presumed to be Husband Number Two. But there was one sepia-toned photo of a young family that made me yelp.

Everyone in the picture—father, mother, brother, sister—was Caucasian, except for the little Asian girl in her father's arms. New York State law be damned, I grabbed the photo and squinted at it. The family was posed in front of a pickle store on Essex Street and, judging from the make of the cars in the photo, it had been taken about seven decades earlier. Samantha had been adopted! Adopted by people who could have shared gefilte fish recipes with my ancestors, it would seem.

If Samantha had been adopted, then her adoptive family—apparently Jewish and presumably explaining the mystery of her shtetl style—was way ahead of their time; today, in New York, anyway, every other Hannah Schwartz or Esther Goldman originally hailed from some dusty, forsaken town in the farthest reaches of China. But a Japanese kid? While I couldn't even begin to imagine the circumstances surrounding that adoption, I did allow myself a moment of triumph: one, albeit tiny, mystery explained. I put the photo back after wiping away any fingerprints with my shirt.

In the hallway, a door clicked closed. I darted to the peephole and spotted the jollier of the cuckolding women headed for the elevator, a Mets jacket slung over her arm and a cap perched on her head. I wasted a moment considering what I would do with a lover if I was cheating on my husband. If you planned to conduct an affair over a long period of time, you might very well end up doing pedestrian activities like attending baseball games. Did they worry about being broadcast on the JumboTron at Citi Field? Did a gay lover rather than a straight lover make it easier to concoct a lie?

Easier than concocting a lie explaining my presence in room 505. I darted back to the desk and quickly surveyed the contents.

Atop one pile of papers was a receipt for $14.73 from Duane Reade—vitamins, a package of nail files, and a carton of Newman's Own lemonade. Another pile held *AARP, Real Simple, Notary Public Monthly,* and a brochure for RVs. I tried to picture the retrofitting that would need to be done on a Winnebago to accommodate a driver of such staggeringly short stature. Raised seat, raised pedals. On the plus side, the interior would probably feel roomier to her than to the average occupant.

The Sprint bill at the top of the third pile offered evidence that Samantha had not, in fact, just stepped out of another century in her silk stockings. Below the cellphone bill, part of a Chase bank statement was visible, and a number caught my eye. A number that took up a lot more space than any number ever had on one of my bank statements.

$500,000.

I looked closer.

One. Two. Three. Four. Five zeroes.

I considered the stack of paper, studied it from a few angles. Hands clasped tightly behind my back again, I bent down and gently blew on the Sprint bill with a force a little harder than that of, say, the air-conditioning suddenly coming on but lighter than if a pigeon had flown in through the . . . closed window. Oh hell, I'd already broken the law by touching the picture frame. I removed the Sprint bill and was treated to an unobstructed view of Samantha Kimiko Hodges's transactions over the past thirty days.

Most of the items were not that different from my own. Debits of $7 for MetroCard purchases at MTA kiosks; $10.32 for a meal at B&H Dairy, where dill was put to generous use in all soups; $5 for a very short taxi ride; multiple voluntary admissions of $1 to the Met, which must have irritated the ticket sellers; two purchases at the Museum of Sex that I tried not to ponder for too long; and a debit of $2,500 from the Greenwich Village Hotel, an excellent housing deal in Manhattan if ever there was one.

And then there were the credits: two from the Social Security Administration of $1,200 each; two of $1,400 from a Vanguard money market; and then the one stand-alone transfer into her account of $500,000, the source of which was posted as "Summa, Inc."

My hands began to shake. I tried to straighten the papers but instead sent them flying, tornado style, to the floor.

Don't cry, Zephyr, don't cry, I warned myself as I crouched down and gathered everything up. Some of the bills had stayed together, but most had slipped out of order. There was no time to guess how they'd been organized. I slammed the documents on the desk, making sure the bank statement was back under the phone statement, and fled.

I raced down the stairwell, the word "Summa" flashing from the wall of every landing. I threw myself against the lobby fire door and slipped behind my computer at the front desk.

"Whew!" said Asa, drawing his hand across his forehead. "Now, can we all just please stay put for a while?" He unwrapped a chocolate Zone bar and settled his elbows onto the counter to enjoy it.

I clicked out of EZ-CheckIn and Googled "Summa." Thousands of results popped up—including "Strengthening Underrepresented Minority Mathematics Achievement," a couple of entries for summa cum laude, and the thoughtful question, "did you mean sumo wrestler?"—but nothing that was helpful to me. I pressed my fingers to my eyes and tried to recall the details of my initial briefing with the McKenzie paterfamilias.

On the day I began work at the hotel, Ballard and I had met at Eisenberg's Sandwich Shop at 6:45 A.M., a place utterly foreign to him and a time then unfamiliar to me. He was a very sweet Santa Clausian man—even told me with a hangdog look that he'd always wished for a daughter, too—but very long-winded, and somewhere between a cataloging of his wife's pottery achievements and recollections of truffle hunting with his son, I'm afraid my attention may have wandered. He'd mentioned his nephew Jeremy only briefly, saying that he loved him dearly even though he was only an adequate squash player and a so-so scientist who ran an outfit called Summa. I was almost certain he'd said Summa, but my notes were back in my cubicle.

"Asa," I said hoarsely. "Do you remember where Jeremy works?"

He studied his snack and licked some chocolate from the wrapper.

"Who's Jeremy?"

"Asa!" I hissed. "*Jeremy* Jeremy. Jeremy Wedge. Jeremy the McKenzie cousin who left on a stretcher on Saturday night?" I looked at him incredulously and wondered whether it was time for him to cut back on the Deadhead soirées.

"Oh, him. Because I went out with a Jeremy last week, but he's not out of the closet at work and I don't *do* closeted so I told him—"

"Asa!" I put my fists at my sides to keep from taking a swipe at my friend. "Do you or don't you remember the name of the place Jeremy works?"

"He's head of the parks department tree-counting prog—"

"Asa, I'm going to try this one last time. Jeremy Wedge. Do you or don't you remember where he works?"

"Um?" Asa searched the ceiling. "Some kind of genetics-institute thingy. Probably trying to figure out a way to weed out the gays."

"Institute, right!" I refined the search and, sure enough, up popped a link, which took me to a single page featuring a series of pink and purple swirls suggestive of, in my opinion, douche packaging. Beneath the logo was the tagline "Investigating Intelligence." There was a Manhattan phone number but nothing else.

The smart thing would have been to go back to the SIC to check Summa's LUDS and MUDS, search Better Business Bureau records—hell, start with a background check on Jeremy Wedge. Instead, just as an emaciated blonde sailed through the doors clutching about twenty Takashimaya bags, I dialed the number on the screen.

It rang as the bride-to-be positioned herself in front of the desk and pretended to look patient.

"Asa?" I said sweetly, showing him that I was on the phone. "He'll be right with you," I told the woman, who was so painfully hip that she most definitely lived in a 3,000-square-foot converted meatpacking plant on Stanton Street. When the weather turned cold, she'd wear a below-the-knee, quilted nylon coat, frayed jeans that dragged in the dirty snow, and a knit Peruvian hat with the strings hanging down the sides of her face. When she finally gave birth, she would, naturally, push a Bugaboo with latte holder attached. She was as far from being a Sterling Girl as a woman could be.

"Summa," sang a female voice on the other end.

"Oh." My stomach sank. Had I really just dialed without a plan? Was I so tired and so confused by what I'd found upstairs that I'd gone ahead and called?

"Um, I was wondering . . . um . . . what . . . where—" I fumbled.

"Ms. Herman! Did you have an easy flight in?"

My brain somersaulted. Why was that name familiar?

"Mmm, yes, yes, I did, thank you. How did you know it was me?" I shut my eyes against the spiraling screen saver, which was making me seasick.

"Well, I can see you're calling from the hotel. We do have caller ID here in New York, you know!"

Herman. Zelda Herman. Somewhere along the way I must have missed a step.

"Ha-ha, of course," I chuckled weakly.

"You're confirmed for two today, my dear. We're very much looking forward to seeing you again."

"Oh. Me, too. Absolutely. Um, could you remind me . . . the closest subway stop?"

"A Rhodes scholar but probably can't remember your own address, right? Typical, my dear!"

"Huh."

"The One to Canal. Go west, young woman, cross Canal, and you'll see Desbrosses. Number twenty-five. Even after a year, I'm certain you'll recognize it. Listen, sweetheart, catch a nap, relax, and we'll have dinner at Capsouto Frères afterward. You *know* there's nothing to be nervous about."

I scribbled the address on a piece of hotel stationery. "Well, *that's* good," I bellowed, suddenly afraid I was going to start laughing uncontrollably. I was so far out on a limb, there was nothing to do but jump. "I'm really looking forward to this!"

"You are?" The voice on the other end seemed to falter.

"You betcha!" I cheered, and hung up.

"So please make sure that the vegan snacks go to the *younger* Zurlansky room and not the older. Because the *older* Zurlanskys are very hostile toward vegans," the bride warned Asa, chewing on her lower lip. She would have been a great candidate for No Divas.

"They *are* often a bit sickly looking," Asa agreed.

The bride looked surprised.

"Vegans, I mean. I don't know the Zurlanskys," Asa explained.

I still had my hand on the desk phone when my cellphone buzzed in my pocket with a text. Two texts. We weren't supposed to use our phones when we were on duty, so I held mine below counter level and read them.

> <Leaving your place. Our place? I don't know what we're doing, but I want to keep doing it. Love.>

And the other:

> <2 bad u cdnt come to the stn lst nite. 2nite? (Delt)>

There was no way for Delta to know how much I loathed texting abbreviations, that I considered them dangerously close to the end of civilization. He couldn't know that even a missing apostrophe was enough for me to consider—however unfairly—dropping a person as a friend, at least in the short term. Gregory, of course, knew exactly how to send a message that didn't drive me to despair for the human race.

I chucked the phone into my backpack and sank down on the round leather stool we were allowed to use as long as no guests were in the lobby.

"Zephyr," Asa chided, shocked at my multiple breaches in protocol. He tilted his head dramatically toward the bride.

"Oh, and one other thing," she said, her voice strained from trying to sound like a relaxed person. "Make absolutely sure that the bag with the black-and-white ribbons on it goes to the Voldmans. They have a four-month-old and they said that, at that age, black-and-white shapes are excellent for the baby's cognitive development."

Asa and I stared at her.

I watched her mouth move, but the blood pounding in my ears drowned out her voice. Summa, Jeremy, Samantha. And maybe Zelda Herman. I was tangled in a massive knot of string and couldn't figure out which thread to grab on to first to unravel it. How the hell was I going to cram in another visit to Bellevue, attempt to follow Zelda Herman to Desbrosses Street at 2:00 P.M., *and* be on a train to Hellsville at 5:10? Not by perching here like a seal at the aquarium.

For the third time that morning, I fled my post, promising a wailing Asa that I'd make it up to him in the form of a dozen 800 calls on his behalf.

"We'll haul in everything from Swedish Fish to Post-its," I called over my shoulder. "An afternoon you won't soon forget!"

Chapter 8

I finally stopped shaking somewhere around Tarrytown: By 125th Street, I had already downed one of the pear ciders that Macy had thoughtfully provided as onboard refreshment, and at Yonkers I popped a second and that had done the trick.

My first death threat and I couldn't breathe a word to the friend beside me, carefully affixing first-class postage to a stack of wedding invitations. At least, I was pretty sure it had been a death threat. It turned out that threateners don't always spell out the threat as clearly as the threatened might hope. There's a lot of room for interpretation, misinterpretation, and ensuing paranoia, but I was almost positive that Jeremy Wedge had threatened to kill me that afternoon, right there in the ammonia-scented halls of Bellevue Hospital.

He hadn't been in his bed. His old roommate, he of the culinary wrath, was gone, and in his place was a man who seemed pleasant enough. One glass eye but otherwise apparently normal.

"Do you know where Jeremy is?" I'd asked hesitantly, knowing that even the most pedestrian of questions was a potential land mine in this place.

"Rec room, most likely," answered the roommate with a grin.

"Thanks. And which direction . . . ?" I pointed toward the corridor.

"I'm trying to get to Iraq. Do you think you could write me a check? My name is Sandy Miller, two 'L's."

"Um," I said, backing out of the room. "Great. Thanks."

"Okay," Sandy said cheerfully. "Bye, now."

Three men sat in the grim rec room, each keeping his distance from the others. One was reading a ragged Bible, another was sleeping in a chair—I hoped he was only sleeping—and Jeremy, once again impeccably dressed, glared out the window, his arms crossed. Even from behind, I could tell he was seething.

"Uh," I said by way of a greeting. Jeremy turned his head sharply.

"God fucking dammit—you again," he snarled.

Three years earlier, this salutation probably would have caused me to burst into tears. I reflected that I must be improving as an investigator—or at least hardening—because it only made me flinch.

Despite himself, Jeremy was obviously desperate for someone to talk to, or at least rail against.

"You gonna say anything, Helen Keller?" Now, that just didn't even make any sense. "Because my goddamn family doesn't believe it wasn't a suicide attempt and signed me up for another week in this resort. I'm being transferred to some other floor, like a fucking convict or a sales manager. So unless you're here to sign release papers, get the fuck out."

He turned back to the window.

"I believe you. I don't think you tried to kill yourself."

His back went rigid and I knew I had his attention. I stepped closer to him so we wouldn't be overheard.

"Jeremy," I whispered. "Why did Summa give Samantha Kimiko Hodges half a million dollars?"

He put both palms against the window and I braced myself for an eruption.

"Who?" he said carefully.

"The Summa Institute, your comp—"

"No." His voice was ice. "Who got the money?"

"The woman who gave you your love potion," I said to his back.

Jeremy whirled around. Beneath his freckles, his face was gray. His eye sockets seemed to sink while his eyeballs bulged.

"What the fuck are you talking about?" he snarled. He was either an excellent actor or we were on ground much wavier than I'd anticipated.

I took a step back. The man with the Bible glanced up at us. I gathered my courage and did my best imitation of someone with authority.

"Your institute gave the old woman on the fifth floor five hundred *thousand* dollars, and three days later you find yourself taking a potion of hers that did in fact contain lethal amounts of Ambien. So. My question is: What kind of business was she doing with Summa? With you? And why did she try to kill you?"

Now take a breath, Zephyr.

Jeremy narrowed his eyes and set his jaw. When he spoke, his voice was calm. "Who else have you told about this?"

"No one," I said, surprised that it was his first question. A small part of me anticipated a little thank-you for identifying his alleged would-be murderer.

"Not even your fat friend at the front desk?"

"Asa?" What did he care about Asa? "No."

Jeremy balled up his fists as if preparing to slug me. He released them, then leaned in close enough that I could feel his stale, institutional breath on my face.

"Who do you work for?"

This time I didn't even flinch, which I thought was progress.

"I work for your uncle."

"I don't believe you."

"The fuck I care what you believe."

Ever so gently, he gathered my mandarin collar in one hand. It was the most violent gesture ever bestowed on me, or at least as violent as having a gun pointed at me for twenty seconds during the nadir of Roxana Boureau's previous professional endeavors.

"Stop playing detective, Zephyr." I felt the warm exhalations from his nose and wondered whether I could safely wash my face in Purell.

"I'm not—"

"I don't know what you know or how you came to know it, but I suggest you leave. I will give you a healthy incentive, you chirpy little blackmailer. So tell me how much you want. To go. The fuck. Away."

Even I recognized it was not the time to be offended by the descriptor "chirpy."

"I . . . I'm not blackmailing you," I whispered. "I just want to help—"

He tightened his grip on my collar, which brought my whole body closer to his. Under other circumstances, it could have been a step in a dance of passion.

"You're a fucking liar. Think of a number right now or you *will* regret it."

A devil on my shoulder wondered, for a fraction of a second, what it would feel like to give my Roth IRA a healthy boost.

"Can I . . ." I didn't even know what I wanted to ask or how to stall for time.

"No, you cannot. Shall I count to three?" he sneered.

"No!" I realized that if I didn't pretend to be what he thought I was—a blackmailer—his suspicions might begin to veer closer to the truth. "I'll tell you what I want." My voice cracked like a newly adolescent boy's. "Oh, I'll tell you. I want . . . I want what you gave her. Half a million."

He pulled me so close I could see nose hairs.

"Two fifty?" I amended.

"You understand," he growled, "that I don't have ready access to my checkbook in here."

"That's okay," I croaked. "No rush."

"And then you go away and don't ever let me see you again." He shoved me back on my feet, hard. I rubbed my neck where the collar had dug into it.

"No problem. This isn't my idea of a grand destination," I spat at him.

"No. I mean quit the hotel, you moron."

"Excuse me?" I laughed incredulously.

"If I see you standing there when I get out of here next week . . ." He shrugged as if he wouldn't be responsible for his actions.

Which is why I was left unable to parse the exact details of his threat. And although I'd been quivering, standing there in Jeremy's clutches, I was thrilled, too. Jeremy had no idea how much he'd given away by threatening me. Of course, neither did I, but I would soon. I hoped. Actually, it wasn't yet clear that Jeremy's five hundred grand had anything to do with Ballard McKenzie's one hundred grand, but it seemed fair to assume that there might be some connection.

It was high time to bring Pippa up to date, but each time I'd called in that day, she'd either been on the ferry or on another line. I was irritated with my boss; if nothing else, I'd needed someone to tail Zelda Herman for me while I interviewed Jeremy, and there was no one I could ask except Pippa. Outside the hospital, I tried to reach her once more and failed, tried to hail a cab and failed, and wound up jogging to 42nd Street and over to Grand Central, blowing off some steam on the way.

I spotted Macy waiting for me at track 30, her back to me. I was about to call out when I looked down and saw I was still in my hotel uniform. Gasping, I turned on my heel and fled downstairs to the bathrooms. Inside the stall, I shoved my sweaty uniform back into my knapsack and tied my sweater over my soaking T-shirt. With a groan, I realized I'd been so distracted by my sleepless reunion with Gregory, followed by my dawn interview in the park with Samantha, followed by a search of her room, followed by my bewildering telephone exchange with the receptionist at Summa, followed by the tête-à-tête with Jeremy, that I'd forgotten to pack anything for my trip north.

* * *

"So what made you call the dermatologist?" I asked Macy as the train hurtled past Peekskill. Although the two pear ciders were partly to thank, I was impressed by my ability to compartmentalize my life. Here I was, carrying on a conversation as though I hadn't been on the receiving end of a death threat not two hours earlier. *This,* I thought, this is what allows otherwise great (and lousy) politicians to preach morality while carrying on affairs with interns, assistants, and Argentineans.

Macy put down an envelope and stretched her fingers. "Because the last guy, the one with the sprained ankle—"

"There were two sprained ankles: Is this the fertilizer mogul or the sculptor?"

"The sculptor—thank you, Your Tactfulness. He had had an ugly divorce."

"You can't hold that against him."

"Well, I can, actually. I never told you his whole deal. He was an artist-retreat cheat. He goes to Yaddo for a few weeks to finish stuff for his exhibit, sleeps with some woman who blows up video cameras while filming the explosions—hello, amateur irony hour—and poof goes his ten-year marriage. Kind of like the videos," she added with mock thoughtfulness.

"And he didn't live happily ever after with the exploder?"

"She went trotting back to her girlfriend of seven years. She'd wanted to sample men again and see if she was missing anything."

"Verdict?"

"Not even a little bit. So now he's out in the cold with only his lead sculptures to keep him warm at night."

"He didn't cheat on *you*," I pointed out.

She peeled the backing off a picture of a great horned owl. "Please. Once a cheater, always a cheater."

I tried not to think about whether Gregory had been with anyone in our time apart—not that it would in any way qualify as cheating. I just had a knack for torturing myself.

"How does a cheating sculptor inspire you to call a dermatologist?" I asked, gathering the discarded wax paper from the stamps and crumpling it. "Or are you finally willing to admit that you're not cursed?"

"No. I am not saying that at all. What I'm *maybe* saying . . ." Macy tucked a loose hank of hair behind her ear. "Okay. I might be willing to admit a tiny bit that maybe I would like to be with someone. And it *was* only a couple of sprained ankles."

"It is killing you to say I was right." I nudged her knee with mine.

"I thought it was sweet that the guy's mom was pimping him out," she continued, ignoring me. "A guy like that probably wouldn't be a cheater is what I'm thinking." She turned to me suddenly and pointed, her finger like a gun. "But I'm bringing an Ace bandage with me on the date."

I swatted her hand away. "Stick it in your bra and let it do double service."

She allowed a grudging smile.

I intercepted a rolling bottle with my foot as the train pulled in to Garrison. Did she honestly think she was cursed? I still couldn't tell how much of Macy was shtick. If, as Lucy had once hypothesized, Macy was truly afraid of intimacy and eschewed parenthood because it was easier for her to give of herself to strangers, did that matter to me? Certainly her reasons were more laudable than mine.

"How long do you think we have to stay tomorrow?" Macy tucked the stamped invitations into her duffel bag.

I shrugged, feeling anxiety begin to seep through me. The closer we got to Hillsville, the more trouble I had recalling why I thought I could spare this time away from work.

"I was hoping at least one of my clients would need me in the city," Macy mused. "Do you think I'm minimizing weddings to the point where I'm putting myself out of business? Oh my God, look at the leaves turning!" She sat straight up in her seat and jabbed at the train window. The passengers on the Garrison platform looked at her with alarm, but she didn't notice. "Hey, let's go apple-picking while we're up there. That's a kid-friendly thing to do, right? And we could build a fire and drink apple cider! Do they make cider before October?" In mere seconds, Macy had talked herself through a 180 so that she was now champing at the bit to get to suburbia. I smiled at her like a proud mama.

"What?" she asked.

"Nothing. I just like your attitude."

The train began to move again, and I leaned forward in my fake-leather seat to watch the river. It was dusk and I had to work hard to see through my own reflection to the view outside. For the most part, I had willed myself out of work mode and into supportive-friend mode, but one small, niggling thought remained: I was almost definitely sitting on an attempted-murder case, and it was critical that I find a moment to steal away and call Pippa. If Samantha Kimiko Hodges was to dole out any more lemon-flavored philters in the next twenty-four hours, I could be out of a job and on trial well before Jeremy ever got around to laying a hand on me.

Chapter 9

The evening had begun well enough, with Lucy racing down the stairs, flinging her arms around our necks, and proclaiming her undying gratitude before the door had even closed. Leonard had picked us up at the train station on his way home from work, and although conversation with him was often hampered by his shyness and ear-tugging, he seemed more confident and forthcoming than I'd ever seen him in the city. Perhaps returning to his native environment had been good for him. Too bad Lucy perceived his happiness as disloyalty.

The signs of distress hadn't been immediately apparent. We hugged and cooed and the kids were squealing and squeaking, so it took a few minutes to realize that the busy street sounds we were hearing—sirens, honking, the rhythmic *thump-thump* of traffic going over a steel plate, the occasional rumble of a storefront security gate being pulled down—didn't match the serene road outside. It turned out that Lucy had been so homesick for New York that she'd called Dover Carter with a specific request. He had called a sound guy he knew and come up with a custom sound track that we now had the privilege of enjoying over the centrally wired sound system Leonard had so innocently installed.

But the babies were even cuter than I remembered, toddling around, bellies first, in footie pajamas. They had become pretty, actually, with their high foreheads, generous eyes, and pillowy, kissable lips (glistening with drool, but still). In the bright, warm kitchen that smelled promisingly of butter and garlic, watching Leonard and Lucy expertly prompting Alan and Amanda to issue forth seal-like giggles, I had one tenth of one second of doubt about my decision to keep my eggs on the shelf. I felt a tug of longing for the glass jars of pasta neatly lined up on the counter, the fresh spider lilies in the living room, the copper umbrella stand by the front door, and the enormous farm table set with cloth napkins.

There was no reason I couldn't have these things, I reminded myself, pulling Amanda onto my lap. One didn't have to wait to have children, or even to be married, before one could equip oneself with a cobalt-blue KitchenAid mixer, but in truth they were all of a package. Part of the mixing *experience* were the rosy little faces covered in flour peering into the bowl. Just then, Amanda sneezed, and her rosy little face erupted with more snot than I imagined could be contained in such a small cavity. I handed her to her father, and as I washed my hands at the deep porcelain sink with the swan-neck faucet, I realized that my longing for a mixing experience could easily be satisfied with an occasional cookie-baking party.

After just twenty minutes of the Amanda and Alan show, the twins were hustled off to bed: The household was currently under tight rule by an absentee monarch, the author of a sleep guide that Lucy referred to no fewer than three times as her bible. As soon as the family disappeared upstairs, Macy and I found the audio closet and shut off the city sound track, right in the middle of the heavy clank of a bike messenger's chain hitting the sidewalk.

"Ahhh," Macy said of the ensuing silence, spreading her arms wide. I followed her into one of the two living rooms to wait out baby bedtime. We poured ourselves San Pellegrino and dug into the rosemary crisps and caviar from Eli's Vinegar Factory, courtesy of Macy's grateful clients, the ones she'd dissuaded from walking down the aisle to U2's "I Still Haven't Found What I'm Looking For." We had curled up on the couches—the ugly brown plaid was, unfortunately, still in residence—and were concluding that we preferred this to reading *Goodnight Moon* for the seventy-fifth time when the front door opened and someone called, "Yoo-hoo! Anyone home?"

We looked at each other, startled. Lucy hadn't mentioned anyone else coming to dinner.

"Well, *hello* there!"

"Mrs. Livingston!" Macy jumped off the couch and greeted Leonard's mother with her best professional smile. I had met Lenore Livingston only once before, at Lucy's wedding, and had steered a wide berth around the small, hard-looking blonde scowling her way through the proceedings.

"So nice to see you again," Macy sang. "You remember Zephyr, one of Lucy's old friends?"

"Zephyr, of course, you're the janitor. I remember you, dear." She embraced me in a falsely tight hug, as if someone had told her she should try to be more affectionate. Her perfume, a cloying, fruity scent, was instantly familiar, though I couldn't put my finger on why.

"Super. Former super," I said. "I'm a detective now." I got ready to don my modest "yes, really" smile in response to the inevitable exclamation of excitement and barrage of questions my job title usually elicited.

"Oh. Well, who's looking after your parents' building? Do they have to pay someone now?"

I halted my smile halfway so that my face felt like a jack-o'-lantern.

"Uh, well, they paid me before, so now they pay someone else."

"Oh, I didn't realize they paid you. How awkward for all of you!" She walked over to the bookshelf, where she adjusted two framed photos, then shook off her coat and draped it across the back of a chair. Macy and I glanced at each other, realizing at the same moment that any therapeutic benefits of our visit were going to be canceled out by Lenore's unexpected appearance.

"I see you girls are making yourselves at home. Good, good. And I assume the babies are going to sleep right now, at precisely seven-fifteen?" She tried to laugh, but it came out a snort. "Have you heard about this 'sleep training'?" She made quotation marks with her fingers. "It's absurd. I *never* let Leonard cry."

"And now I have chronic insomnia. Hi, Mom," Leonard said, darting down the stairs in his twitchy, slouchy way and dutifully allowing himself to be embraced by his mother.

"Your insomnia is because you work too hard and don't eat well, not because of anything I did."

"No, of course not," Leonard said with a tired half smile. "I assume you're staying for dinner?"

Macy looked at me, alarmed.

"Only if it's all right with you and your wife. I did bring couscous and your favorite brownies."

Without waiting for an answer, Lenore headed for the kitchen. "I'll make sure the chicken doesn't dry out. You are having garlic chicken, right? That's what Lucy always makes for company. . . ."

Macy and I turned to Leonard at the same time and fired off identical glares. He took a step back, startled.

"Leonard!" Macy snapped, as if reprimanding a child.

"Now, wait a second, Mace," I warned.

"No, I'm sorry, but this is not okay. It's not as if Leonard doesn't know that Lucy needed a night alone with us. She needs to vent. You do know that, Leonard, don't you?"

I was horrified and thrilled by Macy's daring. Her question was based on the assumption that Leonard knew exactly how his wife felt about his mother, and while Lucy assured us he did, there could easily be a large marital gap between what she told him and what she thought she was telling him.

Leonard flicked at his ear and searched the ceiling. "I know, I know, but . . ."

Lucy bounced down the stairs, a huge smile on her face. "Let the fun begin! I am soooo hap—" She stopped short, as if she'd run into a wall. She pointed to the coat on the chair, then turned to Leonard, her eyes wide and her lips mashed together.

"Honey, I'm sorry, she just—"

"Oh, hello, Lucy, sweetie!" Lenore sailed in, wiping her hands on a dishcloth. "I hope you don't mind, I added a little more olive oil to the marinade. It was looking gluey. How are my babies? Sleeping soundly? Did you see the new jammies I bought for them yesterday? I left them on your bed."

Lenore put Lucy in an armlock that only distantly resembled a hug.

"Thank you, Lenore," Lucy said stiffly, her voice shaky.

"She simply will not call me Mom!" Lenore singsonged to us. "Lucy, honey, sit down; you must be exhausted. Let me wait on you, and you enjoy your friends." She returned to the kitchen. Leonard gave Lucy a pleading look that said, *See, not so bad?*

"Oh, please," Lucy spat. "I'll be paying for this largesse with my *very blood*." She sniffled.

"Well, I think that's a little bit of an over—"

"Leonard," she snapped, "go help your mother in the kitchen so I can complain about you *and* her to my friends. More efficient," she muttered, leaning over the coffee table and scooping caviar straight into her mouth. "God, that's good," she breathed as Leonard slunk off.

"Luce," I rebuked. "Give the poor guy a break! He's on your side."

"If he were on my side, I'd still be talking to Mercedes via semaphores over Perry Street, not having my soul disemboweled by that black-hearted, money-obsessed control freak. Why didn't she come, by the way? Mercedes, I mean."

"Concert," Macy answered, curling up on the sofa again and pulling Lucy down with her, her arm around her shoulder. "See, so you couldn't have been flashing handwritten messages like a couple of ten-year-olds, not tonight."

"I don't think I can get through another dinner with her, I really don't," Lucy moaned, leaning into Macy. "Watch. She's going to dominate the conversation with stories that are alternately boring, nasty, or incomprehensible, while playing up what an involved, self-sacrificing grandmother she is and what a subpar mother I am and how the babies—"

"Oh my God," I exclaimed. "Sorry, but I just realized . . ."
My friends looked at me.

"Her perfume," I whispered, starting to laugh. "I just figured out where I've smelled it before. One of . . . one of Roxana's prostitutes, the only one I ever met. She used to wear the same scent as Lenore!"

Lucy opened her eyes wide and raised her eyebrows. She took a deep, cleansing breath. "Thank you, my love. I believe I will now survive dinner."

* * *

In fact, none of us emerged unscathed and, in the end, I managed to take Lucy's relationship with her mother-in-law a notch lower than it already was. Lenore was in fine form that evening, veering, as Lucy had predicted, from a story about the travails of mastering "suzuki" puzzles—boring—to a gleeful story about a formerly wealthy neighbor who'd lost his home—nasty—to a complicated tale about a friend of a friend who had dated a rich man who had treated her to lobster every single night for a year as a successful incentive to lose fifty pounds, after which he dumped her—incomprehensible.

The dishes were cleared and the brownies were presented, but it didn't look like Lenore was leaving anytime soon. Leonard's father was working late—it was no mystery why Maxwell stayed at the office whenever possible—and she was in no hurry to get home. Lucy, in a desperate attempt to have a conversation that did not include Lenore, mentioned that she wanted to bring the kids to my apartment the next time they visited New York, to play with my rabbit.

"Hitchens?" Lenore interjected, dabbing at the corner of her mouth with a napkin. "What a funny name for a bunny rabbit!"

I just smiled, but immediately a mental tocsin sounded, alerting me to dangerous territory. Even Leonard sensed it.

"Mom, these brownies are amazing. Did you use extra chocolate?"

"Why did you name him Hitchens?"

I glanced at Lucy, who looked nervous. "Oh, just a guy I know. These really are fabulous brownies."

"He's not named for that atheist, is he?" Lenore laughed, a short, hard honk.

I looked to Macy for help, but she stretched her arms high

above her head and settled back in her chair, as though the evening's entertainment was finally beginning.

"Uh, well . . ." *Stand up for your convictions outside the safety of the four liberal boroughs, Zephyr. Be a man.* "Yes. Yes, he's named for Christopher Hitchens," I said proudly.

"You're not an atheist, are you?" Lenore put her hand to her chest. Macy snorted, and immediately I saw that this couldn't end well, so I might as well enjoy it.

I licked brownie off my fingers with a loud sucking sound. "In fact, I am. An all-American atheist."

I watched Lenore's face contort as she prepared to hold forth. To my knowledge, her own son, in time-honored tradition, had not set foot in a synagogue since the final amen of his bar mitzvah, so I didn't know why she was getting all huffy. And then I remembered that she was a convert with all its attending zeal and, in her case, a limited perception, perhaps even a fear of, the tribe's protean nature.

"Well, you know," I reminded her brightly, "Judaism can be an ethnicity or a religion. It doesn't have to be both."

"It is both."

"Nooo. For me, it's an ethnicity. The way you can be an Italian Catholic or an Italian . . . okay, well, say a Spanish Catholic or a Spanish Jew or a Spanish atheist. I'm a Jewish atheist." I felt like I was talking to a five-year-old.

Macy leaned forward and put her freckled elbows on the table. Leonard looked at the floor and tugged vigorously at his ear. Lucy covered her face with her hands.

"So you don't believe in God?"

"Seriously?" I asked before I could stop myself.

She sat back as if I'd slapped her.

I tried to think of a way out of this Religion for Dummies conversation without veering into the "well, I *am* spiritual" realm. I didn't owe this woman any kind of explanation.

"I just feel religion is for those who need it."

Lenore pushed her seat back from the table. I glanced at Lucy but couldn't tell whether she was going to laugh, cry, or cheer.

"I don't mean that in a mean way," I explained quickly. "I only mean I don't need religion to feel gratitude or to compel me to be good. Though I realize I'm in the minority," I sputtered in a vain attempt to save Lucy from some incalculable aftermath.

Lenore stalked out and, a moment later, the front door clicked closed.

Leonard looked at Lucy, his lips and brow contorted with anxiety.

"Oh, go," Lucy said, and Leonard shot out of his chair. "Go make nice with her. God knows Zephyr can't."

* * *

Seven hours later, I crept downstairs and shuffled in the dark toward Lucy's kitchen. I was feeling around for the refrigerator when Macy's voice came at me from the direction of the marble-topped island.

I gasped and fumbled and accidentally turned on the bright overhead lights.

"Turn it off, you idiot! Turn it off!" Macy yelped as I hit the switch and returned us to obscurity, my heart pounding. The insomnia I'd been suffering was now guaranteed to last another few hours.

I clutched at my chest with one hand and blindly took aim with my other, successfully clocking Macy.

"What was that for?"

"You scared the hell out of me," I spat. "I thought I just left you upstairs in the bed."

"You didn't notice I wasn't there? Great work, detective."

"It was dark," I protested, "and there was a big mound of covers. I thought you were under there."

"As if I could sleep after that train wreck of an evening."

By the collective light emanating from the digital clocks on the microwave, the stove, the coffeemaker, and the refrigerator, I could begin to make out Macy's hunched shape, sitting on a stool at the counter. She was eating something, and as my eyes adjusted, I could see it was the cake Lucy had made in honor of our visit.

"You're not even going to get a plate?" I commented, taking the fork out of her hand and helping myself to a bite. "Oh my God," I said, my mouth full. "Even when she's homicidal, infanticidal, and suicidal, she still makes a better chocolate cake than I can on my best day."

"I might have to fake a client call," Macy moaned. "Especially if that woman from whose loins Leonard sprang is planning on joining us at the orchard."

"It would be a little like a fairy tale, though, right?" I mused, shoveling in more cake. "Evil witch, poisoned apple."

Macy took the fork back and gouged out another bite. She was wearing a billowing fuchsia T-shirt bearing the logo of her favorite florist. Since Lucy and Macy were both about the size I'd whizzed past at the age of ten, I'd borrowed a shirt from Leonard to sleep in. I was hoping that no one would notice or smell the fact that the next day I'd be wearing the same clothes I'd arrived in.

"When did Lucy learn to cook?" I asked, opening the fridge to size up the state of the leftovers.

"Since moving to a town where all the restaurants have 'fine dining' on their signs," Lucy said from the doorway. She turned on the lights and dimmed them to a tolerable level.

"Jesus!" I slammed the door shut. "The two of you should have bells around your necks."

"You've gotta be the jumpiest detective in all of New York," Macy observed.

I swatted the back of her head on my way to giving Lucy a hug.

"Zephyr, you're thirty-one," Macy complained. "Stop slugging people."

"Thirty. You okay?" I asked Lucy.

Lucy sank down on the stool next to Macy's and shrugged. "I think I married the wrong guy."

I froze. Macy whipped her head around.

"I do. I mean, I'm not going to do anything about it. I'm just accepting it," she said with theatrical resignation.

"Luce," I began. "I can tell you objectively that your mother-in-law would test any marriage."

"Of course she would, but don't you think I'd be able to laugh it off, at least occasionally, if he and I were stronger?"

"But everything's so hard with kids. You have to think back to when you guys were first dating—try to recapture that." It was embarrassingly facile advice but valuable nonetheless.

"You know how I first decided I was in love with Leonard? We went to Rocco's for a black-and-white cookie one night—"

"Oooh, the ones with the raspberry jam under the icing?" Macy asked.

"We went to Rocco's and I only wanted the vanilla half and he only likes the chocolate half and so I decided he was the one. How pathetic is that?" Lucy dropped her head onto her arms.

"I'm pretty sure that's not the only reason you married him."

"It is," she moaned from under a curtain of blond hair. "I chose my husband based on *pastry*."

Macy rolled her eyes at me. Despite the patience that had been shown her in her time of need, she was not always one to reciprocate in equal measures.

"Lucy," I said, squeezing her bony shoulders. "Until you moved to Wisteria Lane with less-perky boobs, you guys were fine. You'd probably be fine here, too, if you could get a handle on the monster-in-law."

Lucy lifted her face hopefully. "Do you know any hit men?"

Samantha Kimiko Hodges crossed my mind briefly. Was she for hire?

"Sorry, sweets. I meant more like, can you get Leonard to help set some limits?" I asked lamely.

Lucy gave me an impatient look. "Says the woman who couldn't just name her stupid rabbit Thumper!"

"Okay, well, look, what about moving back to New York? Is that such a crazy idea? I'm sure Leonard doesn't want you to be miserable."

"I'd still have the kids."

"Oh, for fuck's sake, Luce," Macy crabbed. "The kids are cute! They're warm and soft and they'll miss you when you're dead. What the hell is wrong with you?"

"Ear wax is warm and soft, too. If they're so great, why are you and Zeph leading the charge in population control?" She jumped up and dragged her stool to the refrigerator. I was sure she was going to pull out a bottle of Stoli, raising the curtain on yet another demon in her life. Instead, she opened a cabinet and extracted a Tupperware full of primary-hued gewgaws.

"Look at this. *Look* at this."

Macy squinted at the pile of plastic and sequins and sparkles.

"These," Lucy explained, "come out of party-favor bags. I do not know what they are. I do not know why people think that one-year-olds need party favors. They would choke on them or poke each other's eyes out or clog the toilet with them. What *are* they?" she pleaded.

"These?" I said, picking up one of the mysteries. "These

are pre-garbage. These were manufactured in China specifically to be put right here." I flipped open the trash can and swept the entire pile onto their rightful place atop scraps of garlic chicken. "They're not a reason to hate your kids."

Lucy kicked at the can. "I don't hate them and I don't hate Leonard. I do hate Lenore and I really miss my job. And I love that you guys are up here, but I'm so damn jealous, it's almost hard to have you."

"Excuse me?" Macy said, sitting up straight on her stool. I could see her calculating what we'd spent on train tickets in recent months.

"You try to make me feel better, but you get to go home to a life where you can distinguish the weekend from the weekday, where the most exhausting thing you do on a Sunday is choose between Danal and Grey Dog for brunch. I miss that. I wish I hadn't done . . . this." She gestured vaguely around the catalog-perfect kitchen.

"You know, people in New York have kids, too," I reminded her.

"Maybe I should have an affair," Lucy said, grabbing a sponge from the sink and wiping at nonexistent crumbs.

"Excellent plan," Macy said, sliding off her stool. "Very original, too. Call me when you need help deciding between the butcher and the lawn guy. I'm going to bed." Macy blew us each a kiss and wandered out of the kitchen.

Lucy watched her go and then looked at me pleadingly. "I feel so trapped, Zeph. Sometimes, in the middle of the night, I imagine jumping in the car and leaving them all for good. I'm never going to do it, but the thought calms me down. Better than yoga breathing. How sick is that?"

A thought crossed my mind, but I censored myself.

"What?" Lucy said.

"Well, and I'm only asking, and I don't want to make you mad—"

"Just ask."

"Do you ever . . . do you think sometimes you don't connect with your kids because of, you know, the genetic thing . . . ," I trailed off, certain I was going to spark a tempest.

"Because they weren't my eggs?" Lucy asked with genuine surprise. She laughed with relief. "God, no. I think about the donor out there as one of the gajillion technicians who helped me have my babies. They're mine and I'm stuck with them, and the fact that I sometimes wish I'd never become a mother has nothing to do with it."

I pulled the plastic wrap over the cake and tucked it back in the refrigerator. "Honestly, Luce? I don't know what to tell you to make you feel better."

"I know you don't. No one does." She wrapped her arms around her tiny body, a body that had gotten worryingly thin. "I just need to get down to the city more. Go to one of Dover's glittery events and forget myself for a few hours."

"Oh, hey!" I remembered as I rinsed off the communal fork. "Come down this Monday. He's hosting a non-Oscar party, where people are reading the speeches they didn't get to read at the Oscars."

Lucy's mouth hung open. "*People?* You mean *people* who were nominated and didn't win?"

I nodded. "It was supposed to happen back in February, but it took a while for them to all coordinate their schedules."

Lucy laughed for the first time since Lenore had mucked with her marinade that evening. "You think? Can't imagine why!" She placed her palms on the countertop and pushed down until her feet left the floor. "Why is that prospect still so damn thrilling? I can finally have a normal conversation with Dover, but the thought of eating pretzels with the cast of

High Dudgeon is exciting enough to carry me through to next week."

"Maybe because you know for sure that Mercedes would never let your mother-in-law in the door." I laid the fork among its gleaming brethren in the silverware drawer, which was free of the grit that mysteriously accumulated in my own. "Can't you send Lenore on a cruise or something? Don't you people with a lot of money do that?"

"I still think a hit man would be the best solution." Lucy stretched her neck, tilting her head from side to side. "But a cruise. That *is* intriguing. . . ."

Chapter 10

Having an ambulatory meeting with Pippa Flatland ranked low on my list of preferred activities, requiring as it did the lung capacity to keep up with her redwood-length strides while carrying on a coherent conversation as well as the forethought to bring to work a change of unsweaty clothes. If Pippa was angry or excited, her pace increased, and on this Thursday morning she was one or the other, but I didn't yet know which. I forsook my dignity and broke into a light jog.

"So after the cousin threatened you—"

"Well, I don't know if it was *really* a threat," I puffed. The jog was not helping the stomachache I still had from gorging on apples in an upstate orchard.

"Don't split hairs, Zephyr. What did he do when you confronted him about the money transfer?"

I had begun my briefing in Pippa's office, but as soon as I got to the part about Samantha Kimiko Hodges and her potion, Pippa hadn't been able to sit still. I had assumed we would head to the ferry but, instead, we charged up Pearl

Street. By Wall Street, I was gasping for air. Pippa wasn't even breaking a sweat.

"He acted surprised, as if he didn't know about it. As if he didn't know Summa had paid Samantha."

"What makes you assume he was acting?"

"Well," I gulped, "the fact that he immediately wanted it covered up, forgotten. I mean, if someone else hired Samantha to kill him, wouldn't he want both her and that person arrested? Also, it would be a free pass out of Bellevue, clearly attempted homicide, not suicide." As we sailed past Maiden Lane, I thought longingly of the MetroCard nestled inside my backpack.

"Any chance he was trying to stage his own murder, for whatever reason?"

I shrugged. It was all I could muster.

"Otherwise he's a victim unwilling to reveal he's a victim—equally mysterious."

A few yards in front of us stood an earnest-looking man wielding a clipboard. Normally I resented having to summon the energy to deflect petitioners—I'd put my cellphone to my ear and feign conversation—but today I hoped the do-gooder would offer me a chance to catch my breath.

"Do you have a moment for the Democratic Party?" he asked.

Pippa practically ran him over. I glanced back apologetically.

"And what is this Summa place he runs?"

"Not sure. Genetics something. Going to visit," I wheezed.

"And no guesses as to why this hotel guest had an appointment at Summa?"

"Zero," I admitted.

On the next block was another petitioner. I started to slow my pace, but Pippa plowed ahead.

"Do you have a moment for the environment?" pleaded a chubby Goth volunteer.

"Oh for God's sake!" Pippa sniped. "The rain lets up and you people are out like worms!" We crossed John Street.

"All right, look." Mercifully, Pippa came to an abrupt stop on the corner. "Where is the Hodges woman right now?"

I shrugged sheepishly.

"You asked her too many questions," Pippa reproached me. "Does she suspect anything about you?"

"I think she just thinks I'm a nosy pain in the ass."

"Still." Pippa started walking again. I groaned out loud, but she didn't even notice. "I'm concerned for your safety, Zephyr."

I was concerned with keeping my Jonagolds down.

"Right," she said, when I didn't bother answering. "I'll give you a chance to visit Summa, but then I'm inclined to bring some other folks in on this—"

"Do you have a moment to save the children?"

"NO!" Pippa bellowed. "Christ, we ought to have taken the ferry. Zephyr, for the next twenty-four hours, I want hourly updates from you. Call me when you're going to sleep, and call me when you wake up. Meantime, I'm going to see whether I can dig up anything on the Hodges woman." She stopped again and looked up at the street sign. She seemed surprised. "Brilliant, we've got you partway to the hotel."

I raised my eyebrows, as if I, too, were pleased by this discovery.

"Speaking of which," she said casually, brushing her hair back from her face. "Do you have any idea whether this is connected to Ballard McKenzie's missing hundred?"

I blushed. Pippa may as well have said: *I think we're both relieved that a month of work has resulted in* something *(even if it was entirely accidental), but, by the way, have you entirely forgotten the case I assigned you?*

"I don't know," I admitted. "I can't figure out how, but I'm going to keep looking."

"Yes, do, Zephyr. It would be rather agreeable to make a dent in the case, don't you think?"

* * *

I tried not to strangle Asa as he squinted at the ceiling.

"Let me think." He tapped a pencil against his doughy chin. "It was a moving van, that company that employs artists and actors. The van was reddish—mmm, maybe more like brown with red overtones? And there were two guys. One was a gym rat." Asa wrinkled his nose in condemnation. "The other was much more my type. A little something to grab on to, you know?"

"Asa?"

"Hmm?"

"Did she tell you where she was going? Did the movers tell you? Do you have *any* idea?" I asked from between gritted teeth. I glanced around the lobby, trying to tune out the echo of Jeremy's threat in my head.

"Hey, you're not supposed to be here on your days off. You know what? I think you actually have a thing for Hutchinson."

I closed my eyes for a moment and wished that I was familiar with some kind of breathing technique other than huffing with exasperation.

"Excuse me?"

"He hates you, and that intrigues you. Turns you on. Speaks to some sub-, post-, anti-feminist self-loathing."

"Asa."

He frowned, apparently having confounded even himself.

"Asa, *please*. Do you know where Mrs. Hodges went this morning? It must have taken an hour or two to move her out. You didn't ask? You didn't make small talk with the out-of-work, love-handled actor?" I wasn't even bothering to hide the desperation in my voice.

"Why do you care? Did you develop some kind of *Tuesdays with Morrie* thing with her?"

"Yeah, she's my mentor. My godmother. My fucking spiritual guide. Asa, *think*!"

Asa finally looked genuinely concerned and I almost felt bad for him, he of the absent sarcasm detector.

"Oh jeez, Zeph, lemme see." He put his chin on his fist. With anyone else, I would have thought they were putting me on, but Asa was all in earnest. I wouldn't have been too surprised to see smoke curl from his ears and an animated chipmunk perch on his shoulder. Suddenly he looked up, his eyes wide.

"Local! They said it was a local move!"

"Local like in the neighborhood or the tristate area?"

Asa looked like he was going to cry.

"Okay," I said reassuringly, "you don't know. How was Mrs. Hodges acting? Angry? Nervous?" I realized this was a lot to ask of him.

"She gave me a box of matzoh ball mix and said she wouldn't need it where she was going."

What did that mean? The afterlife? Riverdale?

"Anything else?"

"She said to say goodbye to the zaftig busybody, but I didn't know what she was talking about. Maybe Mrs. McKenzie? She gave me a note for her."

Luckily, I was not yet in possession of my Glock.

"Asa," I said calmly, "she left a note?"

Asa dug around in the drawer beneath his computer terminal and came up with a neatly folded piece of hotel stationery, taped closed. I grabbed it from him.

"Hey, that's not for you!"

"Look up 'zaftig,'" I muttered, slitting open the note. In

a spidery hand, that aberrational Asian had written, "I am now interested in talking to you. I am at the Hudson Street Nursing Home. Not for long."

Minutes later, I was hurrying along Greenwich Avenue, picking my way through a garden-variety street fair, where one could buy roast corn and tube socks, among other essentials. I stopped to purchase a lemonade, my only nourishment since a handful of animal crackers off Pippa's desk a few hours earlier. Between my race to Grand Central on Tuesday, the morning's speed walk with my boss, and this sprint to Abingdon Square, there was no way I wasn't going to lose a few pounds and, with it, the adjective "zaftig." *Shallow, Zephyr, shallow. We're talking about attempted murder and you're thinking about a few pounds no one has ever complained about.*

I passed the Jefferson Market Garden, where a women's prison used to stand, and wondered what could possibly have happened in the past two days to make Samantha Kimiko Hodges go from an independent widow who loathed me to a nursing-home resident who wanted to chat. Was this going to be a deathbed confession? Or was it a trap? The thought made me stumble. Was someone going to pick me off on the corner of Hudson Street? I picked up my pace, energized by the idea that I actually needed backup protection, that, for once, my life was in enough *real* danger to concern my pragmatic boss.

There was that rescue fantasy again, I chastised myself as I crossed 10th Street. I needed to run this by the Sterling Girls and Macy to see if they thought I needed a remedial course in feminist thinking. When my phone rang, I flipped it open, distracted by visions of what form such a course might take: a male volunteer with whom you practiced divvying household chores? *Listen, Bill, merely putting the clothes in the washing machine does not constitute "doing the laundry."*

"You're not dead," said a male voice.

"Excuse me?" My knees suddenly felt rubbery. *Jeremy?*

"You don't answer invitations to eat meat with heroes."

"Delta," I said in a rush of relief.

"You know any other heroes?"

"Oh God, I'm so sorry."

"For which part?"

I blew out my lips. I couldn't help thinking that if he really wanted to pursue me, he shouldn't tire me out with this sarcastic variety of flirtation, which I didn't care for in the least.

"All of it. Work has been nuts."

"Is that all?"

I tried to think of an honest but not too honest answer.

"I'd like to see you again," he said. "But if you're not interested or if there's someone else—"

"There's no one else!" I blurted out, to my utter dismay and surprise.

"Meaning?"

"That there is," I admitted, too embarrassed to meet my own gaze in the window of Lafayette Bakery. "But there wasn't anyone—I mean, he wasn't in the picture—when you and I went out."

"That was Saturday. Ouch."

"No, I knew him from a long time ago."

"When did he come back?"

"Do we really need to go into details?"

"Good point. To summarize: You're unavailable."

"I guess so," I said reluctantly.

"Zephyr?"

"No, I am," I told him, irritated again with Gregory for showing up and complicating everything. If we weren't getting back together—and why the hell would we?—then I was being forced to pass up Lieutenant Fisk and any number of other possibilities. Textile designers, architects, pastry chefs, entomologists. This episode with Gregory might very well only serve to set me back three months of my life.

"Okay, well," he said, and I heard the deafening blare of an alarm in the background. "Gotta run. Listen, give the reunion two weeks and if it doesn't work out, call me."

"And if it's two weeks and a day?" I asked.

"Then no guarantees."

"You're very odd," I told him, because I had nothing to lose.

"But you had a great time with me," he reminded me.

"I did."

"Zephyr?"

"You really have to go."

I flipped my phone closed and turned onto 12th Street, passing right by my building. Why two weeks? It was so bizarre, yet so appealing. Imagine scheduling a closing for any unresolved issue in your life—even a romantic one. What a relief that would be! If I limited the duration of my reunion with Gregory to two weeks, then I wouldn't have to be angry at him for his jarring reappearance. We could even, I thought, crossing Bleecker Street, revisit our relationship once a year for a two-week stretch, provided no one was involved with anyone else at the time. A designated period to upend our hearts, with the knowledge that the upheaval had an expiration date. Brilliant. I'd propose it to him at dinner that night. We were scheduled to meet at Barbuto for a reverse date, during which we would back up to have the conversation we should have had at Bar Six.

Two weeks to sort out whether we could make a go of it. Two weeks to resolve our different opinions on parenthood, differences we hadn't been able to resolve over the course of a three-year relationship. Surely Gregory would see the merits of this rational and levelheaded approach. He'd be so impressed that he'd remember I was much more important to him than an imaginary child. I could even suggest taking the twins for a week every month, thereby killing two birds with two stones—we'd dabble in temporary parenthood while giving Lucy and Leonard a break. I'd seduce Gregory with sanity, flabbergast him with phlegmaticness.

What man could resist?

Chapter 11

I'd passed the Hudson Street Nursing Home countless times on my way to and from the Hudson River Park, but I'd never gone inside until I began volunteering with Macy. Since then I'd grown strangely comfortable with the aroma of cold eggs and denture cream. And instead of feeling dread and sadness, as I initially did (after all, I was the daughter of Ollie and Bella Zuckerman, both of whom regarded aging as a personal affront), I found it a relief to have so little expected of me, to be in a place where my mere presence was more than sufficient to satisfy the task at hand.

I nodded at a few residents who were sitting on the benches outside, their white faces turned up to the sun while their black aides thumbed through magazines. Inside the glass door, I jogged up the five steps to the front desk. The perpetually harried director, Arturo, greeted me with a frown.

"I don't have volunteers scheduled for today," he said, gathering up a stack of papers. The phone rang, but he ignored it.

"I'm not here to volunteer. I'm here to visit a resident."

"Not the same thing?" He jabbed at the keyboard in front of him with his free hand.

"She just moved in this morning. Asked me to come by."

"Name?"

"Hers or mine?"

"Both. I can't remember all you volunteers."

"I'm Zephyr; she's Samantha Kimiko Hodges."

Arturo traced the two sides of his pencil mustache with thumb and forefinger and sighed heavily.

"Sign in. Show ID," he relented.

I fished out my driver's license, remembering that Macy had asked me to run the dermatologist through the DMV database before their first date.

"Miss Zuckerman!" I felt a gentle hand on my arm and turned to see Alma Mae Martin flashing her bright red grin at me. *Miss* Alma Mae Martin, as she insisted on being addressed, was a nonagenarian who wore flapper dresses and spiky heels that added a good three inches to her not inconsiderable height. The staff at the nursing home had, in vain, urged her to relinquish the stilts, weaving ominous scenarios involving fragile bones and wet floors. She refused and had even signed a waiver saying she would not sue them for any incident that occurred while teetering in her preferred footwear.

Alma Mae Martin maintained that it was her long legs atop tall shoes that had helped secure spots in the beds of the Kennedy brothers and the former secretary of defense. She wore the flapper dresses out of perpetual mourning for the Roaring Twenties, which she'd missed, coming of age as she had during the Depression.

"What brings you here, darlin'?"

"Hi, Miss Martin," I said, sliding the clipboard back to Arturo.

"Not 'hi,' sweetheart. A lady always says 'hello.'"

I wanted to point out that I was not a lady and neither, according to her purported track record, was she.

"Hello, then."

"What brings you to this neck of the woods on a Thursday mornin'?"

"A friend of mine just moved in," I said after a moment's hesitation. I indulged a quick imagining of her initial meeting with Samantha. It would be a matter of adoration or loathing. I predicted that there could be no indifference between the two of them.

Arturo hung up the phone and nodded curtly at me.

"Mrs. Hodges said you could go up. Third floor, room 308."

"Is that the short one?" Alma Mae asked, her lips twitching to avoid a snarl. So they'd already met.

"How have you been?" I asked her, changing the subject and walking slowly toward the elevator so she wouldn't trip.

"Oh, honey, I've been evah so busy," she said, fanning herself as though she were on a porch in Savannah. "I've been sorting through my old love letters. The ones from Jack, those are easy. But there were two Bobbies! In private, Mr. Secretary let me call him Bobby, so it's tricky, you know, to tell which beau is which—"

"You're from the South, Miss Martin, right?"

"A lady never interrupts."

"My apologies. But you're from Georgia, yes?" We stepped into the elevator, where the metal walls distorted our reflections like so many fun-house mirrors. I pressed the button and hoped Alma wasn't planning on escorting me all the way to Samantha's room.

"Oh, a long, long time ago, sugar. I've been up north for ages."

"Any suggestions on how to get a stubborn Southerner to change his mind about something?" I asked, embarrassed for myself.

She laughed, a long-practiced but contagious birdlike laugh. "You have a Southern gentleman caught in your womanly web?"

"I do, but he's . . . presenting some problems."

We stepped off and Alma Mae pointed past some birthday decorations wilting along the wall to Samantha's room. She was lady enough to know when to say goodbye.

"Well, I've never taken a fancy to Southern men, myself. I prefer Northerners. Catholics from Hyannis Port, in particular." She smiled and winked and I watched her saunter away, a swing in her achy hips. Fantasy lovers notwithstanding, I hoped I had her self-assurance when I hit ninety. I hoped I had it when I hit thirty-one.

* * *

Samantha slammed shut a drawer in the modest-size bureau. There were only two boxes and one suitcase in the room.

"Where's all your stuff?"

"You see room for it here in this postage stamp? Storage."

"So why'd you come?"

"I got tired of fine carpeting. I had a yen for linoleum and cheap cabinetry. Brings back my childhood." She tugged at the suitcase on the floor. I reached down and pulled it onto the bed for her.

Without acknowledging my help, she unzipped it and began removing items. Old age didn't mean you had to be obnoxious, I thought. Look at Alma Mae Martin. No more kid gloves for this woman.

"Okay, so answer this: Why did you ask me to come here? To clear your conscience? Because I already know you got paid to kill Jeremy," I said casually, and then held my breath.

It did the trick. Samantha froze, her hands on a hanger. She pointed her finger at me, but the gesture was tempered by the uncertainty in her voice.

"I did not try to kill that man."

"That's a lie," I told her flatly.

"I *pretended* to try to kill him. So I'd get paid. But I called 911 right away. And I went and got you. *And* I left the bottle so they'd know what he'd taken."

I thought back to Saturday night, to Delta's insistence that someone had called for help at least ten minutes earlier, not two minutes. Samantha had called well before I told her to go do it.

"The bottle with the crossed-out label? Under the bed?"

"I left the name of the drug showing, so they'd know," she said defensively.

"Hold on." I allowed myself a quick doglike shudder to clear my head, which was reeling from the fact that she hadn't denied my accusation of attempted murder. A week ago, I'd been eating Asa's trial-size SnackWell's at the front desk, and Samantha Kimiko Hodges had been a sweet old lady with a dress-by-numbers wardrobe. "Let's start with the person who paid you to kill—"

Samantha jabbed her extended finger at me.

"—sorry, to *not* kill Jeremy." I wasn't sure how long I'd be able to play along with Samantha's interpretation of events, but for now, I had to resist pointing out that poisoning someone with an entire bottle of Ambien was not, by any definition, pretending.

"I don't know her name."

Her. It surprised me, though it shouldn't have. Add it to the remedial feminist lesson plan: Women are capable of hiring murderers, too. Of hiring female murderers, in fact. Female murderers who were active members of AARP. I wondered if the criminal world was outpacing legitimate businesses when it came to progressive hiring practices. I sat down on the bed.

"How . . . ?" I tried to find the question that would get me to the beginning. "Why . . . ? How did you meet her?"

Samantha resumed unpacking. "She found me through the Bernie Madoff list," she said, as easily as if we were having a conversation under dryers in the salon.

"Excuse me?"

"The list of Bernie Madoff's victims is everywhere on the computers. This woman found me that way."

My brain tripped over the unexpected name. "You lost money to Madoff and so you agreed to kill someone to get some more money?" I asked incredulously. Surely my imagination was, once again, taking giant liberties.

"*Pretended* to kill! That's very important! *Pretended!* Swindling the swindler." Her face turned red. "And not just some money. My husband lost everything to that shmendrik and then he goes and has a heart attack, leaving me with bupkes."

I pinched the bridge of my nose, wishing I could take a notebook out of my backpack.

"Why did you call me here?" I asked again.

"Because someone needs to catch this woman before she hires someone else to try again," she said self-righteously.

I declined to point out that Samantha herself might yet be of interest to any number of law-enforcement agencies.

"But why me? Why not go to the police?"

"Please. You *are* the police. This way I don't have to waste my time sitting next to trannie hookers and talking to some shmegegge sitting behind a desk and breathing his coffee breath on me."

"I'm not a cop," I said, snorting too loudly.

"You're not fooling anybody." She waved me away.

My fingers and toes went numb, and a wave of nausea undulated through me. My first undercover job and I'd blown it. Completely and utterly blown it. How long had she known? Where had I screwed up? I wondered just how many people I wasn't fooling. I couldn't exactly request an exit interview. Samantha continued to unpack, seemingly unaware that she had thrust a dagger through my professional future.

I took a shuddery breath and tried to chart a new course. Was it worth expending energy to attempt to restore my ruse? If anything, I realized after a few seconds, the fact that I had a badge seemed to be a point in my favor at this moment.

"Okay," I acknowledged, chucking a month of apparently fruitless undercover work. "So you want to lead us to the woman who hired you. Are you hoping for immunity?"

She looked at me scornfully. "I don't need immunity. I didn't do anything wrong. I made sure he lived."

Wow. I thought about Alma Mae and her insistence that she'd really entertained JFK, RFK, and McNamara in the boudoir. You could almost look forward to aging if this was the kind of rock-solid certainty it bestowed on you. Of course, in Samantha's case, reality would necessarily throw a wrench in that certainty in the rudest way.

"Let's back up—way, way up," I said, grabbing a pad of paper off the peeling laminated desk. If my cover was blown, I might as well get the facts right. I looked down and noticed she'd taken the hotel's stationery as a parting gift.

She sighed impatiently, as though it was my fault we were stuck there, keeping her from proceeding with her day.

"You gave him the lemon drink full of Ambien at the bar?" She nodded.

"And he drank it right there or took it somewhere?" I wanted to see whether Jeremy and Samantha would offer corroborating scenarios.

"Right there. I remember Geraldine, the bartender, telling him he was lucky he was the owner's nephew, otherwise she never woulda let him bring his own drink."

"Then what?"

"Then he goes and starts talking to a pretty little shiksa at the bar. Men have no idea when a woman is out of their league. Egos like you can't believe."

"You stayed at the bar?"

"Of course! I was *watching* him," she said pointedly, as if to remind me of her virtuous concern for her victim. "He and the girl were chatting it up, and I almost felt bad for the schmuck."

"Almost," I muttered.

"You want I should not tell you anything?" she snapped. "So then he suddenly stops talking to the girl."

"He looked sick?"

She squinted at a corner of the room. "No, actually. You know the couple who'd been staying in the room you found him in?"

I looked up from my scribbling.

"The Whitcombs?" I asked, surprised.

"You think I bother with the names of everyone who comes in and out of that place? All I know is that they were a lot quieter than those idiot Australians."

"New Zea—never mind. What about the Whitcombs?"

"They were checking out and saying goodbye and thank you to Geraldine. Why the guests all love Geraldine, I do not know. She smells like diesel, but everyone thinks they've had some kind of authentic experience after a conversation with her."

"The Whitcombs."

"You're too pushy, you know that?" Samantha took her time folding a silk scarf, making the most of her captive audience. "So he—you know, *him*—he seemed pretty interested in them. Maybe he was starting to feel not so hot and figured he could run to their empty room if he needed to be sick?" She shrugged, unconvinced by her theory.

"So then what?"

"He excused himself and went straight up to their room."

"Did he ask them their room number? How did he know it?"

"He didn't say a word to them."

I frowned. I'd figure that out later. "So you said he didn't look sick yet?"

She put her hand to her cheek and shook her head as if remembering her disappointment. "Not really. Surprising, since I used the whole bottle."

I steadied myself against her detached affect, which was grotesque.

"You followed him."

"Until he went into the room. Then I went and called 911. And then I came and got you."

"So how did you get the empty prescription bottle under the bed?"

"I tossed it in after you opened his door."

A shot of horror rippled through me. She had been carrying out her crime right in front of me. I looked at my notes to help maintain a blank expression, a feat of Everest proportions for me.

"Tell me about the . . . your employer," I said, trying not to make it sound like a joke.

"Never met her."

"You spoke on the phone?"

"What, you think we did the e-mail?"

She certainly didn't *sound* like a novice.

"How many times did you talk?"

Samantha slammed closed the top drawer of the dresser. I'd have to hurry; she was getting agitated.

"Maybe half a dozen times."

"Did you move in to the hotel before you were hired or *because* you got hired, to be near Jeremy?"

"Because."

I filed this away; if I paused to consider the appalling extensiveness of the plot, I'd lose my line of questioning.

"Did she tell you why she wanted to kill Jeremy?" Sometimes I couldn't believe the words that crossed my lips in the course of doing my job. Until now I'd thought interrogating the nail-salon owners in Queens about whether they'd bought a dozen bottles of Sex Hair or Vigorous Love (both shades of pink) was a highlight.

"Nope." She hung a bright orange silk—Fridays—in the closet, then zipped closed the suitcase. It was still half full of clothes.

"And you didn't ask?"

"Nope." She wrestled the suitcase into the closet. This time, I didn't bother helping.

"Did you know that the money came from the victim's—I mean Jeremy's—business account?"

Samantha let go of the suitcase and stood up straight. An expression approaching surprise crossed her face. "So she's his business partner and she wanted him dead," she concluded with a satisfied nod. "See, I helped you! That was easy. Go arrest her and get some sleep. You don't look good."

I ignored the last comment. "Mrs. Hodges, I wouldn't exactly say you've helped me yet. I'm going to need a name, a number—"

"What do you mean I haven't helped? I told you this whole big thing, this murder plot. So I don't know her name and I don't know her number—big deal. You're smart, you'll figure it out."

"She called you—you obviously know her number!" I exploded.

"She called me from pay phones. I didn't even know any pay phones still worked," she added, just as I had the same thought. "So did you decide to bear your lover's children?"

I looked up at her, startled. Did she really think she was off the hook? Her face was expressionless.

"We're not done," I said tersely.

"You'd better make up your mind, missy; otherwise you'll spend your whole life, *ping pong ping pong,* patschkieing around until you're an old lady without him *or* kids." She bopped her tiny head from side to side.

"I mean we're not done here, you and me," I said, feeling whatever authority I thought I'd gained in her eyes slip away. At what age could you earn and hold on to the respect of people older than you? Would it happen on my thirty-first birthday? Fortieth? Seventieth? Surely by the time I was seventy . . . "I'm giving us two weeks to reconsider," I added haughtily.

"You think you can give a man a deadline?" She laughed, which I'd never heard her do before. It was hoarse and unpleasant. She reached for her coat. "What you can do is walk me out."

I stood up, certain I had enough to arrest her but knowing that I wouldn't, not at that moment. Besides being shy one essential pair of handcuffs, it was clear to me that Samantha's murderous employer would be wise enough to keep an eye on her freelancer. I didn't want to do anything that would make the nameless, numberless, utterly unidentifiable woman bolt.

"Mrs. Hodges!" I blocked her path. "You haven't told me why you're here. Are you sick?"

She pressed her lips together. "He made me come here."

"Who?"

"The one we've been talking about," she said in exasperation. "The carrottop."

"*Jeremy* made you come here? How is that even possible?"

Samantha looked uncomfortable, which was intriguing. She tried to sidestep me, but I blocked her again.

"How did Jeremy make you come here?"

The pretend murderer-for-hire scowled at me, and even though she was a foot shorter than I was, it was still unnerving being at the receiving end of so much disgust.

"If I didn't, he was going to call the cops on me."

"Ha! So you didn't call me out of civic duty! You don't care if this woman makes another attempt. You just didn't want Jeremy to have you arrested!"

"Get out of my way," she blustered, and it occurred to me that it had been imprudent to identify Samantha to Jeremy as his attempted murderer. I didn't need the various players taking justice into their own hands. It was one of many details I hoped would be overlooked if this case ever came to any kind of satisfying conclusion.

"But why here, in a nursing home?"

"Some mishegas about 'see how you like being trapped somewhere against your will.'"

"Wouldn't prison have been a better trap?" I asked.

She slipped past me and put her hand on the doorknob.

"Maybe *he* did something illegal and doesn't want to tangle with cops. I don't know. I don't care. I've got my money and he's still alive. I figure this boss lady who hired me has enough problems that she's not going to shell out another half million to have *me* killed."

And with that flawless logic, the little old would-be murderess headed out into the city, free as a bird.

Chapter 12

A lengthy phone call to Macy, followed by a quick visit from Mercedes, clad in rustling black silk and en route to Lincoln Center with her viola, had resulted in the most carefully considered outfit I'd worn in three years. To the uninitiated, it might look like I was wearing jeans and a T-shirt, but my friends had helped me weigh the complicated and unusual conditions surrounding my forthcoming summit with Gregory, and they knew what a long, challenging path I would be navigating that evening.

Under their wise, patient direction, I had finally selected the Levi's that were almost torn at the knees, which had won out over the brand-new Levi's and the ones with the paint stain. The new jeans would have been at odds with the familiarity between Gregory and me, but the paint-stained ones would indicate that we were jumping right back to the level of intimacy at which we'd left off.

Even more arduous had been the issue of the shirt. It couldn't be so snug and sexy as to prohibit the occasional slouch (which would result in visible tummy roll or, worse, back roll), as this might be a tough evening and I had to be comfortable, but obviously the shirt couldn't be so loose as to be classified as baggy or sloppy. Color, collar, cut—the possible interpretations of all were painstakingly identified and assessed, and by the time I chose the white, slightly stretched out, long-sleeved, V-neck cotton shirt, I realized I was in an outfit nearly identical to the one I'd worn three days earlier, when I'd set out to see Delta and wound up at Bar Six with Gregory.

"Take a deep breath," Mercedes reminded me as I escorted her and her finery to the door. "Drink some juice. Put your feet up. You still have over an hour. You're *fine*."

"It shouldn't be this hard," I said, unable to keep the whine out of my voice. "It's so easy for you and Dover. Why can't I fall in love with someone who wants what I want?"

She shook her head, sending her mini-dreads bouncing. "Maybe you should have given yourself more than three months to find an alternative."

I shot her an injured look.

"But that's why the two-*week* cap is a great plan," she added.

"You really think it is?" I said hopefully.

"For all of us."

I socked her. "You'd tell me if this was a dumb idea, right?"

"First in line," she assured me, picking up her viola case. "Seriously, this way you can get over him and find someone who fits the bill."

I felt my vital organs seize up at the suggestion.

"You think that's how this will turn out?" I said shakily.

She looked at me sharply. "Does the thought of losing him again make you nauseous?"

"Completely."

"And he still insists on kids and you still refuse?"

"Last I checked."

She opened the door and tapped her fingers against it, unconsciously performing an excerpt from the evening's program. "This really sucks. Just as much as it did in June."

Embarrassment made my face grow hot. "I hope my problems aren't boring you, Mrs. Movie Star with the perfect husband who could afford to hire someone to wipe away his drool every time he looks at you."

Mercedes was unfazed. "Movie star is the one thing that keeps him from being perfect. And I'm not bored, toots. It's just hard to see you struggling all over again. *Really* hard. For all of us."

I rubbed at my brow with both hands. "I know. And I'm sorry to drag you guys into this again."

"Don't be sorry," she said brightly, giving me a quick hug. "That's what we're here for. But, like I said, it's also why we're enthusiastic about the deadline."

"What deadline?" said a breathless voice. My mother appeared, Lycra-clad and red-faced, on my landing. "Mercedes, *darling*! How are you!" she cheered.

Mercedes curtsied from her great height.

"I'd hug you, Bella, but not in the silk."

"Oh, I know, I'm all ick," my mother said, pulling at her silvery French braids in an incongruously schoolgirl gesture. "Ollie and I kickboxed and then jogged back. He stopped off at Chelsea Market for ciabatta and some kind of pumpkin spread he read about on a spread blog: He's discovered how to make technology work for him. So what's on your menu tonight?"

"Brahms, Haydn, Mendelssohn, Vivaldi."

"Smorgasbord!"

"All that's missing is a roast ham and some mead," Mercedes agreed. "Okay, ladies, I'm off. Good luck," she said quietly as she hugged me again.

My mother and I watched her glide carefully down the stairs.

"I love that girl," my mom said, snapping her shirt against her skin. "Always have. I hope that Carter Dover guy is treating her right."

"Dover Carter," I corrected her. "And he adores her."

"Excellent news. Only the best men for my Sterling Girls. I'm so glad they're all finding the right partners."

Eject! Eject! Escape hatch! Locate parachute!

"Okay, well, I've got some work to do and then I'm gonna go meet Macy," I lied.

"Uh-huh." My mother put her hand on the banister, lifting my hopes for her quick departure. "Hey, you know who I saw the other day?"

I waited, raising my eyebrows in a simulation of interest.

"Gregory. He seems to be back."

Subtlety, thy name is not Bella Zuckerman.

"Uh, yeah, I guess I'd heard he's back in New York." I could match her parry for parry in the battle of the absurd.

"Back in your apartment."

"Mom. Stop. Just stop."

But *clonk* went the drawbridge.

"Zephyr, we can't go through this again!" she cried dramatically.

"We?" I inhaled through my teeth and strode into my living room. She followed me inside and closed the door. "This is not your problem, last I checked!" In a far corner of my brain, though, I thought of my dating-by-committee approach and conceded that I would do well to thin out my army the next time I waged romantic battle.

"Okay, maybe that wasn't the best choice of words, but, you know, we get attached."

"What, the royal 'we'?" I spat, plopping defiantly onto the

sofa and crossing my arms. I glared at the dying fern sitting on the floor, its brown leaves brushing the cushions.

"Zephyr." She perched across from me on the coffee table and put her hand on my knee. "You can act like I have no right to feel anything about this, but that would be childish. We've opened up to Gregory, we love him, and we're trying to see your side of things, but honestly . . ." She trailed off.

I stared at her, incredulous, and as nervous as if my toes were curled over the lip of a canyon: We hadn't ever directly broached the subject of her genetic legacy, though she'd made her feelings abundantly clear.

"Honestly what?" I said coldly.

She moved her jaw from side to side, deciding how far she would go.

"Honestly? Honestly, I didn't object when you dropped out of Hopkins—"

"Ha!"

"And I kept quiet when you decided not to go to law school—"

"Revisionist history!" I declared to imaginary spectators.

"The point is, I let you make mistakes. I do, Zephyr. Because I respect you. And because you can go back to med school at the age of sixty if you want. But this? This you can not undo if you change your mind." She squeezed my knee. I moved so that her hand flopped off.

"I'm not going to—"

"Yes. You *are* going to change your mind."

I swayed back as if she had struck me.

"You're acting as if I'm a child," I said quietly.

"Well, you're acting like one. And if you never become a parent, you will always be one."

I blinked slowly at her.

"You did not really just say that."

"I probably shouldn't have, but I did." She stood up and rubbed hard at her temples. It irritated me to recognize how many of her gestures I'd inherited. "Zephyr, do you see any limitations Daddy and I have had to accept because of you and Gid? Did we not travel? Do I not have a career? Do you think he and I aren't romantic—"

"Gross," I said, and immediately regretted it. The epitome of a childish reaction.

"Are you afraid you're not selfless enough? Is that it? Because, honey, every parent is worried they won't be able to give enough, but I know you. I know what a big heart you—"

"See, no, right there!" I interrupted. "Of course I could be selfless enough. It's that I don't *want* to be selfless."

My mother shrank back in horror. I'd never imagined being sucked into such a riptide of parental disappointment, but, to my surprise, I kept breathing and the clocks kept ticking and the horns outside kept honking.

"Then I really don't understand," she whispered.

I plucked a dead leaf off the plant and traced its veins, trying to find the perfect words. "It's not just the sleepless nights and the whining and the getting sick. I could probably handle that. It's that they're always there. Forever. You have to dress them in weather-appropriate clothing and feed them on a regular basis and get them playdates and make sure they don't become Hitler or someone who goes on *Wife Swap*. There's homework and there's social backstabbing: I don't want to live through the cruelty of thirteen-year-old girls again." My insides lurched at the very thought. "Your life as you know it is gone. No spontaneity, not enough money or time for plays and concerts and trips." I resented her for making me spell it out; it sounded so shallow, broken down into its parts. "It's a kind of death," I concluded.

"Jesus, Zephyr, I'm not talking about evangelical reproduction. I'm talking about one or two kids." A vein in her forehead was pulsing.

I shook my head.

"So what are you going to do instead?"

I held my palms upward in an angry question.

"You have to *give*, Zephyr. There are no free rides on this earth."

"I *do* give," I protested, thinking of my occasional visits to the nursing home, though even I knew I couldn't count this last one—an interrogation—as community service.

"You know, it's actually easier to give to your own kids than to try to save the world."

"Those are my choices?" I crumbled the dead fern in my palm and wiped it on the cushion. I thought enviously of Macy, with her long list of volunteer organizations. Macy had a better sense of responsibility than plenty of parents. Whatever her character flaws and mysteries, she was a certifiable grown-up.

"You're a loving, giving person, Zeph. I'm glad you devote so much to your work and to your friends. But I think—no, I *know* that there's going to come a day when you'll wish you had given more. And gotten more. You have no idea, Zephyr, what you'd be missing." Her voice cracked.

I shook my head, bracing myself against her tears. "Are you going to give Gideon this hard a time?"

She pressed her fingers against her eyes. "If he comes up with the same stu—I mean the same idea, yes. But as far as I know, he hasn't ruled out parenthood."

"Would you leave me alone if he popped out a few grand-kids?" I asked, and began weighing potential incentives. When I was in fifth grade and Gideon was in second, he got me to pay him fifty cents every day to make my lunch. Surely we could work out a deal now.

"No. It's not about giving Daddy and me grandkids."

"Bullshit."

"It's not, Zephyr," she said softly. "It's about your happiness."

"I'm so done with this conversation," I informed her.

"As am I," she sighed, heading for the door. She had never, not once in my entire life, left me without a hug. But now she simply let herself out and shut the door behind her, which stung more than anything she'd just said.

I toppled facedown on the couch, feeling my throat ache and my eyes sting. A few tears slipped out, tears of anger, self-doubt, and anger about the self-doubt. There was a light tap on the door. I sat up quickly and wiped my eyes, trying to look merely angry.

"What?" I yelled.

"Honey?"

Maybe she wanted to apologize. Or at least open the door for a hug.

"What?" I yelled again.

"Can I make a suggestion? Change your clothes before you go out. Those jeans look ragged and that shirt is all stretched out."

Chapter 13

Gregory had arrived with flowers—lovely—and announced that Barbuto was booked—understandable—but that a restaurant was kind of a boring date and since he had two more punches left on his ten-visit card to the Polish–Czech baths on East 6th, why didn't we go there instead? While I tried to hide my disappointment, he reminded me that the two owners operated on alternate weeks and that his card was valid only for Stanislav's weeks. This being one of Stanislav's weeks . . . Gregory spread his arms as if to say, *Well, the stars are aligned.*

I recognized that look of oblivious optimism—my dad had invented it—and knew I'd be spending my evening surrounded by two thousand pounds of hot stone in an Eastern European establishment that prided itself on not being overly solicitous of its customers. And so here I was, at nine o'clock on a coed night, crammed alongside eight sweaty strangers with only my Miraclesuit to remind me that I was not on the subway.

But it turned out that a schvitz in a dark down-at-the-heels spa, punctuated by a few buckets of icy water over my head, was exactly what my scrambled brain and shaky heart needed. Between trying to wrap my head around the fact that I had an attempted murder case on my hands and trying to calculate who was less likely to flee their respective institutions first—Samantha or Jeremy—while trying to recover from the stour with my mother and also avoiding thinking about how extensively I'd blown my cover at the hotel, I was feeling as though all roads had arrived at the same intersection. It was an intersection jammed with stalled cars, blaring emergency vehicles, smashed traffic lights, and even some honking geese. If I didn't proceed with great caution, I'd definitely have some human casualties to answer for.

The darkness and nearly unbearable heat calmed me, as did having a crack NYPD detective with whom to dissect the case. I told Gregory everything, forgetting the sweat pooling in my cleavage, dripping behind my knees, drenching my scalp. It was a relief to unload, especially after the effort of keeping my mouth shut around Macy and Lucy. I began with Ballard McKenzie's missing money, my inability to find anything unusual in the hotel's accounting, and Hutchinson McKenzie's inability to tolerate my presence. Then I recounted the night of the drunken Kiwis, Jeremy's brush with death, my enlightening trip to Samantha's hotel room, and her subsequent confession—if you could call a meeting yielding precious little information a confession—at the nursing home. I told him about Jeremy's genuine surprise upon learning that Samantha had received half a million dollars from his company, and I described Jeremy's threat and Pippa's concern for my safety. I also mentioned Zelda Herman, the hotel guest who had had an appointment at Summa earlier that week, even though I wasn't sure it meant anything; Jeremy might have been throwing some business to his family by recommending the hotel to people doing business with Summa—whatever that business might be. The only detail I omitted was the date with the fire-fighter immediately following Jeremy's egress in an ambulance.

And even though a hirsute woman was being slathered with Dead Sea mud in a far corner of the room, and even though a former mayor was (willingly) being beaten with a *platza*—a broom made of oak leaves, dripping with olive oil—just ten feet from us, Gregory gave me his full attention. He listened like no other person I knew, besides my parents. It was genuine listening, not the glazed-over kind some men perfected after being accused by ex-girlfriends of not listening. He interjected with questions, but not too often, and they were questions that helped me think, not just intended to showcase his smarts. He reassured me that I wasn't taking too long to collar Samantha and reminded me of the case that had brought us together: His nervous-nelly boss had been so anxious for Gregory to make an arrest on a small bid-rigging scam that Gregory was thwarted in his pursuit of an entire crime family.

"So one other piece in all this," I continued as the mayor turned onto his back with a grunt, "or it might be a piece, I don't know, is some garbage Jeremy was holding when the ambulance came."

I didn't admit that I'd forgotten the two receipts and the crumpled hotel stationery until an hour earlier, in the women's locker room. The jeans that my committee had selected with such care (time wasted given that I'd be trading my pollo al forno and pinot grigio for some cherry pierogies and a bowl of borscht) were the same ones I'd changed into after my shift on Saturday night. I'd shoved the scraps into a back pocket, where they'd remained until they appeared on the damp floor in front of locker 120. In addition to mishandling potential evidence, I was also guilty of pushing the boundaries of acceptable laundry behavior.

"Garbage? From the room you found him in?" Gregory uselessly wiped his chest with a soggy towel.

"It seems like it, but I don't know. No, wait, it definitely was. The pharmacy credit-card receipt had the husband's name on it—Martin Whitcomb."

"And Samantha said Jeremy headed straight for their room after he saw the Whitcombs say goodbye to the bartender?"

I held my hands up: I had no idea if these pieces made a complete puzzle.

"Receipt and what else?"

"Two receipts. And some hotel stationery with a phone number I traced to Large Tomato Walking Tours. Nothing suspicious."

Gregory stretched, leaning away so that his armpits wouldn't be staring me in the face. Ever the gentleman.

"Well, clearly you need to pay Summa a visit while Jeremy's still trapped at Bellevue—"

"Maybe call Zelda Herman and see what she can tell me first?"

"Yeah, that's what I was gonna suggest. So you don't go in blind."

"And take a look at the Whitcombs' reservation," I added, making a verbal to-do list. "See if there's anything in the notes about what they were doing in town."

"And tell your boss you need twenty-four–seven on Hodges and Wedge," he reminded me as he stood up. He pretended to pant. "I think I need a break."

The mayor struggled into a sitting position and waved to us as we headed unsteadily to the door. He was utterly unembarrassed to have his former constituents witness his pouchy, speckled body, a body that was no longer called upon to lead a city.

"Jewish acupuncture!" the mayor wheezed, pointing to the *platza.*

"There is no superego in this town," Gregory murmured as he headed for the bathroom.

I sat down on a damp bench beside the cold-plunge pool to watch the half-naked parade: saggy, perky, wrinkled, taut, some with hints of mud still clinging to them. And if I'd ever wondered what Humpty Dumpty looked like in a towel, I now knew. An ostrich egg of a man brushed past me, turgid belly protruding over a small towel, and reached for the can of shaving cream chained to the communal sink. As he began to draw a razor across his jowls, I wondered what it was that inspired men to take me on dates whose pleasure quotient was not immediately identifiable. Five days earlier, Delta had treated me to an evening that involved a harness and raw fingertips. Not *un*fun exactly, but not *clearly* fun. Now this. Last I checked, shaving in a towel was something reserved for the privacy of home or at least the men's room.

I dropped my own towel on the bench, inflated my lungs with warm air, and jumped into the cold pool. My screams drew only a few cursory glances. I willed myself to stay in and, after a few seconds, I felt as though I'd drunk a triple espresso after a twelve-hour slumber. Floating on my back and examining my unpedicured toes, I sized up the evening. My interaction with Gregory so far appeared to be an exercise in false comfort: We were reverting to our old, easy way of respectful, thoughtful exchanges, slipping into the grooves we'd so lovingly worn over the years. That wouldn't be a bad thing save for the subject we were avoiding, the bomb we weren't detonating.

But now, I thought—my mind racing from the cold with optimistic, practical, and ultimately specious certainty—now it seemed we had lit on a brilliant new possibility. In fact, I couldn't believe the idea hadn't occurred to me sooner.

Friendship. We could be great friends. Amazing friends. If this date—comfortably discussing work in our bathing suits, wandering around under fluorescent lights and surrounded by dingy white tiles—was a sign that the romance had taken leave of our relationship, then I might not even need two more weeks to decide on a course of action. I would call Lieutenant Fisk that evening and fully embark on the next chapter of my life, one in which Gregory and I looked on at each other's weddings with a kind of sibling love and pride. It would be a friendship admired for its rich history and mature resolution, nothing short of a brilliant way to handle our fatal fertility flaw. It had been absurd to think two people could come to a happy agreement about whether to become parents! I almost laughed out loud at the childish fool I'd been until thirty seconds ago.

And then.

Right behind two men whose concave chests and goatees screamed liberal arts came the perfect, luminous face that made everything around it fade to black and white. The strong chin, the long cheekbones, the full chestnut hair—all of that was beautiful and in the right place and in the right proportions, but what was it about him that made him shimmer, that made everyone else around him recede into two dimensions?

I watched him scan the room. His hazel eyes, bright with flecks of gold, held back until he spotted me. And then he gave me the look that I'd never seen him give anyone else, the look that I hadn't had the good fortune to receive until we'd been together for a year. It let me in, all the way in, even now, after months of being apart and, before that, months of heartbreak and painful disintegration. At that moment, in a room that shared all the best characteristics of a morgue, I was elated and terrified. It's not that I feared no one would ever look at me that way again. It's that I didn't want anyone else *but* him to look at me that way.

With only a slight shudder, Gregory eased himself down the steps of the pool and floated next to me. We watched Humpty Dumpty pat his face dry, study it in the mirror. What did he see? What did his wife see? Since starting at the Hudson Street Nursing Home, I had become painfully aware of how my gaze dismissed the elderly on the street as uninteresting. The thought of being rendered invisible in just a few decades had sobered me, and now I made a point of seeing past the old to the person. Unfortunately, my train of thought still degenerated into a cataloging of all the ways gravity could exert its fierce force and wondering which of my features would go south first. But I was working on it, training myself to wonder who had been a food scientist, who was a taxidermist, who had translated the Arabic of royal families, who had recently discovered an unknown sibling from a parent's long-ago dalliance, who had won a Pulitzer, who had just buried her best friend.

The shaver caught us watching him in the mirror and grinned, a big grin that showed a mouthful of gold. He rattled the chain on the Barbasol.

"Good ting dey tie dis down—I mighta wanted to tuck it down my trunks!" He chortled, gathered his things, and, with great effort, made his way toward the stairs.

I gazed at the stained ceiling and savored the awareness of Gregory's half-naked body floating beside mine. His long fingers grasped mine and, despite myself, I relaxed.

Thirty minutes later, we had showered and dressed and were sitting beneath the clanking pipes of the reception area/café while we sipped at our celery-apple-beet-carrot juices and waited for our food to arrive. For a while, we said nothing, just watched Stanislav grunt and toss locker keys at his clientele. Gregory traced the tendons in my hand, then leaned down to kiss each of my fingers. I was thinking that

I should go easy on the potato dumplings—first cousins to cement—if I wanted to fully enjoy the imminent bedroom acrobatics.

"I have a proposition," he said as a narrow-faced girl plopped plates of yellow-beige food in front of us. She glanced at him. "Not for you," he said, a faint blush coloring the tips of his ears. She shrugged and slunk away.

"A proposition," I repeated, biting into a pierogi and immediately letting the scorching mouthful fall back onto the plate. "Yikes!"

"Lovely. Yes, a proposition." He wasn't eating, just watching me intently. I took a sip of cold juice and swirled it around my burned tongue. "I'm proposing that you not say no right now."

"Not say no to what? Sour cream?"

"Kids."

I swallowed my juice, feeling the evening come to a screeching halt. I wanted to delete that four-letter word and start over.

"Why did you even call me?" I asked him tiredly. "Last week, I mean. Why start this again?"

"Wait, Zephyr. Please listen," he urged. "*Listen* to what I'm saying."

I put my chin in my hand, bristling with impatience.

"What I'm saying is that I want to be with you and take a chance that you'll never want kids—"

"What do you mean *chance*? Where the hell have you been during this yearlong argument—"

"Would you please shut up? I'm willing to be with you and take the chance that you'll never want kids, if you'll agree to just *think* about it once a year."

I stared at him.

"Once a year we revisit the subject. That's it."

"Until?" I felt like I was talking to a drunk. I'd humor him, pretend we were having an intelligible conversation, bide my time until I could escape.

"Until you change your mind or we're too old to reproduce."

My head began to throb.

"Unbelievable," I concluded.

"It's not."

"No, actually, what it is is insulting."

His eyebrows shot up. "Zephyr, I'm *conceding*. You win. Hooray. Fireworks. We can be together. How is this insulting?"

The waitress appeared and thrust a small metal bowl onto our table.

"Sour cream," she grunted, and left again.

"Insulting," I told him, leaning forward, lowering my voice, "because it's infantilizing."

He slammed his palms on the table. "*Infantilizing?*" he growled.

"You're assuming I'll change my mind, right? You think I'm selfish and immature and soon I'll see the light. Just like my mother does." I wondered why this sounded like a childish comeback.

"Well, now you do sound childish," he confirmed. "What is the fucking matter with you, Zeph? Have you changed your mind about me?"

My chest closed in. "God, no," I whispered. "But you're humoring me."

"How?" he pleaded. "By asking you to revisit the subject once a year?"

I thought of the schedule I'd planned on proposing that evening, the one that called for checking in with each other annually if we were still single. The two proposals were alarmingly similar, but his made me realize that both were, at best, absurd and, at worst, futile.

"Because you're assuming if I just get a little older, I'll change my mind."

"Not assuming. Hoping. *Not* assuming," he emphasized.

"Why can no one accept that this is not a phase?" I asked the clanking pipes.

"Why can't you see past your stupid, idiotic, misplaced pride?" he asked.

I shook my head, scrounging around for the right words. "Even if we followed this ridiculous plan, what's to keep you from becoming bitter and resentful in ten years when I still don't want kids? Because I'm not going to want them," I said, more certain than ever.

I thought about Jeremy Wedge and Zelda Herman and Samantha Kimiko Hodges and the hotel and how thrilling my work was—okay, at the moment, a little too thrilling—and I thought about how good it felt to see my beloved city clearly and freshly, not myopically, with stroller brand names and mashed-up organic vegetables clouding my vision. To not have anyone else to worry about if I lost my job. To be able to give myself entirely to a man, a partner, a fellow adventurer, not be part of a tired, diluted, stressed relationship. I was saving money and I planned to see the world, not Disney World.

I thought about what my mother said, about the other option being saving the world. Maybe she was right about that part. Maybe that *was* a condition of deciding not to raise kids. Certainly it would be easier to, say, start fighting climate change if I had no progeny to suffer the consequences of a lost battle. I could throw myself into planet-changing struggles and have adventures and have the freedom to put myself in danger without worrying that I might leave a child motherless. Hell, I wanted the freedom to contemplate suicide if times got rough. Not do it, just keep it as a reassuring ace up my sleeve.

People who had children would always think there was something unfulfilled about my life and I would always think the same of them. Eternal détente.

Gregory shook his head at me. "I'm doing this because I love you, Zephyr, and I want to marry you. Why can't you believe me when I tell you I won't be bitter?"

"Because," I explained quietly, "if you're so sure I might change my mind, then it's entirely possible you might change yours. I can't risk you hating me for this."

Gregory poked holes in his pierogies, his eyes bright with tears. "So you're saying no? You're actually saying no to this, Zephyr? To me?"

Chapter 14

Early the next morning, because I was distracted by grief and because I had run out of ideas and was spinning my wheels, I hunched over my desk and dialed Large Tomato Walking Tours. I tugged at the blue tailored shirt I'd let Macy talk me into buying, in an attempt to look like I had moved beyond college, wardrobe-wise.

"Special on the gay and lesbian tour this weekend!" someone answered, just as Tommy O'Hara thumped on my cubicle wall. I hung up.

"You learnin' some history?" he accused me, peering at Large Tomato's website on my computer screen. He was wearing a gray suit that set off his rosy face, making it shine even pinker than usual. "Hey, I hearda these guys. They oughta hire me—I could give some tourists a run for their money. Heah? This heah's where we nabbed that superintendent sellin' jobs to principals outta her car. And ovah heah? This bar, this is where the deputies at County Health used to meet during taxpayer-funded work hours to place their bets on the horses—and by the way, ladies and gentlemen from

Omaha, the bookie doubled as a college guidance counselor!"
He chortled fondly, recalling pleasant memories.

"What can I do for you, O'Hara?" In truth, I was glad for
the distraction.

"Aw, you got such good manners, Zepha. It's what I can
do fuh you." He bowed low. "I'd be honored if you'd let me
drive you and Alex to your WAC."

I looked up at him blankly.

"Your weapons acquisition ceremony. Ain'tcha gettin' yuh
piece today?"

I hadn't forgotten. Not exactly. Well, one part of me knew
it at some point, but the other part had definitely forgotten.
Or not gotten around to believing that all my hours logged at
Rodman's Neck, shooting paper people in pouring rain and
scorching heat and sneaking up the stairs of the tactical
house, ready to be fake-assassinated by a fake drug lord,
would actually result in someone handing me a lethal weapon
and a license to use it. Early on in my employment, I had
asked Pippa whether I could forgo this part of the job. She
had regarded me steadily and then suggested, for the sake of
my reputation, that we pretend I'd never asked.

I puffed out my cheeks and exhaled. "Yes. Yes I am."

"What's wrong witchoo?"

"I don't know. Weren't you sort of a little nervous when
you first got your gun?"

Tommy grabbed each of his elbows and gazed into the for-
est of corkboard-lined cubicles and swivel chairs.

"Nope."

"Great. Well." I eyed the pad of paper on my desk, which
bore Summa's phone number and address as well as Zelda
Herman's cellphone number. Regardless of whether I wanted
to go get my weapon—and I didn't—I had no time for a ceremony and an oath-taking. Not today. It was a formality held

every month; I'd reschedule. I needed to get to Summa, find the person who'd hired Samantha, and start making some arrests. I hadn't yet had the guts to tell Pippa my cover was blown, but I had a feeling that, once I did, she'd want to move quickly.

"I can't do it today. I need to find Pippa right now." I stood up.

"Chicken."

"I am not!"

"*Bok, bok.*"

"I'm sorry, how old are you?"

"Old enough to know a scared little girl when I see one." He tore a corner off a piece of paper and put it in his mouth to chew.

"Oh, ouch, kick me where it hurts."

"You're a funny kid, Zeph," he said. "Can I call you Zeph?"

"Now you ask?" I tried to walk past, but he put his hand on my shoulder.

"Seriously, I want to drive you guys. It's a big deal, and you and Alex are my favorite probies."

"Because we laugh at your jokes."

"Because you buy me green bagels on Saint Paddy's Day and Alex does backflips in my office."

"I appreciate it, Tommy, but, seriously, not today. Next month. I'll do it next month, and you can drive me."

"Aw jeez, really?" He clasped his hands in front of his chest and let his knees buckle slightly. "So when are you and Poker P gonna let me in on yuh secret case?"

Tommy didn't even need a weapon; he had his timing. I summoned my own best poker face way too late.

"Don't even try, Zepha. I know you got somethin' good. I just wanna know when you ladies are gonna let me in on it." He spit the wad of paper into my trash can.

I looked at him with what I hoped was a patient, empty expression.

"Awright, awright, you keep yuh little secret for now. But you go tell the commish I want in when you take it down."

"You don't even know what you're talking about," I said lamely, grabbing the notepad off my desk.

"Yeah, well." He winked at me. "I know the commish is wearing a dress that looks like one of my wife's oven mitts. Put a burn mark on her ass and it's a dead ringer."

I groaned. "And so that's all I'm going to be able to think about when I go into her office."

Tommy grinned and waggled his fingers at me. "I play dirty, Zepha Z."

* * *

Pippa spritzed a clear liquid across the three Lucite handbags she kept on display in her office. I suspected she periodically rotated them in and out of her home collection, though I couldn't be sure, since they all looked the same to me. As I tried to keep my eyes off her polka-dotted butt, which did indeed resemble an oven mitt, I wondered why anyone would collect sea-green Lucite handbags—why, really, anyone would intentionally amass anything. I spent an ungodly amount of my time trying to fight the natural accumulation of stuff, probably in reaction to a childhood of near engulfment by the detritus of my parents' hobbies. Perhaps one day I'd work up the courage to ask Pippa why she was drawn to these handbags.

"Who else knows?" Pippa asked sharply, her back still to me.

"I don't think anyone, but . . ."

"You didn't think Hodges was on to you, either."

I looked out Pippa's window. We were on the thirty-second floor, and even though our offices were nearer the west side, the island was narrow enough down here that I could see out to the ferries coasting up and down the East River. I allowed a moment to wish myself away from this meeting and onto one of those boats.

"All right, here's what we're going to do. You've got that Zelda woman's phone number?"

I nodded.

"Ring her."

"Right now?"

"Right here, right now. Then, after the WAC, we'll head straight to Summa. I'll drive you myself."

"I don't need to get my weapon today," I assured her.

Pippa tapped a fingernail against the smudgeless handbag and looked over her shoulder at me, eyebrows slightly raised.

"Okay, okay," I muttered, reaching for Pippa's phone. I glanced down at the pad of paper in my lap and dialed. "Any particular questions you want me to ask?"

"No. Casual conversation being your unparalleled strength." She began spraying another one of her polymethyl methacrylate beloveds.

"Oh, hi," I said too brightly to the voice that answered the phone on the first ring. "Is this Ms. Herman?"

"Yes." She sounded suspicious, and I remembered the edgy beauty who'd thrown Hutchinson off his game and checked out just forty-eight-hours later. If she was already back in California, she was probably exhausted from her whirlwind trip.

I tugged at my shirt. "This is Zephyr Zuckerman from the Greenwich Village Hotel." Pippa and I had discussed the pros and cons of using an alias while I was at the hotel but agreed that I would have enough to worry about without having to remember to answer to a fake name, the benefits of which were minimal. "We found a red silk scarf in the corridor outside your room and were wondering if it was yours."

"Oh." I heard her voice relax. "Nope, not mine. But thank you for call—"

"May I ask how your stay was?" I chewed on my bottom lip, studying the pigeon that had landed on the air conditioner outside the window.

"Uh, fine, fine. Nice place." A truck horn sounded in the background. "Look, it's hard to hear—"

"Can I just ask you one sort of odd question, nothing to do with the hotel?"

A pause. "Um . . ."

I jumped in, grabbing on to nothing more than my brief exchange with the Summa receptionist.

"I'm about to . . . do some business with the Summa Institute myself, and I'm a little . . . nervous. Could you tell me what to expect?" Pippa turned slowly, rag aloft, and stared at me. Apparently this was not her idea of a subtle approach. I squeezed my eyes shut.

On a street in California, Zelda gave a hard laugh. "The anesthesia made me puke, but the money, well, you know, the money's amazing."

My eyes flew open. Pippa sat down and watched, still holding the bottle of cleaner and the rag. She pressed speakerphone.

"What . . ." I squeaked, and then cleared my throat. "What else?"

"Well, you're taking the injections already, right?" she asked.

Deep breath through the nose. "Of course."

"Are they making you nauseous? Bloated?"

"Very," I told her, suddenly so calm I almost laughed. Before Lucy had resorted to borrowing DNA, she'd tried every method under the sun to get pregnant, including harvesting her own recalcitrant eggs.

Money + injections + nauseous + bloated = Alan and Amanda.

"Well, then, you've survived the worst of it. They knock

you out for the retrieval, so that part doesn't hurt," Zelda assured me.

Pippa leaned forward, nearly knocking over her coffee mug, which read *Don't Lose Sight of Your Lucite*.

"Just some puking when you wake up," I confirmed smoothly.

"Not just some. But like I said, the money . . ."

"Did you tell your family?"

"God, no."

Pippa looked at me with downright admiration, and suddenly I felt comfortable in my button-down shirt and black linen pants. I imagined myself behind her desk one day, modestly downplaying my career highlights as I mentored another young colt, who would sit where I now sat. There would be no strange collection of women's accessories on the shelves behind me. What would I put in their stead? What physical item defined me? Maybe that was why people collected and then displayed their collections, as a shortcut to making themselves better understood. What did it mean that I could think of nothing to exhibit on my imaginary shelves?

"I couldn't tell them I needed money," Zelda confided. "It would break their hearts. They named me Zelda hoping I would be a great artist—minus, you know, the over-shadowing husband and schizophrenia. My dad, especially, has this . . . this paradigm in his head about Eastern European immigrant generations in America. . . ." Pippa sat back, startled. Personal information, divulged under any circumstances, made her uncomfortable. "The immigrants come over and work their butts off. They own shops and do physical labor, work long hours. They send the next generation to law school and medical school. And then the third generation are supposed to be artists."

"And what's the generation after the artists supposed to be?" I mused, forgetting my mission for a moment.

"I've wondered that myself," Zelda said agreeably. Pippa looked at me as though I were speaking another language. "So after I went to Oxford, they just figured I . . . I was . . ."

"Done?" I suggested.

"Exactly. Not in a goodbye way but in a great-she's-all-set way."

"What do you do, if you don't mind me asking?"

"I write. Articles, essays, ghostwrite op-eds. Whatever pays. But it never pays enough, so I found Summa. It's the fastest way to make a buck besides prostitution."

I waited.

"Not that I've ever done that," Zelda added breathlessly. She had apparently resumed walking. "I'm just saying. Summa pays really well."

"So you've donated your eggs before?"

"This was my third time," she admitted after a moment. "I hope it was my last. I've got a shot at doing a speed bio on Lady Gaga's new girlfriend, and that would be great money."

"Is that what you want to be writing?"

Pippa frowned at me and made a circular motion with her finger: *Wrap it up.* She thought this wasn't necessary. I thought the more information the better.

Zelda snorted. "Are you kidding? I'd rather be working on my biography of Deborah Garrison."

"The poet? Did she die?"

"God, no! She's only in her forties. I'm trying to get in on her early."

Pippa snapped her fingers at me.

"Okay, listen, Zelda," I said, watching the pigeon on the air conditioner flap its wings and resettle. "Thanks so much for telling me all this. I feel better knowing what to expect."

"Good luck," she said generously. "It'll be fine. Paulina is a little weird but fine."

I hung up, and Pippa and I regarded each other.

"So Summa is an egg-donation business," I concluded. I felt reassured by how much sense it made for a genetics researcher to go this commercial route. "I'll pose as an egg donor, find this Paulina person or whoever hired Samantha. And if she's really the payer of the half mill . . ." Then I could wrap up this case before the end of next week. The thought of being done with Hutchinson McKenzie forever was extremely appealing.

Pippa stowed her cleaning supplies in a cabinet that bore the SIC's shield and slogan: *Getting Graft Out of Gotham.*

"First do a dry run elsewhere. Some other clinic."

I raised a corner of my mouth. Why waste our time? Why risk another hour that Jeremy or Samantha might flee?

"We just don't know enough yet, Zephyr, and we are talking about attempted murder. Unpredictable suspects, one of which, I hasten to remind you, we haven't actually ID'd. I'd prefer that you go in there playing the role well."

As opposed to hotel concierge, which had been a flop. I wasn't in a position to argue. I stood to go.

"I have a friend who used donor eggs. I could go to her place."

Pippa crossed her arms and tilted her head.

I sighed and dropped my shoulders. I would never be the commissioner. Not that I really wanted to be, but it had been an appealing minute-long ambition.

"Right, unwise to bring a friend into this," I said, heading for the door, fueled by irritation with myself. "I'll cold-call somewhere else."

"And, Zephyr? Meet me downstairs in fifteen minutes. There's a revolver at One Police Plaza with your name on it."

Chapter 15

All of which is how I came to be sitting in an overstuffed armchair in the offices of Ova Easy, decked in apathetic black with a brand-new Glock strapped to my belly, trying to persuade an adenoidal gatekeeper to give me more information about her business for my pretend younger sister, the producer of fictionally fresher eggs.

Reluctantly, St. Peter of Noho had wasted two more minutes of her precious time on me, during which she allowed that a donor could expect pain and money.

"And the joy of giving life to a barren couple?" I couldn't resist adding.

"Well, *obviously*," she growled as the elevator door glided closed between us.

This blooper-filled meeting was a fitting conclusion to a workday that had begun with a call to Zelda the tattoo-eyed lady of California and proceeded to an oath-taking in lower Manhattan, during which I had managed to drop my gun in front of forty other newly armed colleagues—all while trying to put Gregory out of my mind. By the time I hauled myself up my stoop that evening, I was mud-in-my-veins exhausted.

Certainly the last place I expected to wind up was in the tattered lounge of Engine Company 14, shoulder-to-shoulder with the rock-climbing, Melville-reading firefighter, he of the baby face and obscenely long eyelashes.

Tired as I was, I hadn't been able to sit still at home—being there only made me miss Gregory more. So after a quick con-fab with Macy, who required some cheerleading before her date with the maternally pimped dermatologist, I left my apartment again. Outside, it was a breath-seeing night, a steep drop in temperature from that afternoon, and I pulled my gray fleece jacket tighter around me as I headed south on Seventh Avenue. I was clad in old running shoes, yoga pants, and a ratty NYPD T-shirt that I had stealthily appropriated over years of cohabitating with Gregory. I planned to walk for a long time.

I headed past the chipped September 11 memorial tiles that hung where many believed the diner in Edward Hopper's *Nighthawks* once stood, a juxtaposition that turned Mulry Square into a palimpsest of two wartimes. I kept going, past fortune-tellers that, mysteriously, could afford expensive storefronts and past Chinese massage parlors that couldn't and so were inevitably relegated to basements or second floors. I kept my head down along the tourist stretch south of Bleecker Street, home to restaurants that advertised by driving skeletons around the city in a retrofitted hearse.

I turned at Houston, hoping something engrossing was playing at Film Forum. *Shaft*, part of the Subtle Seventies retrospective, had already started, so I continued east. I paused briefly by Billy's, the outdoor furniture explosion that might be mistaken for a shantytown, before selecting First Avenue as my conduit north: excellent serendipitous food possibilities.

I began to enjoy the snippets of conversation that surrounded me, relaxing as other people's lives and thoughts supplanted mine. I halted for a moment to marvel at a woman in a suit and sneakers who was walking while also reading by streetlamp. Read/walk, scan a few yards ahead, resume read/walking. Read, scan, read.

Behind me, a conversation approached, too loud and too close, violating the unwritten rules that governed ATM lines, bus queues, and sidewalk etiquette.

"Are you disappointed you have to wear it?" the distaff half of a stooped couple asked her bald mate. They were arm in arm, their careful pace blissfully out of sync with the plowing crowds.

The man rubbed her hand and shrugged. "I have brown things on my head. So now I have a brown thing in my ear."

On I went, past fruit vendors packing up for the day, when, at 18th Street I suddenly turned left, succumbing to a powerful desire for City Bakery's mac and cheese and a shot of their viscous hot chocolate.

Officer, I swear, that's how it happened.

The door to the fire station was wide open at Engine 14, the gleaming truck encircled by pairs of boots with pants dropped around their ankles, as if lewd ghosts were haunting the place. Thick-muscled men roamed and smoked and leaned, and one of the leaners was Delta. I saw him before he saw me, and my first thought was that there was no way he'd believe this was a chance encounter. Even I didn't believe it.

I considered hurrying past, but if he caught me, this would become even more awkward than it already was.

"Delta," I said weakly. I grabbed the attention of nearly everyone but him.

"Hey, Delt!" one of his colleagues yelled helpfully.

It was absurd how sexy he was, how sexy all of them were, just because of the firehouse. I tried to picture Delta sitting behind a desk, a pocket protector tucked into his shirt, saggy with leaky pens, no helmet in sight. In a million years, I wouldn't have kissed him. At least I was admitting to myself that I was being jobist—attracted to him for his career. When Gregory and I met, he'd been posing undercover as an exterminator, and he accused me of caring what his profession was; now that the accusation was true, I suspected this guy couldn't have cared less. In fact, I wouldn't have been surprised to learn that many of the men there went into the business of saving people from flaming buildings precisely because the ladies loved it.

"Zephyr. It's Zephyr. Zephyr whose last name I still don't know," Delta said, a genuine smile spreading across his bright face. "You missed dinner, but we've got leftovers." He didn't leave his leaning post by the office door. He was going to make me sweat.

"Oh, that's okay. I was out walking and . . ." I gestured weakly in the direction I'd been heading.

"You just happened to pass by."

"That's what I thought, but my subconscious probably had other plans," I conceded.

"Hey, she's funny," one of the men proclaimed. I did a double take. The guy had to be close to seven feet tall. He was clutching a paperback that seemed to disappear inside his palm. He probably didn't even need to slide down the pole, just put his feet out and he was down.

"No, I believe you," Delta said. "Look at what you're wearing. That's not what we usually get around here."

I glanced down at my baggy pants, fleece, and sneakers.

"The women who hang around firehouses usually dress to kill," he explained.

"Women who hang around firehouses?" I repeated dumbly. "What, like groupies?"

"Exactly. Like groupies. Except they're not here for the music."

To look shocked would have been to expose myself to merciless mockery. I did my best to hide my surprise.

Delta finally took pity and gestured me inside. "Come on, Zeph. I'll give you the grand tour." A tiny part of me twinged with discomfort at the familiarity implied by "Zeph." Names of endearment were earned. But, as I approached, he flung his arm around me easily, and it felt good. Warm, solid, good.

As I joined Delta by the office, the giant guffawed, and it sounded like a foghorn, but the rest of the men returned to their leaning, talking, smoking. I noticed that most of them wore wedding rings, and I wondered how that fit in with the female groupies.

"I really don't know what I'm doing here," I told Delta as he led me up a narrow flight of stairs. The walls were cement, painted a dingy red.

"Decided you didn't need to wait two weeks?" We stepped into a small kitchen. A fireman with his suspenders hanging down so that they outlined his plum-firm butt was carefully crimping tinfoil over Pyrex dishes. It was a discordant image, like a prizefighter arranging a dollhouse.

"Pretty much," I hedged. We passed through the kitchen and into an adjacent black-ceilinged lounge containing three lumpy sofas, a battered coffee table, and an enormous, gleaming flat-screen TV.

"Taxpayers foot the bill for that?" I asked.

He gestured for me to sit down. "Can I get you something? Soda, water, juice?"

"Water would be great. Is it from a hydrant?" I added lamely.

He grabbed a bottle of Evian from the refrigerator and flopped down beside me.

"Are you always this charming? The sweatpants, the smart remarks. I really do believe you came here by accident."

I grimaced in apology.

"But now you're here," he said.

"Now I'm here." I took a sip of water, then realized how

thirsty I was and guzzled the rest. I came up for air to find him grinning, and before anyone said anything else, he was kissing me. Our first contact had been hands-off as we hovered over Brooklyn. Now he ran his fingers through my hair—as best he could. It was pulled into a knot on top of my head, and an hour and a half of street escape had turned it into a tangled, sweaty nest. He cupped a hand around my neck—also sweaty, I now realized—and pulled me tighter. I squirmed.

"What's wrong?" he said, pulling back enough to look at me without going cross-eyed.

"I'm just . . . this is not how I'd want to start something." I fanned my fingers toward my gymlike state.

"Are we starting something? You still have two weeks to decide."

"Well, so, what would you call this?" I asked.

"Fun."

Sweet nothings could not have been more persuasive. I lunged at him, reminding myself that he was used to contact with people who were not at their best. At least I wasn't covered in soot.

I kissed him hard, determined to forget everything— Gregory, my mother, unproduced children, unhappy friends, death threats, unwanted guns, unsolved cases. He wore a peppery cologne, a scent that made him even more of a stranger than he already was. Straddling him, I savored the outside of his hard thighs pressed against the soft insides of mine. My hands wandered to the back of his smooth neck and then his face, my thumbs tracing his cheeks.

"So," he said, catching my hand as it started to explore what lay beneath me. "Am I part of a revenge plan?"

"You make that sound bad."

"No. I just want to know where we stand. I'd like more

from you, but I'll take this for a couple of weeks. Thirteen days to be exact."

I wished I could shut him up. Talk was not what I wanted.

"Why?" I said, letting myself fall off him and onto the lumpy cushion beside me. A button dug into my elbow. "Why do you want more from me? You don't even know me. How do you know I'm any better than the women who usually come in here?"

"I didn't say you were better. But I think you're different."

"Well, of course I'm different," I snapped. "Everyone's different." I watched the steam of our encounter evaporate into the dim light.

We were silent for a moment as the colossal colleague lumbered toward the bathroom at the far side of the lounge with his book, which I now saw was *The Fountainhead*. He stopped and turned back to us.

"Don't start, Rousakis," Delta warned. "Leave the woman alone."

Rousakis ignored him. "Have you ever heard of Ayn Rand?" he asked me, and I nodded, trying to hide my surprise. "She changed my life. That's all I wanted to say," he told Delta defensively, and continued on his way.

"Sorry," Delta said.

"If only all proselytizing were that painless."

He ran his arm along the back of the couch and tugged gently on my earlobe.

"Hey, so I have a question," I said quietly.

"Yes, my real name is Delta."

"That's not my question, or, I mean, at one point it was a question, so thanks."

He grinned at my confusion.

I tried again. "Remember when I asked whether you wanted kids?"

"How could I forget? That's what I mean by different."

"Do you?"

"Want kids?" He sighed, conceding that we had fully left the kissing arena. "No, actually, I don't want kids."

"Why not?"

He brought the corners of his lips down in an upside-down smile. "Look at my job. I don't want to make orphans."

"What about widows?"

"Are you proposing?"

"Just asking. Most firefighters and cops seem to come equipped with wives and kids."

"I'm different."

"So we have that in common."

"I've been married, Zephyr. I don't think I'll try it again." He ran two fingers down my neck. "What's with this kid thing?"

I shrugged. What did it say that our shared disinterest in procreating didn't crash open any floodgate of affection for Delta? Here was a guy: sexy, funny enough, smart, and without the land mines I had with Gregory. And yet the sparks fizzled rather than flared with that realization. This was not the man with whom I wanted to be strolling up First Avenue in fifty years discussing hearing aids.

The Brobdingnagian objectivist passed through again, and this time he merely nodded at us.

"You want kids," Delta guessed, "and the guy who showed up again this week doesn't."

"Wrong. Sexist assumption."

Delta raised his eyebrows. "Interesting."

"Not really. Tragic and painful, in fact."

He kicked his feet onto the coffee table. "Zephyr, let's either have some fun or let's say goodbye. I don't want to do therapy."

I sucked in my breath. "You're big on ultimatums."

"I told you. I'm almost forty."

I stood up and smiled helplessly at him.

"Don't be mad," he said kindly.

"I'm not." And I wasn't. But hanging out in a grungy room above a couple dozen swashbuckling carnivores was no longer where I wanted to be.

In the pocket of my fleece, my cellphone rang: Macy. I sent it to voice mail, wondering why she was calling during her date with the dermatologist. I hoped he hadn't stood her up. Talk about therapy.

"I'm really not mad," I assured him. "Just disappointed. In myself."

Delta hauled himself off the couch. "I'll walk you downstairs; otherwise you'll never make it out of here alive."

"Why, is this place a firetrap?" I said as my phone rang again.

"Don't quit your day job," he said. "Whatever it may be."

I flipped open my phone as I followed him out past the kitchen.

"Mace, what's up?" I said. "I'm kind of in the middle of something here—"

"Zephyr!" she wailed, and in the background I heard sirens. "He's dead!"

Chapter 16

Macy hunched over her empty coffee cup, staring with hollow eyes at the King Charles spaniel attempting to hump a foamy-mouthed Newfie. I glanced at my watch, anxious about my impending surveillance of the Summa Institute but equally anxious about Macy's mental health. Even though I'd spent the better part of the weekend at her side, I'd felt compelled to keep our dog-park date. She had begun pining for her parents' couch again, recalling it with outsize tenderness.

"The man went volcano boarding in Nicaragua," she groaned for the umpteenth time. "Not a burn. Not even a bruise. But one date with me. Dead. *Dead!*" She smashed her cup and began to cry again.

The date had begun with great promise. Macy and the dermatologist—Rudy Feinstein, by name—lingered over their bolognese at Tanti Baci and shared an entire bottle of wine. They had a lot in common—a love of camping, anything with garlic, Virginia Woolf—and he was making her laugh. An understated humor, her favorite kind. They had both been eager to continue the date, so they wandered for a while and then

hopped the F train to Chinatown so that Macy could introduce Rudy to what she felt was the best bubble tea on the East
Coast. It was there, inside a closet-size, brightly lit tea parlor
on Baxter Street, that Dr. Feinstein met his end. A clump of
high-velocity tapioca bubbles shot through his straw and into
his throat, where it lodged, resistant to all ensuing Heimlich
maneuvers by staff, paramedics, and even Macy herself.

"Can you possibly look me in the eye, Zephyr, and tell me
I'm not cursed?" she said, after her tears had subsided into
staccato sniffles.

I shook my head, finally convinced.

She nodded with dull satisfaction.

"Do I go to his funeral?" she asked. "What's the fucking
etiquette on that one?" She released her hair from its ponytail
and dug her fingers into her scalp, letting flaming sheets of
red cascade around her face.

"Macy, what do you have going on today? What are you
gonna do to keep yourself busy? Talk to me." I peeked at my
watch again. I had to stop by the office to get wired with a
camera and mike and make it to Summa by ten. But I was determined to steer her back to the land of the living. Literally.

She laughed harshly. "I'm supposed to meet my divorcing
bride for lunch at Elephant and Castle."

"Excuse me?" The Newfie loped off to the far end of the
run, while the spaniel leaped in circles around him.

"One of the couples where the bride didn't die? They're
getting a divorce."

"Why is that your problem?"

"Because they're getting divorced for stupid reasons," she
spat. "He's convinced a child should only be raised in Park
Slope, like he was, and she insists Upper West is best. This
boy is the Elgin Marbles of offspring."

"And you think you can talk her out of it?" I asked,
aghast.

"I do. I did. Now I don't give a shit. Maybe I'll tell them to go on a cruise like Lenore, work things out."

To our amazement, in the space of four days, Lucy had not only persuaded Leonard that she—that they—were in dire need of an immediate break from Lenore, but she had found a recession-achy cruise liner that was more than happy to take her money and her in-laws on short notice for a two-week sail around the Seychelles Islands. The trip had been billed as an apology for being subjected to an evening with Zephyr the Godless.

"Why don't *you* go on a cruise?" I suggested.

"And sink the whole goddamn ship? I'm already a murderer, Zephyr. I don't need to add 'mass murderer' to my résumé."

A woman in a bright purple jacket on the bench near us was pretending to read, but I saw her eyes go round.

"Okay, what else are you going to do?" I needed some reassurance she wouldn't be headed for New Hampshire by sundown.

"Sit here and hope none of these dogs drops dead."

The woman gathered her newspaper and moved to another bench.

"Well, that's a good plan," I said, momentarily distracted as the mayor of the dog run approached the newspaper reader. Acquiescing to the overnight arrival of cooler weather, he had traded in his orange Lycra bike shorts for a billowing black leather coat, and it wasn't by any means a given that he had clothes on beneath it.

"Excuse me, Miss. Miss?"

The woman looked at us first, keeping the murderer in her sights, then realized the voice was coming from the bald *Matrix* wannabe.

"Your doggie did a poopy over there. Were you planning on cleaning it up?"

She glanced over his shoulder, searching for evidence.

"That's not mine. I mean, that's not my dog's."

"You have the husky, do you not?"

"Yes, but that's not his poop."

"Oh, but it is. I saw him make it. You were busy reading. We remind doggie caregivers that this is not a library. You need to pay attention."

The woman blinked at him. "Who's 'we'?"

The mayor held up his palms to her. "Don't even."

I was about to catch Macy's eye, hoping this sideshow might be palliative, when she suddenly streaked past me. I clutched at her sleeve, but she shook me off.

"Leave her alone!" she shrieked, her voice cracking. "Life is too fucking short, so stop harassing people! Stop making everyone's day just a little more unpleasant. Hand out dog treats or poop bags or volunteer at the pound or even just shut up. Just shut the fuck up!"

The woman sat stock-still, shifting her gaze from Macy to the mayor, who were now locked in each other's livid glares. She carefully placed her newspaper on the bench and rose slowly, as if to avoid being noticed. Ten seconds later, she and her empty-boweled husky were gone.

The mayor's shoulders shifted beneath his coat. He inhaled through his nose, his nostrils turning white and rigid.

"Do you think," he snarled, "that I have not noticed your state of doglessness? Do you think that salient fact has escaped me all these months? Do you not wonder why it is that you and your equally dogless friend are permitted to remain on the premises?" His forehead was turning an alarming shade of pink.

Macy took a step closer. I envisioned cop cars, ambulances, tearful confessions of temporary insanity—none of which I had time for.

"Why *do* you let us stay here?" she asked with genuine curiosity, her voice dropping suddenly into a strangely normal register. I held my breath, wondering if the mysterious truth that had been kept from us for so long, that had been flavoring our visits with a pinch of uncertainty, would finally be revealed.

The mayor looked nonplussed. "Because I'm a *charitable fucking person,* you java-swilling breeder."

* * *

Eventually, after dragging her across six lanes of traffic and all the way to Seventh Avenue, I got Macy to swear she would meet me at Mercedes's and Dover's non-Oscar party that evening. I reminded her that Lucy was escaping Hillsville and motherhood for the occasion and that her level of enthusiasm was bordering on psychotic. Even as she teetered at the lip of her personal abyss, Macy would not leave me to handle Lucy by myself under such circumstances.

I tried to shake her at the entrance of the Christopher Street station, but she started down the stairs behind me.

"Macy," I said, stopping. She crashed into me. "You need to go home."

"Can't I come with you?" she asked, her voice wavering. "I'll just sit in your office. I'll read a magazine. I won't bother anyone. They can shoot me if I do."

I started to laugh, but she looked so forlorn that I stopped. "I would let you. I really would. But I'm not going to my office," I admitted.

"Well, where are you going?"

I was reminded of the stalker stance she had assumed with Lucy when I'd first met her a few years earlier.

"Well, I'm stopping at the S.I.C., but then I have to interview someone."

"I won't say a word, I promise."

"C'mon, Macy. You know I can't have you there."

"No, I don't know that. Pretend I'm your assistant."

"It's not that," I said, pressing my back against the railing as a mother hefted an occupied stroller past us.

"You're scared of me, aren't you?" she whispered.

"Oh, for God's sake, *no*. I just . . ." I glared at the sky, trying to think of a way to get rid of her without hurting her feelings. I only had time for the truth. "Macy, I'm undercover. Some other day, I promise, you can come sit in my cubicle."

I did enjoy the rare satisfaction of being on the receiving end of dumbfounded admiration.

"Seriously?" she shrieked.

"It's not a big deal," I lied. "It's a nothing case." Just a hit woman and death threats and hundreds of thousands of dollars in play.

The truth worked. An hour and a half later, Macy was nowhere in the vicinity of me or my thoughts. Pippa let me off on the corner of Watts and Washington Streets in Tribeca and I walked as calmly as I could toward Desbrosses Street. A sizable camera had been glued to my collarbone, camouflaged as a heavy jade pendant and purfled with fake diamonds that hid a microphone. The knowledge that every grunt and sigh was entertaining both Pippa and Tommy O. was immeasurably helpful in keeping my breathing under control.

To his great delight, Tommy had been brought in on the case out of concern for my safety, but it seemed to me that I would be paying for that security with my sanity.

"So you're in," I'd said to him when he pulled the car around Hanover Square.

"I'm in, baby, I am *in*. Not that you broads have much in the way of, ya know, *information*, but I'm in." He bared his teeth in a crazy man's grin.

"Did he really just say 'broads'?" I asked Pippa as Tommy slid over and she got in behind the wheel.

"Did he really just get cheeky with a superior?" Pippa wondered back.

Tommy immediately looked contrite. "Commish, I was just joshin'—I didn't mean nuthin'—"

"Quite finished, O'Hara?"

Tommy pressed his lips together and nodded, though he wasn't even close to finished. He ran his mouth the entire short drive over to Summa, telling a true story (he claimed) about a porn producer, a weights-and-measures inspector, and a ferret named Rhubarb. I didn't realize how grateful I was for the distraction until it came time to set out, alone, for 25 Desbrosses Street. I had only the walk around the corner to start sweating.

I'm a prospective egg donor, I reminded myself, touching the necklace nervously. Shopping around. For this mission, I had forgone the smoky grad-student garb and instead donned jeans, a V-neck T-shirt, my thigh-length sweater to hide the Glock, and hiking boots, which was more along the lines of what Zelda had been wearing (minus, presumably, the firearm). Since I had exactly no one with whom I could consult for this particular date, she'd served as my unwitting fashion plate.

The building was a five-story brick affair on an industrial-turning-condo block whose metamorphosis had been halted by the recession. Grimy scaffolding encased half a dozen façades, with no signs of activity. I took a deep breath, exhaled, and rang the buzzer.

"Abigail, dear?" crackled a voice in response. Again I wondered at my inability to invent a name out of whole cloth. At least this time I'd used a Sterling Girl on the West Coast rather than an ex-boyfriend. Non-ex. Yes, ex. Yes. Ex, for sure.

"Abigail Greenfield?" the voice repeated. Okay, I could have at least used a different last name.

"Yes," I croaked. "This is she."

"Love it! You're our girl!" I was buzzed into a tiny foyer, making it the first time in my life I'd gained entry to a place by virtue of my good grammar. Never mind that Tommy would crucify me. I closed the door and was thrust directly onto a creaky, curving staircase.

"Right this way!" sang the voice, and for a moment I had a presentiment of being tortured in a Tribeca death trap. An executioner wearing black would blend right in in this neighborhood.

On the landing was a bright-eyed, dark-featured spark of a woman. She was slightly shorter than I was and bursting with an energy that was coiled in her legs, her arms, her shoulders. Her nose was sharp, but everything else about her was fleshy, warm, inviting. She was dressed in a beautiful but convoluted style whose dictates I could never decode—things were draped and wrapped, and there was a scarf and a knee-length jacket/sweater thing involved. She was exactly the kind of woman who could talk you into handing over an ovum or two.

She ushered me through the open door, past stenciled douche swooshes I recognized from the website, and into a sedate, carpeted office lined with bookshelves and dotted with plants. As I passed her, she grabbed me by my shoulders and kissed me on each cheek.

"I am Paulina!" she declared joyfully. "I am so happy you have found the Summa Institute! Sit, sit. Can I get you a tea? Pellegrino?" I caught the merest touch of an Eastern European accent.

"Coffee would be great," I said, settling myself on the edge of a burgundy suede sofa and wondering how this one-room operation tucked behind the entrance to the Holland Tunnel constituted an institute.

"Uh-uh." She wagged a finger at me. "Only decaf, right?"

"Righto," I said brightly. While Paulina busied herself at a small galley at the far end of the room, I pivoted my torso slowly, getting a panoramic shot. A Dalí print, a replica (I assumed) of a Fabergé egg, and an uncluttered cherry desk that gleamed under the recessed lighting, bearing only a printer, a fax machine, and a laptop.

I bent forward at the waist to pan the coffee table in front of me, which held a neat pile of brochures bearing the "Investigating Intelligence" slogan. I skimmed the first page and a number jumped out at me, a dollar figure that was a galaxy away from the dollar figure on Ova Easy's website. Before I could fully register the glaring difference, a single-page insert slipped out of the brochure. It was printed on heavy purple stock and resembled a menu of spa services. In flowery script, it read:

Truman . . . . $2,000 extra
Marshall . . . . $3,000 extra
Rhodes. . . . . $5,000 extra
Documentation required

"So." Paulina carefully set a tray in front of me bearing coffee, a crystal pitcher of milk, and an ivory bowl of sugar. "You know we are doing this the backward way? I usually interview *after* I review the application, but we do so love Zelda. I made an exception." She held my gaze and I understood that I was to express gratitude.

"Thank you so much," I obliged.

"You are most welcome." She sat down and folded her hands in her lap. "Now, tell me, how do you young ladies know each other?"

I had given this question some thought. College and childhood were out, since Paulina obviously knew Zelda better than I did. I poured some milk in my coffee and hoped I sounded at ease.

"We're just acquaintances. We met in the Loehmann's dressing room the last time she was in town. We both reached for the same pants." I hid behind my coffee cup and watched her reaction. She broke out in a big smile.

"Fabulous! I love it! What a town, no?"

I nodded.

"So." She extracted a folder from a drawer in the coffee table. "I will leave you to do all the paperwork in a moment, but, first, tell me about yourself. We are like a family here and I like to know my girls."

It reminded me of the way Roxana referred to her former brothel employees. I shook off the thought.

"Well," I began carefully, "I'm twenty-four." I waited. Just a happy nod. Hooray! I was still officially young! Or I could still pass! Or something! "And I'm healthy."

"Of course. The blood work will confirm that. And you went to school . . . ?"

"Uh, yes."

She laughed, and her laugh was surprisingly sharp, an unpleasant contrast to the rest of her mien. "Well, of course, you did. Where?"

And then I remembered the remarks about the Rhodes scholarship and the slogan and the list of rarefied fellowships on the purple menu and it occurred to me to lie.

"Princeton?"

"Brilliant. Magna cum laude? Summa?"

Ah, as in the *Summa* Institute. I decided not to push my luck.

"Magna."

"Ah, well, that is fine."

"Can I ask you . . . ?" I began.

"Anything, dear. Ask me anything."

Are you the one who hired Samantha Kimiko Hodges to kill Jeremy Wedge?

"I see the fees here are twice what other fertility clinics offer. How do you manage to do that?"

A frown flickered across her brow. "Well, as you know, dear, we are very much *not* a fertility clinic."

I very much did *not* know that. My insides solidified and sank. "Of course, I didn't mean to use that term. What I meant was . . ." I had no idea what I meant. I was just glad I had a gun.

Paulina's face softened a bit. "I understand. So many of the girls have been looking around at the clinics before they hear about us. They forget. We have grants, dear; that's how we pay fifteen thousand when the fertility clinics typically pay eight thousand. So many grants. The Institute of National Health, for instance, is using some of our data for a study right now. And then many of our girls do wonderful things with the money they get from us and feel so grateful to us that they give back. We are a big happy family." She nodded at the brochure I was still holding. "After Sarah Palin was saying those terrible things about the polar bears, one alumna began a rescue mission for them and now she herself is greatly funded."

"Polar bears?" I repeated, willing myself not to laugh or panic.

"Polar bears. People very much want to save them."

"They *are* cute." I was pretty sure I could hear Tommy roaring with laughter in the vast silence that followed. "Um, why is there extra for these?" I waved the purple insert.

"For the INH study, specifically. It is for the link between intelligence and genetics."

"Isn't that eugenics?" I asked, alarmed.

"How's that, dear?"

"Nazis?"

"Oh." Paulina waved away the comparison and chuckled. "It is marvelous how you girls think so much. No, no, nothing like that, dear. Look, Abigail. It is win–win. You girls, you get lots more money to do your wonderful projects, plus the peace of mind—you need not have strangers making babies out of your eggs. Right? No unknown progeny running around. It is our way of rewarding the brightest minds in the country."

I tried to digest this. It actually sounded like a pretty good deal. "Who else works here?" Paulina's eyes went slightly dark, so I added, "I mean, you said, '*our* way of rewarding.'"

She pointed to a door behind the one I'd entered, which I hadn't noticed. Did *two* rooms make an institute? Didn't an institute require white lab coats, rooms with red lights above the doors, and at least one elevated walkway?

"Imogene is our lab technician. It all happens back there."

"So it's just you and her. I guess that keeps costs down."

Paulina drummed her fingers on the folder and straightened her back. "I have a business partner, but he is out sick at the moment." She gave a brief, exaggerated grimace. "Hopefully he will grow better soon. Let's get you started on your paperwork. It takes a long while. Or would you prefer to do your bloods first?"

"That would be great!" I said too eagerly. "I mean, needles make me nervous, so if I could get it over with . . ."

She stood up briskly, and I had the uneasy sense that she wasn't completely pleased with me. Still, she knocked on the door and opened it.

"Imogene," she sang, "we have another lovely candidate. This is Abigail Greenfield. Abigail, Imogene. I'll be right out here, Abigail, if you need anything." She sailed out, her various flowy garments billowing behind her.

It was a standard physician's examining room, with

fluorescent lights, padded table, sink, labeled drawers. A stout sixtyish woman with a pillowy face and eyebrows that didn't line up put down her *Martha Stewart Living* and peered up at me from her swivel stool.

"Hello, deah, welcome to Summa," she said in the unhurried, heavy rhythms of deepest Queens. My shoulders backed off slightly from their embrace of my ears. She rolled out fresh paper and patted the examining table. "How are you feelin' today?"

"Good." I sat down.

"Nervous?"

"No. Yes. Why? Should I be nervous?"

"No, deah, not at awl. I'm just gonna draw blood. If all your credentials check out, you'll schedule a full checkup and then you can begin the injections."

My relief at not having to undergo a pelvic exam while wearing a camera made me guffaw out loud. Imogene gave me a strange look. She was probably under orders to assess mental states, I reminded myself.

"So," I said, "about how long altogether until I could begin giving eggs?"

"Depending on your cycle, it could be as soon as a month."

"And you do the checkup?"

"Everything but. I do bloods and extraction. A doctor does the exam. Are you right-handed or left-handed?"

"They care about *that*?" I asked incredulously.

"For the blood," she reminded me, tapping my wrists. "Which arm would you like to use?"

I held out my right arm and tried to sound casual. "So, after you take out the eggs, what happens? Who picks them up?"

She swiveled over to the counter and began unwrapping a needle.

"The other owner. Jeremy's the scientist. Paulina's the business."

I breathed in as quietly as I could through my nose. It was the first solid confirmation of Jeremy's connection to Summa.

"Oh yeah, my friend mentioned there was another guy who worked here." Imogene turned her head to look at me for a moment. I gave her an innocent smile. She turned back to her needle. "What's his last name again?"

She hesitated. "Wedge. Jeremy Wedge."

"That's right, that sounds familiar. So he takes the eggs. The places studying them never pick them up?"

"Honey, I just do my job. Roll up your sleeve, please, and make a fist."

I gave her my forearm while my mind reeled with new possibilities of dirty money and motivation. All I knew was that a woman had given Samantha her killing orders. Samantha didn't know her name, which didn't give me much to go on. Would I now have to pursue witnesses at the Institute of National Health? I squeezed my eyes shut against the needle. Forget witnesses; would I have to investigate the highly questionable ethics behind a study by a federally funded entity into genetics and intelligence? *First deal with the hit woman,* I reminded myself. Still, I couldn't resist indulging in a quick fantasy: me being congratulated by Barack and Michelle at a private ceremony in the West Wing. No, I didn't even need that, maybe just tea in the Oval Office. Or a club soda squeezed in between his other appointments. That would be fine.

In one move, Imogene pulled out the needle, placed my left hand over the bandage, and bent my right arm.

"Put pressure on it," she instructed me. Then she sat back and froze her face in a bizarre fake smile, teeth bared.

"What . . . what's wrong? What are you *doing*?"

"Smiling for the camera."

I felt my own face freeze in a garish smile. This was not happening, not again. Made by two grandmas in less than a week. I licked my lips and willed my voice not to abandon me.

"What are you talking about?" I finally squeaked in a falsetto fit for a boy's choir.

She shrugged and pointed at my necklace. "I wasn't born yesterday."

"I have no idea what you're talking about," I protested. But I was already off the exam table, my sleeve rolled down, one hand on the doorknob.

"Look, deah, I don't care what you're up to. I like this job. It's easy. It's pleasant. It pays good. I wanna keep it."

"I really don't—"

"Oh, stop it," she said, not unkindly. "Jeremy never comes when the girls are here. I don't know why and, like I said, I don't care. But your friend never met him, that I know. If you had some lover's quarrel with him, that's not my business. Just don't mess with my job."

I threw pretense to the wind. "Believe me, he's no lover of mine."

Imogene laughed easily and stuck my blood in a centrifuge. "Don't be too hard on him, deah. He's a nervous boy. Needs more fiber."

At any moment Paulina could come charging through the doors to kick me out, or worse. "It's just...," I persisted desperately. "Are you sure you've never seen any paperwork, anything, from the INH or anyplace that takes the eggs? A name? A folder? Anything?"

She shook her head at me and started the centrifuge. I couldn't tell if it was a refusal or a statement of genuine ignorance.

"Okay, well, thank you."

"I don't suppose we'll be seeing you again," she mused, turning to the machine.

"Uh," I said, unsure of anything but how much I needed to get away from the Summa Institute. "Yeah, no, I'll be back," I croaked unconvincingly.

"Rechurch."

"Excuse me?"

Her back was to me. "I see a lot of that name on the papers. Rechurch. Never seen anything else, in fact."

"Rechurch?"

"Rechurch."

"Thank you," I breathed.

"You tell whoever's watching that this better not cost me my retirement."

Paulina was tapping at her computer when I bolted from the exam room. I told her I was feeling light-headed from the blood draw—no breakfast, I apologized—and assured her I'd return with the completed paperwork the very next day. I fled the office, the pounding in my ears drowning out her concerned queries.

I raced around the corner and flung myself into the backseat of Pippa's car, where, predictably, Tommy's honking laughter greeted me.

"Oh shit, Zepha, you suck at undercovah! Pardon my French, Commish."

"Oh yeah, what would you have done differently?" I snapped, approaching hyperventilation.

"She made you so fast, man!" he howled.

"Maybe the techs should have used a necklace that was smaller than a fucking planet!"

"Dooohh, look out, Zepha's maaad."

I slapped my palms against the leather seat.

"Are you two finished?" Pippa asked from the driver's

seat. She refused to let anyone drive her around the way every other city official did. Not appearance of impropriety, she liked to say. *Actual* impropriety.

Rechurch. *Rechurch?* Was there a megachurch involved? Were there megachurches in New York City? Where was there room for a megachurch? "Do you think this is some evangelical thing, some God racket?" I wondered aloud. Maybe it really was a eugenics project. How many more spin-offs to this case could there be before I saw any kind of resolution? "What in God's name is 'Rechurch'?"

"Sistah Michael Bernard taught me that at Our Lady of Smack Me Silly," Tommy said, "but she beat the crap out of me every day, so I fuhgot it all."

"Yeah, blame it on the nuns," I said reflexively, looking out the window onto Watts Street.

Pippa started the car, then turned. I straightened up in an attempt to lose the air of sulking adolescent.

"You did fine, Zephyr. It's too bad you got made, but we need to move really quickly now."

"I'm moving as fast as I can," I protested.

"Faster."

Chapter 17

Certainly, when Pippa said "faster," she didn't mean racing west on Perry Street at seven that evening so that I'd beat my cursed, depressed friend to a non-Oscar party. In my defense, I'd spent the entire afternoon glued to my computer, surfing every database and search engine Pippa, Tommy, and I could dream up, trying to find a Rechurch, trying to make that fit with the Summa–Jeremy–Samantha–poison-lemonade–money-transfer pieces. Pippa had called her fellow Lucite collector and confirmed that Jeremy was still alive and well and being held against his will at Bellevue. I checked in at the nursing home and was told that Samantha was making enemies right and left but was still in residence.

I needed a break. My plan was to fill up on hors d'oeuvres, hear a couple of speeches, ogle the guests, and go back to the office. I'd work all night, but I needed a break.

Mercedes answered the intercom.

"'Tis I!" I announced, giddy with exhaustion and remnants of fear. In the silk-lined elevator, I tried to switch mental gears. Out with the murderous, in with the glamorous.

I stepped out onto the twelfth floor and into an oasis of

hushed, elegant activity. Where Lucy had insisted on college-era decor for her twin apartment across the street, Mercedes and Dover had a legitimately adult home. Low sofas, muted carpets, and sleek brass floor lamps created three cozy nooks scattered in front of the floor-to-ceiling windows. Along the interior wall was a series of nearly life-size bold composer portraits, some by Avedon, some by Platon. Mercedes's practice area was in a far corner of the apartment, her music stand arranged so that she faced the river as she played.

Tonight there were scores of tealight candles on every surface that wasn't covered with platters of basil-encrusted, arugula-garnished, grass-fed, locally grown victuals. Waiters bustled about importantly, trying unsuccessfully to hide their delight at their evening's assignment.

"I'm really glad you guys are here," murmured Mercedes, in a departure from her genetically unflappable self.

"Even Macy?"

"Even *Lucy*."

"I thought you'd gotten used to all this," I said. I started to take off my sweater, then remembered I was still wearing my gun. Damn! I hadn't had time to go home to change and lock it up. Given that the Hollywood crowd paid top dollar to look like slobs, I wasn't too informal, but I was going to roast.

"I have gotten used to it, sort of, but this is a bit much. Even for me." She glanced out at the crowd from the shelter of the entryway.

Dover Carter had captured the hearts and libidos of women young and old, as much for the fact that he was a confirmed nice guy as for his resemblance to Cary Grant. Regular appearances in front of United Nations humanitarian commissions at the behest of numerous oppressed peoples, fearless stumping for worthy liberal candidates, and a willingness to gain weight for roles (confirming, in his fans' minds, an absence of vanity) made his bachelorhood all the more mysterious and tantalizing.

At the age of forty, he fell head over heels in love with one of my best friends, so much so that when she expressed grave doubts about the yawning chasm between their lifestyles and social circles—he regularly topped Sexiest Man of the Year lists, while she could spend an entire afternoon in the basement of Avery Fisher Hall discussing rosin—he had voluntarily entered semiretirement. And there he had stayed for the three years they'd been together, making only one film a year. He was blissed out living among us mortals, but it didn't change the fact that his best friend was Ben Plank, with whom he'd costarred in all three *Cans of Gravy* films. Ben was married to Aphrodite Jones, the philanthropic sexpot, and while I had been mostly at ease ordering in Chinese with them one evening—a petri dish attempt by Dover and Mercedes to merge their friends the way other couples merged libraries—it was still hard not to be disproportionately titilated when Phrodie (as her friends called her) cajoled me into a game of hide-and-seek with two of their three adopted children.

"Wow, that's really De Niro over there?" I asked.

"Yeah, and that's Streep and Connelly and Moore, except I'm supposed to call them Meryl and Jen and Julie with a straight face. Give me your sweater, Zephyr, I'll toss it in the bedroom." She sounded strange.

"Are you mad about something?"

She fluttered her eyes closed for a moment. "No," she said, trying to convince herself. "I knew what I was getting into when I married him. And he's still my Dover, my guy. And it's just one night and then tomorrow I can sit and do battle with Shostakovich's Fifth all by myself all day long." She looked longingly to where one of her violas sat, displayed in its teak stand at the far end of the apartment. Ed Norton was admiring it. "Give me your sweater," she repeated.

"Nah, it's okay, I'll keep it."

"You'll roast!"

I shrugged. At some point, I would tell my friends and family about my new lethal accessory, but this didn't strike me as the right time.

Dover strode out of their bedroom, his eyes searching the crowd. He wore a button-down over a T-shirt and khakis.

"Does he pay someone to look that good in regular clothes?" I asked Mercedes.

"He used to, but now the home visits by the stylist are limited to red carpet nights."

Dover gave a few quick pats to passing shoulders but visibly relaxed when he spotted his wife. He threaded his way over to us and enveloped me in a bear hug, then slung his arm around Mercedes. The two of them were absurdly tall and gorgeous, and the fact that they were different colors made them even more ridiculous: *Not only are we kind, stunning, talented, and rich, but we're* interracial, *too.* Nobody should have that many bases covered.

"Zeph! I'm so glad you made it. Macy thought you might be working late. She told us you're working undercover. *So* cool."

I choked on plain air. "No! I mean, yes, but please don't say anything! She wasn't supposed to say . . . I wasn't even supposed to tell her, but . . ."

"But she's so pathetic when she decides she's cursed, you feel like you have to toss her a bone," Mercedes finished. "Your secret's safe. Right, Dove? No screenplays out of this?"

He held up his hands. "I leave writing to the writers. Hey,

did you bring Gregory? Merce said you guys might get back together. I wish you would—I miss him."

Dover, in my opinion, still needed a little work in the normal conversation department. After years of being surrounded by toadies, he often didn't vet his comments before they departed his lips. Luckily, Lucy charged over to us, glee flowing freely from every pore. Her eyes and cheeks were bright, and she looked like her old, pre-Hillsville self. I was glad to see her holding a plate piled high with food.

"This is so great!" she squealed.

"You'd be happy if we took you to the West Fourth Street station at rush hour and let you sit on the platform."

"I know, I know," she conceded, "but *this*. This is just. Soooo . . ."

"Great?" Mercedes offered.

"I get into Grand Central and I . . ." She hunched her shoulders up and then let them down generously. "Don't you ever stand on those glam steps and look down at the clock and the bustle and all the lives and feel . . ." She spread her fingers as if listening to an aria.

"Like Mussolini?" I suggested.

Lucy was undeterred. "God, I miss this view," she breathed. "I miss it so much. I miss the traffic. I miss the subways. I miss homeless people. I miss the river."

"You guys live in the Hudson Valley," Dover reminded her.

"Yeah, but you have to drive to see the river. You have to drive to see everything. You have to drive to go for a walk. Don't get me started."

"Too late," Mercedes mused.

"No, I am not going to whine tonight. I promise. I'm enjoying the present. Immensely." She beamed, then turned to me suddenly. "Hey, Zeph, Macy said you're undercover! That is *so* cool! What's the case about?"

A few minutes later, I found my loose-lipped friend deep in conversation with a four-foot-tall woman. I tapped Macy on the shoulder, near bursting with irritation that she was fine.

"Hi, sweetie!" She gave me a quick tight squeeze, all evidence of the weekend's drama apparently having vaporized. "Zeph, this is Madge. Madge, this is my friend Zephyr Zuckerman."

"Hey, that's almost as funny as Madge the midget. What were my parents thinking, right?" Madge chortled comfortably.

"Uh," I said.

"Madge met Dover on the set of *Death and Renovation*. She works as a stand-in for child actors; isn't that *fascinating*? Kids can't work long hours, so she gets paid to stand there while they figure out lighting and stuff. She makes a living at it!" Macy shook her head with satisfaction.

"Wow," I said. "That's. I'm. That's so interesting."

"Better than being bowled," Madge agreed, popping a mini-goat-cheese-and-sweet-potato galette into her brightly lipsticked mouth.

"Madge, can I borrow Macy for a second? I need her to help me with something."

I pulled the redheaded chatterbox into the kitchen, just in time to hear one of the waitstaff say to another, "I could never be a drag queen—waaaay too much work and time. Plus there's all the ass-waxing."

So I pulled her into Mercedes and Dover's carpeted, dimly lighted bedroom, where the mound of coats was now almost shoulder height.

"Why did you tell everyone I'm undercover?" I fumed.

"I didn't tell everyone."

"Oh, don't *even*."

"You're the one who wanted me to get my mind off Rudy," she defended herself.

"Yes, I wanted to get your mind off the dead dermatologist, but not at the expense of my personal safety!" I shouted.

Macy's ginger eyebrows shot into tiny arrows of concern. "Your safety? Is someone trying to hurt you?"

"Actually, yes." It sounded ridiculous, but it was true. "So please, please stop telling people, okay? I'll tell you everything once the case is over."

"I'm sorry, Zeph," she whispered. "I didn't know."

"I know you didn't." I glanced at the clock on one of the bedside tables. "I only came to make sure you weren't New Hampshire–bound. I have to get back to the office."

"Well, now you're scaring me."

"I'm fine, Mace, but this case is picking up steam and I need to finish it." Or start it. Something.

Her eyes suddenly went wide.

"What's wrong?" I glanced behind me, but no one was there.

She shook her head.

"What?" I insisted.

"Are you . . . ? Is that . . . ?" She pointed to my hip, where my sweater had fallen open to reveal the gun's leather case.

"I'm outta here."

"Oh, stay, Zephyr. I swear I won't breathe a word. I won't ask. About anything. C'mon, eat something, listen to some speeches, and then you can go back to being hunted."

As it turned out, I did fall prey to someone five minutes after leaving the bedroom, but—for the moment, anyway—it wasn't Jeremy Wedge or Paulina. It was a woman named Sycamore Dawnsart. Sycamore was a vacant-eyed, silicone-lipped, plunging-necklined woman in towering black leather boots, who was too young to have hair so decimated by platinum dye. Sycamore was an honest-to-God, modern-day wet nurse, and as I stood cornered against a portrait of Rostropovich with only my plate of asparagus-and-quince gnocchi to defend me, she told me all about her profession, which she found endlessly fascinating.

"I started doing it for my sister, who had to start chemo while she was pregnant. It was sooo sad, but she's fine and the baby's fine—her name is Breuckelen, spelled the Old Dutch way—but she couldn't nurse. So I got a breast pump and got myself to lactate. It really wasn't that hard. And oh. My. God. You cannot believe how many calories you burn breast-feeding. I eat cheeseburgers every day and I still look like this." She gestured to her figure, apparently the universal symbol for the perfect waistline.

"It is *awesome*. I eat whatever I want and I make great money, even though I still charge only half of what formula costs." If this was her elevator pitch, she was in the wrong building. "I pump three times a day, during *Good Day, Oprah,* and *Idol.* I thought it would make my boobs huge, but I guess that's just in the beginning. They're actually a little smaller than they used to be, but I have my tricks. And when I give it up, I'll have plenty of money for a boob job. Also, you'd think it would be free birth control, but really it's not. My cousin got pregnant while she was breast-feeding, so I started using my diaphragm again."

I looked over her shoulder in desperation, telepathically willing Dover to start the speeches.

"You cannot believe how many actresses use my services," Sycamore continued, tilting her head to catch my eye again. "They want the best for their kids, right, but they, A, can't take the time to breast-feed and, B, they don't want the stretch marks." She paused for a nanosecond of what was probably her deepest soul-searching. "I'm a little bummed about the stretch marks, but like I said—"

"You'll have the boob job," I finished, wondering whether the much-touted benefits of breast milk to developing brains held up under these particular circumstances. Nothing less than an angel from heaven, Lucy pounced on me.

"Zephyr!" she shrieked.

"Will you excuse us?" I said to Sycamore, who was starting to talk again. "She needs me." I dug my fingers into Lucy's arm and pulled her clear across the apartment, barreling through a cozy conversation between Reese and Drew.

"Thank you," I breathed. "Thank you, thank you, thank you."

Lucy didn't seem to notice or mind that I had probably left fingerprints on her flesh. She was actually bouncing, rocking up and down on the balls of her feet. "Look at this," she crowed. "*Look.*" She shoved her phone in front of my face. I held her wrist to steady the message she wanted me to read:

<Mom and Dad's ship captured by pirates.
CALL ME ASAP.—L>

It took me a long moment to shift from Sycamore the wet nurse to Lenore and Maxwell's adventures on the high seas.

"Can you *believe* it? Do you think it's really true?" Her face held the look of wonder that true believers assumed when they spotted the Virgin Mary taking shape in an oak tree or tea leaves or toothpaste residue.

"You haven't called him back yet?" I asked, shocked.

She waved her hand at me. "Oh, I'll call him, I'll call him in a minute, but, really, what could *I* possibly do, right here, right now? Plus"—an explosive laugh burst from between her lips—"I should probably give myself a moment to practice . . . sounding . . . *worried.*" The pressure built until she was doubled over, convulsing with laughter, tears streaming down her cheeks.

Macy and Mercedes found us.

"What's wrong with her? What happened?!"

Lucy was in no shape to speak, but when I tried, I found myself happily infected by her hysteria. "It's . . . Lenore."

"Is she okay?"

"No!" I yelped, starting to snort. "She's been hijacked . . . by . . . PIRATES!"

In the end, Dover had to herd the four of us hyenas back into the bedroom because, even in that apartment full of people who made a living out of creating spectacle, we were making too much of one ourselves. And because Lucy was still unable to stop laughing, Dover put in a quick call to Leonard on her behalf. Two U.S. carriers and a fleet of Republic of Seychelles coast guard cutters were already engaged in hostage negotiations with the Somali pirates. The media had caught wind of the story, and so there was, in fact, absolutely nothing Lucy could do but eat, drink, and lose herself in the proximity of so much celebrity.

"Let's start the speeches," said Dover.

"Amen!" cheered Lucy. Dover looked at her disapprovingly. "Oh, Dover," she said, casually putting her tiny arm across his broad back. Four fingers of scotch could not have made her more uninhibited. "Really, if you knew her, you'd understand."

The moment the crowd had settled on couches and rugs and bar stools to listen to the speech by a novice director who'd been nominated for his documentary on tiramisu— he'd sampled more than a thousand different versions in an espresso-dusted journey of self-discovery—my cellphone buzzed. I darted into the bedroom to answer it.

"Hi, Pippa."

"You're not at the office."

"I took a break," I admitted.

"Good. You needed one. Any progress?"

"None." I was too tired to sugarcoat.

"Where are you?" she asked as a round of applause and cheers filtered through the door.

I hesitated. "I stopped by a friend's party."

"Zephyr, I'm not joking when I tell you I want to know your every move. You will not get hurt on my watch."

For a strange moment, I thought she was talking about my love life, and the memory of my cheek fitting perfectly into Gregory's smooth, sweet-smelling neck nearly leveled me.

"Sorry, sorry. I'm on Perry Street, all the way at the river."

"Text the address to Tommy, right?"

"I will. Sorry."

"Zephyr, just stay there. There's nothing else we can do tonight."

My throat closed with the pressure of impending failure.

"No, I'm going back," I insisted.

"Let's talk in an hour. Stay there until then. Try to enjoy yourself." She hung up, never one to go in for the finer points of phone etiquette.

I returned to my spot in front of a couch and leaned back against Macy's knees. I tried to listen to the speeches, but my mind kept drifting back to the case. I was sure that, based on Samantha's bank records, not to mention her verbal confession to me, we had enough to subpoena at least some of Summa's financial records, but it wasn't enough. We were all wary of moving too hastily, of letting some other part of the puzzle get away.

Ben Plank got up and gave a seven-minute-long accolade to everyone who had worked on *When the Cows Came Home,* from the AHA set inspector who'd ensured the bovine cast remained blissful to the production accountants. Everyone in the room hooted and cheered Ben's inclusiveness, normally precluded by the parameters of live broadcasts.

Even if we assumed that Paulina and Jeremy were business partners gone sour, I thought, as Meryl Streep charmed the pants off everyone with a speech that veered from witty to poignant and back again for her role as Eleanor of Aquitaine in the musical *Plantagenets!*, there was something about the Summa Institute itself that was weird. It was just so . . . tiny. Its website was so unrevealing. There was a lack of bustle that was eerie: The phone hadn't rung once while I was there. I shifted, recrossed my legs. Not exactly the stuff of search warrants.

Lucy was sitting beside me, whispering animatedly to a rapt Julianne Moore. I strained to listen. She was telling her about her social work, regaling her with stories of meth addicts in Bed-Stuy and speaking in the present tense. For the moment, her life in Hillsville had never happened, and even if the stories she was telling weren't currently true, they were accomplishing the same thing her idly threatened affair would have: They were making her feel worthy again.

"Luce," I whispered as Meryl sat down and Dover prepared to introduce the next nominee. She brushed me off without even turning her head. *"Luce,"* I whispered again.

"What?" She whirled around, irritated.

"Where did you get your eggs?"

She widened her eyes and tilted her head as if to say, *Do you* not *see who I'm chatting with?*

"Are you kidding me?" she choked out.

"No. Where'd you get them?"

"I used to go to the Union Square farmers' market; now I go to Stop and Shop." She turned back to her conversation but added over shoulder, "I still get the cage-free."

I tapped her again.

"Would you excuse me?" she said to Julianne. Julie. "I'm sorry my friend is so rude." She glared at me.

"I meant the eggs that made your children."

She looked confused, and then her whole face went round. "Zephyr, are you thinking of going *solo*?! Or are you and

Gregory getting back together? You're going to join me in my misery? Wait, why do you need eggs at all? Oh, Zeph, you're having trouble getting pregnant, like I did!"

"Calm down, schadenfreude. No to all of the above. Just tell me the name of the place."

"You're not trying to get pregnant?"

"The name, Luce."

She looked at me suspiciously. "Recherché."

My eyes grew tight with the beginning of tunnel vision. I swallowed hard.

"What?"

"Recherché." She tried to turn her back on me with finality, but I pulled her to her feet. She smiled apologetically to the freckled thespian, who smiled back in confusion. "What the—Zephyr, *stop*."

I yanked Lucy toward the bedroom, my brain ricocheting around my skull.

Recherché. Rechurch. It's how I would have pronounced it, too, had I not been the beneficiary of four years of otherwise useless French. Tommy O. could take his mockery of my private-school pedigree and shove it in his soda bread: This entire case might hinge on an accent *aigu*.

In the bedroom, the waiter who was averse to applying depilatories to the farthest reaches of his anatomy was locked in an embrace with the director of an animated film about Karl Rove. I pulled Lucy into the bathroom.

"Why do you think they tiled it with this black marble?" Lucy said as I locked the door behind us. "I can always see up my own dress in here. Very unlike Merce."

"Lucy."

She crossed her arms, still annoyed about her interrupted conversation.

"You're sure it was called Recherché?"

"Are you insane? Of course I'm sure."

"How much did you pay?"

"Zephyr!"

"Lucy, please. I know what brand of dental floss you use. I know you can't go to bed unless your shoes are all facing the same direction. For God's sake, you've even told me how much Leonard earns, so why won't you tell me this?"

She fingered one of the hand towels hanging from a silver ring. "I don't remember exactly."

"Bullshit."

She blushed. "Zephyr, it's embarrassing. Why do you want to know? And why right now?"

"Please, Luce, I'll explain, I promise. Just tell me."

"Two hundred," she mumbled.

"Thousand?" I said, breaking all vows to play it cool. "Two hundred thousand dollars?"

"They're excellent donors," she said defensively, turning the faucet on and off. "They're all Ivy League graduates and some of them are even—"

"Rhodes scholars?"

She looked scared. "How did you—"

"Why, Luce? I'm not being judgmental," I promised her, putting my hand over hers to stop the flow of water. "I need to know why you would go there when other places charge, what, *twenty*?"

"It was important to Leonard. I know that sounds really shallow to you, but he wanted Ph.D. genes. Actually, we paid a little extra for the Ph.D. Well, she was still a candidate, because, you know, the eggs need to be really young, but she had already passed her comps."

I sat on the edge of the tub, the cold enamel a relief beneath my sweaty palms. I pressed my forehead against the tile and closed my eyes.

"Zephyr!" Lucy gasped. "Is that a . . . *gun?*"

Chapter 18

At 9:05 the next morning, I rode to the eighth floor of 561 Park Avenue. My recording studio was around my neck, my gun was on my waist, Tommy and Pippa were in the car downstairs, Letitia Humphrey and Bobby Turato were backing me up in the lobby, and Richie McIntyre stood by the stairwell entrance, his hand resting lightly on his weapon. I looked at him, he nodded, and I pushed open the oak door to suite 807.

Inside was a large reception area with leather couches, a low glass coffee table, raw-silk-covered walls, and fresh lilies whose cloying scent nearly knocked me over. A small rock fountain burbled at the far end of the room. The place hummed with quiet wealth, and I could only imagine how uncomfortable it had made Lucy to come here. Between their decision to use Recherché and the move upstate, I was beginning to reevaluate the force of Leonard's pull within the marriage.

For the occasion, I had borrowed my mother's smoke-gray Dior suit. I had put on her pearl studs, swept my hair up in combs, encased my legs in stockings and high heels, and applied makeup with an unpracticed hand. I had feared the result would look like a child playing dress up, but I realized, as I looked in the mirror, that I'd been deceiving myself. The effect was that of . . . an almost-thirty-one-year-old. A regular grown-up thirty-one-year-old. No less, and maybe a bit more. Tommy had whistled and the others had regarded me with quiet shock. If I'd had more time, I might have indulged a small crisis of identity, but, as it was, a potential bust awaited me.

As I sized up the front desk, I was grateful for the costume. The heavily painted receptionist—the lava lips and bright spots of red on her cheeks reminded me of a Russian doll—was dressed in a crisp gray pantsuit, and she wore her hair in a shiny bob that had not a single strand out of place. She was designed to make people nervous, and I wondered why these places that made a business out of creating people couldn't seem to relate comfortably to those of us who already existed.

I had planned to stride up to her with the confidence of a woman wearing a two-thousand-dollar suit and in possession of two hundred grand to blow on conception. I had planned to request an informational interview and demand a tour of the facilities. But the striding plan would have to wait.

Leaning over the Matryoshka doll's desk was a grimy, gray-bearded, saggy-jeaned man with three cameras dangling off him. Matryoshka's chair was rolled back as far as her carpet protector would permit. A faint look of horror seeped through her mask.

"No, sir. I cannot let you back there."

"But she wants me there. Ask her yourself. She's paying me to be here!"

"And I'm being paid to say no to people like—Look, sir, only the partner is permitted in the procedure room."

The man slammed his hand on the counter. "She's going to be extremely angry. And not with me, let me tell you." Suddenly he brought one of his cameras to his face and snapped a photo of the receptionist. She stood up and backed away.

"What the hell are you doing? Give me that camera."

He laughed gruffly. "Look, lady, I'm the Pembrandt family photographer. I was there when he proposed to her in a hot-air balloon over Provence. I was there to photograph them in bed the morning after their wedding. I photographed all three of their renovations, the last seven Christmas mornings and Valentine's Day dinners, and I was at Tessa's birth. And now Mrs. Pembrandt wants me in that room"—he pointed to a door leading off the waiting room—"to photograph the embryo transfer of Junior. It's extremely important to her. So if you won't let me, then I will photograph the alternate story. She'll like that, yeah. . . ." He nodded to himself as he started taking pictures of the room. I quickly turned my back on him as he spun around, shooting. "Mrs. P. likes when I record the mishaps, too. She's got an appreciation of narrative—"

"Sir, stop it! Stop it or I'll call my boss."

He and I both snapped to attention.

"Oh no, call your boss? Oh please, no, not that." He returned to shooting, taking pictures of the waterfall and the otherwise empty waiting room.

Matryoshka picked up her phone and spoke in sharp, hushed tones. She hung up and addressed me.

"May I help you, ma'am?" she asked, locking her eyes onto mine, anxious for a life raft back to the civility to which she was accustomed.

"Hey, what about me?" demanded the family photographer, hitching up his jeans.

"You," Matryoshka said coldly, "will have to wait. May I help you?" she repeated. I was grateful to the ornery photographer for offering a sharp contrast to me: Any suspicion I might have aroused by my unannounced arrival had been quieted by his performance. The painted receptionist and I were now sisters, and I milked our new bond.

"Yes, thank you so much," I gushed politely. "I'm afraid I'm here without an appointment, but my friend Lucy Toklas insisted you wouldn't mind. I'm just looking for an informational interview, perhaps a tour, and I found myself with a free morning. Is there any chance . . . ?" I smiled delicately at her.

"Of course, of course, I remember Ms. Toklas." Matryoshka immediately started jabbing at her keyboard and peering at her screen. "If you wouldn't mind waiting just half an hour, I can have one of the counselors sit down with you."

"Oh, terrific." If I'd had white gloves I would now be peeling them off finger by finger. "And with whom will I be meeting?" I added lightly as I sat down.

"You'll meet with Sander."

At that moment, Paulina pushed through the door that connected the back rooms to the reception area. The photographer snapped her picture. I was torn between wanting to make sure I got a clear shot of her on my own camera and wanting to hide behind a magazine to buy myself time, so I half-stood, half-turned, and found myself in a bizarre crouch that looked like I was trying not to pee on myself.

Of all the elements that had been refusing to come together on this case, now, *now,* the most concrete evidence of a scam of epic proportions was throwing itself into my arms, and I was paralyzed. Of all the scenarios the team had envisioned at ten o'clock the night before, during an emergency meeting post-non-Oscar party, this was not one of them. No one had predicted Paulina herself would be here.

"Sir, just what do you think you're—" She caught sight of me and froze, but only for an instant. The features that had seemed so inviting the day before hardened, transforming her face into a sinister, nearly unrecognizable mask.

"Please come with me, sir." I tried to catch her eye, but she would not stop looking at the photographer, who tossed the receptionist a triumphant look and followed Paulina back through the door. It *whoosh*ed and clicked closed.

I tried to swallow. I could practically hear my team shrieking over their radios downstairs.

"Unbelievable!" squeaked Matryoshka. "She has never, ever . . . This is most unusual, I assure you. We have strict guidelines about who may go back there. I hope you'll excuse this disruption. Really. We pride ourselves on being extremely . . . Well, this is just very unusual."

"Oh, now, don't you worry," I said shakily, and perched on the edge of the sofa, trying to figure out what to do next. I wished I had an earpiece.

A minute ticked by in silence while I pretended to look at a magazine. I had Paulina cornered. She'd be eager to get me into her office to keep me from making a scene. I'd confront her with our suspicions and get her reaction—either confession or denial—on tape, and then, because her presence here and at Summa was sufficient, I'd arrest her.

Holy shit. I didn't have handcuffs on me, had never made an arrest solo, and my mind froze, drawing a blank as to what I was supposed to do next. Sweat erupted from places I didn't know could sweat. *Calm down, Zephyr. Think*. Think. At the very least, I reassured myself, Pippa was on the phone dispatching officers to the courthouse with a search-warrant request. And maybe, just maybe, Tommy or Richie would burst in with cuffs, reeling off Miranda warnings. Matryoshka had no idea how much activity had been set in motion.

As it turned out, neither did I.

Another minute passed. This was not how I pictured my first career-making bust. My fingers had become so sweaty that the pages of the magazine grew soggy in my hands.

I stood up and approached the desk apologetically.

"Actually, excuse me? Would it be possible to meet with Paulina instead of Sander? I've heard such wonderful things about her."

Matryoshka smiled at me, still relieved the disruption was over.

"Well, I don't see why not! I'm sure she could spare a few minutes for a friend of Lucy's." She put the phone to her ear and pressed a button. "Hmm, she must be on a call."

I sat back down, barely able to swallow. I watched the clock. After a minute, I stood up and approached again.

"Would you mind trying again?"

This time the smile was not quite as big, but she dialed.

"No answer?" I asked.

"Let me go check."

I began to follow her.

"You wait here."

I waited until the door was nearly closed, then caught it and followed Matryoshka as she turned down a short corridor. I peeked around the corner and watched her tap on a door whose brass plate said *Examining Room*. After a quick conference with someone inside, she frowned and moved on to another door that was slightly ajar: *Office*. I tiptoed after her.

The photographer was in there, reclining in a chair and idly shooting pictures of anything that caught his eye: a collection of figurines, a framed MBA from Columbia, a spiky aloe plant. He appeared to be alone.

"Where is Paulina?" Matryoshka demanded, certain that the cameraman had disposed of her boss.

He shrugged and snapped a picture of her.

"Is there an emergency stairwell back here?" I asked.

Matryoshka whirled around, hand clutched to her heart. "What are you doing here? Please return to the waiting room!" Her world was once again topsy-turvy.

"Well, is there?" I demanded.

Furiously, she pointed down the hall to an exit sign above a door.

"Oh my God," I said. "Oh my God oh my God oh my God. She fled!" I yelled into my chest, as if Pippa and Tommy couldn't already hear every breath I was taking. "She fled!" I ran down the hall and threw myself against the door. I looked down the well to the bottom. Nothing. No one. "Dammit!"

I circled down flight after flight as fast as I could and reached the first floor, certain I was going to throw up. I never used to get dizzy—wasn't loss of equilibrium a sign of aging? I ran outside and found myself facing an alley. Pippa and Tommy were parked around the side of the building, on 63rd Street, but without benefit of an avenue or traffic moving in a known direction, I was momentarily stumped. I blindly followed the alley and emerged onto a side street. I spotted an awning and breathed a sigh of relief.

"I'm on Sixty-second. I'm in front of 127 East Sixty-second. Crimson awning on the north side. If anyone's still here . . . ?"

I looked up and down the street. After a minute, the town car came screeching around the corner.

"I'm sorry, I'm so sorry," I moaned, climbing into the backseat.

"I can't believe we didn't cover the fire exit," Pippa grunted, as much to herself as to me and Tommy, who, for once, was silent. "What an utter, monumental lapse. White collar and we assume they won't put on trainers and run. Idiots. Idiots!"

She pulled away from the curb with tires screeching.

"Where are we going?"

"Bellevue. Let's try to catch at least one suspect, yes?"

I sat back in the seat and pressed my fingers to my eyes.

"Zephyr, think. Where does Paulina live? Where might she be going? What the hell is her last name?"

"I only met her yesterday," I nearly sobbed. "I don't know! No, wait." I thought of the diploma I'd just glimpsed. " 'G,' " I concluded lamely. "It begins with a 'G.' "

"Oh, blast it, she'd likely use an alias anyway. Let's alert the airports with a physical description and press Jeremy Wedge as hard as we can."

I watched the city whiz past, feeling like a misbehaved child perched in the backseat. Peering through the windows of the taxis that surrounded us, I briefly wondered what was unfolding in all those other backseats. People on their way to funerals? Coming home from signing divorce papers? On their way to being diagnosed with a fatal disease? Anyone else out there who'd just botched the most important moment of her budding career? Anyone else minutes from being fired? Forget fired. I'd completely bungled my apprenticeship, which meant I'd never sit for the licensing exam the following spring. I wasn't even angry at Paulina. She was doing her job, being the criminal. It had been my job to catch her.

Med school: fail. Law school: fail. Law enforcement: fail. Zephyr: fail. What I wanted was to crawl into Gregory's arms and stay there for a little bit of eternity. But I couldn't do that, either.

As the tears threatened to roll, my cellphone rang. The hotel's main number. The last thing I had time or tolerance for at this moment was Asa and his solipsistic trivialities, but if there was any chance it was Ballard, I had to take the call.

I breathed in a big, snotty breath. "Hello," I sniffled.

"Zephyr, my acupuncturist has an opening in an hour and a half. Is there any way you could cover?"

I thought about hanging up on him, but then I considered my imminent unemployment and began to laugh hysterically. Maybe I could get a permanent job as a concierge at the Greenwich Village Hotel.

"No, Asa, there is absolutely no way, not in a million years, that I can cover for you today."

"You don't have to *laugh* about it. I was only *asking*." He paused. "I'll be with you in a moment," Asa said to someone at the desk, and then to me again: "Excuse me for bothering you with my chronic *pain*. I said I'll be with you in a *moment*. God," he muttered.

In the background, I could hear the familiar tones of an irritated guest.

"I told you, I'll be with you in a mo—Jeremy? No, Jeremy's not here right now. I have no idea when—"

"Asa!" I shrieked into the phone, bolting upright. Pippa and Tommy whipped their heads around. "For the love of God, please, Asa, for once in your life, play it cool. Is the woman you're talking to about five foot six, dark features, dark hair, well dressed? Wearing..." I squeezed my eyes shut, willing my deficient powers of observation to rise to the occasion. All I could see were wraps and swaths and scarves. "Well, I don't know how to explain what she's wearing." Pippa shook her head slightly in disbelief as even more of my shortcomings were brought to light.

"Well, she's wearing a blond wig that doesn't suit her," he whispered. "I don't know whom she thinks she's fooling."

In the background, again, I heard what was definitely Paulina's voice. At least one of my five senses was operative.

"Asa," I said, my mouth dry. "Keep her there. Whatever you do, keep her there. Tell her that you just heard Jeremy is on his way over. He's been released from the hospital and he's headed to the hotel."

"That's great! I'm so glad he's better!"

"Excellent, keep it up. Give her a free lunch in the restaurant, offer her a tour of the rooms—whatever you do, keep her there. Please? Can you do that?"

"Is she famous?" Asa whispered as Tommy opened the window and stuck a turret light on the roof. Pippa turned on the siren, swung a right off her eastbound route, and hurtled south.

"What?"

"Long-lost sister?"

"You know who she is, Asa? She's an undercover scout for Revlon."

He gasped. "What does that even mean?" he breathed.

Hell if I knew. "Just keep her there, okay?"

"You can count on me, Zephyr."

Chapter 19

By five-thirty that evening, I officially liked beer. I was starting on my third Red Stripe, courtesy of the White Horse Tavern and a dozen SIC colleagues who continued to buy rounds even as they mocked me. It was a kind of love I was quickly coming to accept and even enjoy.

"She's yellin', 'Oh my god oh my god she fled,' " Tommy O. told the group in a whiny voice that didn't come close to resembling mine, even under the most dire circumstances.

"That is *not* what I sounded like," I protested, putting both hands on the tabletop to steady myself.

Tommy R. whipped out a small recorder and entertained the group with my earlier panic, captured perfectly by the necklace he'd created. "Oh, that's exactly what you sounded like, Zepha." He grinned and then assumed a thoughtful pose. "Hey, Mikey," he said to the lumbering detective beside him. "How many times you ever drawn your weapon?"

"On my wife?"

Laughs all around.

"Nah, nah, in your entire career. In your twenty years on the force and then at the S.I.C., how many times?"

I let my head drop to the table. It was sticky. The table, but now my head, too.

"Uh, lemme see." Mikey matched his faux-reflective tone. "In twenty-five years, I've drawn three times. Fired it once."

"Three times, huh? So, Zepha, you've had your weapon, what . . . ?"

"Four days," I muttered to the table.

"What's that?"

"Four days," I grunted, as everyone started cracking up.

Pippa had pulled up in front of the hotel entrance and I'd jumped out before she stopped. This time, at least, we had radioed ahead and were confident every single exit was covered.

I bolted through the sliding doors with Tommy O. a few feet behind me. Inside, Asa was alone at the front desk.

"Where is she, Asa?" I shouted.

"Zephyr? Are you wearing makeup? And that suit—Oh my God, is that Dior? You look amazing!"

"Where is she!" I was going to start crying if we'd lost her. I briefly thought of Zelda's tattooed eyeliner.

"Relax. She's in the little girl's room. We're having a very nice chat, though she is *really* playing it cool. Pretending not to know this season's colors. She is an excellent under-cover—"

At that moment, Paulina appeared from the direction of the bathroom, but when she saw me, she turned and headed for the stairs.

"Freeze!" I screamed. "S.I.C.!"

And then I pulled my gun, which, in retrospect, probably wasn't strictly necessary, since Paulina had, in fact, frozen after my command. Asa yelped and dropped down behind the desk, the most sensible move he'd made in weeks.

"Hands in the air," Tommy added.

Paulina did as she was told. So did the unfortunate guests who happened to emerge from the elevator at that moment.

"S.I. what?" Asa asked from beneath the desk.

"You're under arrest," I began, looking at Pippa for confirmation. She nodded, and Tommy produced cuffs. "You have the right to remain silent. Anything you say can and will—"

"What the hell is going on?" Hutchinson strode out of his office. He looked at me, in high heels and brandishing a gun, and did a double take. "Zephyr?" For once, he was speechless.

"Is there a room we can use?" Tommy asked irritably in the direction of Asa, who lifted one finger and pointed at Hutchinson to identify him as the resident authority.

Two minutes later we were installed in a ground-floor room, with Paulina, blond wig in shackled hands, perched indignantly on one of the beds. Pippa, Tommy, and I sat on the other bed, facing her.

I finished the Miranda warnings. "Knowing and understanding your rights as I have explained them to you, are you willing to answer my questions without an attorney present?"

"I don't need a lawyer," she sneered.

"Is that a yes?"

"I'm smarter than any lawyer, and I've done nothing wrong. Ask me anything you want."

I touched the fake diamond digging into my clavicle, restarting transmission. A video wasn't necessary, but as long as I was saddled with the equipment and a conniving suspect, it couldn't hurt.

"Say it again," I instructed Paulina. "State your name and your intention to waive counsel."

She raised her eyebrows: *amateurs*. "And how will that help you?"

I pointed to my necklace. "I'm a traveling show."

Paulina's expression of surprise laced with grudging admiration was extremely gratifying.

"Can I smoke?" Paulina demanded, after we had dispensed with formalities.

"Of course not," I told her.

"Idiotic country," she muttered.

"Want some nicotine gum?" Tommy offered. Paulina glared at him, then opened her palm. She began chewing furiously and then, to my surprise, she let herself collapse sideways against the pillows, keeping her back rigid. It was a pose of resignation.

"Okay," I said, taking my own first deep breath in a couple of hours. "How about you tell us what we want to know."

Paulina was thirty-eight years old, originally from the Czech Republic, and had come to the United States on a full scholarship to Barnard. She went on to get her MBA at Columbia but, even armed with two of the best degrees in the country, she didn't know what to do with herself. So she went to a *What Color Is Your Parachute?* seminar, where she met other highly educated but aimless graduates, including Jeremy Wedge. It surprised me to discover that the laissez-faire Lothario had ever entertained a moment's doubt about his scientific destiny. At one point, he'd considered becoming a tree surgeon. In any case, he and Paulina began dating and fell in love. Or, rather, she fell in love. No, she was certain he had loved her, too. Anyway—she shrugged—it didn't matter now.

No, we agreed, it probably didn't.

With his expertise in genetics and his internship experience at a fertility lab, Jeremy supplied all the technical know-how for their nascent plan. Paulina brought to the partnership a head for business. Indeed, her acumen was astounding. Not only had she identified a commodity for which a certain market was willing to pay exorbitant prices—high-quality ova—and found a surefire way to keep supply plentiful—tell the donors it was only for research—but she'd even come up with the idea of making the eggs go twice the distance: They'd harvest seven or eight eggs from a donor and plant four in one recipient and four in another. So for the cost of fifteen thousand dollars to the donor, they were pulling in not just two hundred thousand on the other end, but sometimes four hundred thousand. They would have made a killing if they'd found only two recipients a year. As it was, they—Recherché—were doing two or three transfers a month.

It was all going swimmingly until Jeremy took an eye to the donors: young, bright, beautiful. He came up with the idea of housing them in the family hotel, as a way to throw some business their way. (I'd been right about one hunch! That was definitely going in the report.) But then he was unable to resist the sight of the intelligent beauties alone at the bar, far from home, and so began hitting on them. Paulina said she didn't care. She was hurt at first but soon concluded the romantic portion of their program and got over him.

The problem was, she said, Jeremy became paranoid. No matter how many times she reassured him, he didn't believe that she wasn't angry. Paulina had shrewdly structured the business so that she was majority owner, and Jeremy grew afraid that she was going to turn him out into the cold world of unemployment. He began to steal from their operation. Nearly a million dollars.

"A million?" I said sharply, glancing at Pippa. If this case didn't connect to Ballard's missing hundred grand, I was going to implode under the sheer force of frustration.

Paulina shrugged. "We had plenty. I figured I'd let him take a bit, pretend I didn't notice, and then maybe he'd feel he had a cushion and would calm down and stop on his own."

"How thoughtful of you."

"Yes, well, he didn't stop, and I started to get annoyed."

"Anyone would," I couldn't resist quipping.

"But then I thought about how to confront him. He was

already so paranoid and crazy, there was no way he'd admit to stealing. I was nervous about what he'd do to me or the business if I brought it up."

"So you decided to kill him."

She flinched and cleared her throat.

"Have him killed," she clarified.

None of us said anything.

"This was maybe not such a good idea," she conceded. "Perhaps a little too far." Then she perked up and said hopefully, "Self-defense?"

"Yeah, good luck with that," Tommy said.

"We'll get back to you hiring Samantha to kill Jeremy in a minute," I said. "I need to ask you why—"

"It was a brilliant idea," Paulina interrupted.

"Your egg scam?"

"I do not like that word: 'scam.' It is a brilliant *business model,* but I meant using the Bernie Madoff list to find Mrs. Hodges. Don't you think? I mean, really, I *do* understand motivation."

Kimiko *Hodges,* I thought, and almost burst out laughing. *Do not laugh, Zephyr. This is anything but funny. This is one of the most ethically vile cases you will ever have the good fortune to encounter.*

"Congratulations," I said, my voice choking with the effort of suppressing laughter. "But here's my question. You could easily have run a legitimate business. You were this close." I pinched my fingers together. "Why the ruse about the intelligence studies? Why not just solicit girls willing to have their eggs fertilized?"

Paulina pushed her gum into her cheek and sneered.

"Because they're so snotty about keeping their precious smart genes to themselves. You can't possibly attain the quantity and quality that we do if they think some nice couple might benefit. Really, what they don't know won't hurt them. We simply took advantage of their selfishness."

"Is selfish worse than greedy?" Pippa asked suddenly, her voice steely with an anger that surprised me.

Paulina looked at her, startled.

"You could have run a legitimate business," Pippa said, "if only you were willing to earn—and I use that term extremely loosely in your circumstance—a bit less. Instead, now we have, what—dozens? scores?—hundreds of young women who will need to be notified, whose lives will never be the same. We have families who will have to know their children were ill-got. It's an ethical and legal quagmire of vast proportions. All because you wanted to make two hundred a pop instead of fifteen."

Paulina squared her shoulders but said nothing. For the first time since the capture, I thought of Lucy. Of Alan and Amanda. How would Lucy and Leonard feel once they learned they'd gotten their eggs under tainted circumstances?

"So there's no INH study? No studies of any kind?" I clarified.

Paulina merely snorted at me.

"Then why not take any woman's eggs—no fancy degrees—and just lie about their credentials? Save yourself the trouble."

She opened her eyes wide in surprise. "That would be dishonest."

I was pretty sure that some scientist, at the INH or elsewhere, would pay a pretty penny to get a glimpse inside Paulina's twisted three-ring circus of a brain. I glanced at my colleagues, who wore identical expressions of stupefaction.

"Let me ask you something else, Paulina," I said after I'd recovered from my own astonishment.

"Please address me as Ms. Glantz."

"No, I don't think I will. Paulina, you're attractive, healthy, and in possession of two excellent degrees yourself. Did you ever donate *your* eggs?"

I felt Tommy and Pippa stiffen with interest.

Paulina regarded me coldly. "*I* didn't need the money."

"Well, but you're so interested in personal motivation," I persisted. "I'd think, in the course of creating your business plan, you might have gone through the process yourself. You know, to understand your clients."

"You'd think wrong."

There was a knock on the door. Tommy got up and returned with Letitia Humphrey and Bobby Turato pushing Jeremy Wedge, hands cuffed, ahead of them. As usual, everything about Jeremy was bright red, but now he had deep circles under his eyes and appeared to have lost some extra padding during his stint at Bellevue.

Behind them was Ballard McKenzie, his bald head shining and his bushy white eyebrows furrowed in anxiety. Hot on his tail was Hutchinson, who'd been lurking in the hall, outraged at his exclusion from our mysterious proceedings.

"Why the hell would you come here, you stupid bitch?" Jeremy spat at Paulina by way of a greeting.

"I figured you had cash. After I saw her," she pointed to me, "I knew our accounts would be frozen." She really was a very bright woman.

Jeremy looked at me and pulled his chin down in surprise. "Zephyr? I didn't recognize you."

That was the other line that would be repeated endlessly at the White Horse Tavern until it was etched into the story like handprints in cement. It was almost enough to make me stop shopping in thrift shops. Almost.

I let Jeremy and Paulina snipe at each other for a while as they perched on the bed. The mattress was so thick that their feet barely touched the floor, making them look like two siblings bickering in their bedroom. Jeremy studiously avoided his uncle's pleading face. If nothing else, the sight of Ballard McKenzie seemed to elicit from him some trace of shame.

Jeremy possessed more business aptitude than Paulina had given him credit for. He had, in fact, used the hotel's accounts to launder more than a million dollars from the Summa–Recherché operation. He'd done it perfectly for months but had finally slipped up and lost track of one hundred thousand dollars. He recorded the debit but not the credit, which was why Ballard noticed it as missing but why none of us could make it reconcile with the final balances. It was why there was no video of anyone tampering with the safe. Jeremy hadn't actually stolen a dime from the hotel.

And while he had made a point of having the lovely young donors stay at the Greenwich Village Hotel, he was careful to make sure the couples never did. So when Mr. and Mrs. Whitcomb of Akron, Ohio, just happened to choose the hotel over all the others in Manhattan, Jeremy kept vigil in the hotel's public spaces to make sure they didn't accidentally start chatting with the Summa donor who was staying there on the same two nights—the donor for whom he had drunk the lemon-flavored love potion.

His conversation with the donor at the bar had been going well—he was over the moon to discover she was a Ph.D. candidate in economics, though he took issue with her adherence to the Chicago School—when he spotted the Whitcombs bidding farewell to Geraldine, the bartender. With a hasty apology to his would-be conquest, he fled to their room—room 502—to clear it of any evidence that might have exposed the purpose of their visit. This included emptying their garbage can. But just as he grabbed the scraps and prepared to return to the bar, Samantha Kimiko Hodges's would-be-fatal love potion took effect.

"Idiot," Paulina muttered, when Jeremy was finished. She

spat her gum into a tissue and put the wad on the bedside table. Out of the corner of my eye, I saw Ballard shift as he absorbed the final insult to this colossal injury.

"Shrew," Jeremy replied.

"Ya both disgusting, so pipe down," Tommy told them.

"I'm done with them for now," I announced. "Let's go downtown."

"What could you possibly charge me with?" Paulina said huffily.

Even Tommy's eyes went wide.

"Are you kidding me?" I said. "For starters, Paulina, you get accessory to an attempted murder. You both get scheme to defraud. There's also larceny by false pretenses, forgery, money laundering, and mail fraud, I'd bet. I guarantee you a charge for each girl you stole from and every couple you swindled."

Jeremy and Paulina, at last, were too stunned to protest. When Letitia and Bobby nudged them, they stood up. Paulina's eyes were expressionless, but Jeremy's were wild, those of a trapped animal. I heard a small yelp come from Hutchinson's direction as his cousin's future disintegrated right in front of him. Ballard pushed his glasses to his forehead and pressed his fingers against his eyes. They shuffled out, gently escorted by my colleagues.

I caught sight of Asa's round, surprised face hovering at the entrance to the room. His mouth gaped as Jeremy passed him.

"What are you staring at?" Jeremy snapped. Asa shrank back like a bullied kid.

"Oh, Jeremy," Ballard moaned quietly to himself, sinking down on the bed we'd vacated.

"I'm so sorry, Mr. McKenzie," I said.

"I promised my sister I'd look after him, and I failed."

"Mr. McKenzie, he's thirty-five years old. I think you can confidently assume that he was no longer your—"

"Oh, Amelia, I'm so sorry!" Ballard wailed, thrusting his forehead to his clasped hands.

Pippa tapped me on the shoulder and nodded toward the door. Tommy came with us and we left the McKenzie men to their grief and betrayal.

"Commish, the last time I was undercovah, you sent me to be an apprentice taxi dispatcha in Floral Park," Tommy said the second we shut the door behind us. "Zepha gets down comfuddahs and mini-fridges. I think yuh playin' favorites."

"O'Hara, how long do you think you would have lasted at the front desk fielding petty complaints from wealthy guests?"

"Awwwww, c'mon, gimme some credit," he chortled, digging his knuckles into my scalp in lieu of making any jovial physical contact with Pippa, which was unthinkable.

Speaking of credit, I was hoping for a tad myself. *I solved a case! I just solved a case!* I wanted to shout. Or had I simply been lucky, managed to be in the right places at the right times, like Tommy and his soda bread? And, really, did it matter? Was the key to some cases just sticking around and not giving up?

"Well done, Zephyr," Pippa said, picking up where my thoughts left off.

I shrugged. "I was in the right places at the right times," I said, hoping to be contradicted.

"No, it was more than that. You persevered. You questioned Jeremy based on nothing more than some garbage scraps and an empty vial. You pursued Samantha and had the sense to search her room before it was too late. You pursued Zelda as a source when others might have dismissed her as irrelevant."

I thought about Zelda standing before me at the hotel desk just days earlier. I thought about all the young women who would need to be told they had biological children running around the world. To whom would that task fall? Certainly not me, and for that I was immensely grateful. Therapists and social workers would need to be enlisted. And who would tell the parents? Was I obligated to tell Lucy? Was I even allowed? For many people, this case would go on forever. The inherent incompleteness unsettled me.

"Samantha!" I said suddenly.

"Indeed," Pippa said.

"We need to go arrest her," I said reluctantly.

"I don't imagine any of us relishes the prospect. I'll have a word with Mr. McKenzie, and then O'Hara and I will go with you to the nursing home." Pippa knocked on the suite door and let herself in.

I finally noticed Asa, still standing with us in the corridor, listening to every word, his hands stuck to his chubby cheeks in shock.

"Zephyr, you're a . . . cop?" he said with wonder.

Tommy guffawed.

"No, a peace officer. I work for the Special Investigations Commission."

"Is that like a cop?"

"Kind of," I relented.

"So . . . so . . ." The squeaky wheels of his brain churned as he revisited our interactions over the past month. "Who knew?"

"Only Ballard."

"But you were so nice to the guests! You worked so hard!" I wished Pippa could have heard this part, too. "And it wasn't even your real job!"

"Well, that's what undercover is," I said modestly.

"You even helped me call Cracker Barrel and Kleenex!"

Tommy's eyebrows shot up in perplexed amusement, and I knew that somehow, someday, once he figured out what it meant, he would use this against me.

"That was part of being undercover, too."

"Woooow."

It was an extremely gratifying reaction.

Pippa returned, smoothing out her red-polka-dot-on-black dress. "Well, father and son need a bit of time to work things out. Junior's not atall pleased that he was kept in the dark on all of this."

"But he was a potential suspect."

"Yes, and you can imagine how that delights him. He does seem awfully . . . attached to his cousin."

The three of us let the implications of this musing sink in.

"You think there was a little . . ." Tommy twirled his fingers in the air.

"Oh no," Asa said firmly, and we looked at him, surprised by the confidence in his voice. "I think Jeremy is the only person in the whole world Hutchinson loves, or even likes. He just hates everyone else, including himself," he said plainly. "It's not sexual or anything."

I wondered from whence this bit of deep insight sprang.

"He's so mean to you, Zephyr, that at first I thought he was covering up some attraction. But then I realized he really, truly doesn't like you."

"Thanks."

"But I wasn't picking up anything on gaydar, either. I mean, we have a lot of hot guests, and . . . nada. He's just a sad, lonely, angry guy."

"You've given this a lot of thought."

"I do more than call 800 numbers. Hey, Zeph?" he said as the four of us headed to the lobby to find a line of guests waiting irritably at the unmanned desk. "I know this isn't your real job, but now that you caught your bad guys, is there any way you could cover for me just one last time so I can go see my acupuncturist? My ankle's really acting up today."

I grimaced apologetically.

"You let someone stick needles in you for fun?" Tommy asked Asa.

I saw Asa begin to bristle, but before he could launch into an impassioned defense of Eastern medical arts, I interrupted.

"She's not just an acupuncturist, right, Asa? She's Wiccan. It's needles *and* spells, and it works for Asa, so, really, that's all that matters." I widened my eyes at Tommy to indicate that he shouldn't pick on such a pathetic target. "Let's go," I urged.

Tommy moved his lips from side to side, weighing his possible responses, any one of which was likely to make Asa cry.

"I got a buddy who's afraid of roller coasters. Could she help him?" he asked earnestly.

"What, he's afraid one's gonna jump out of his closet?" I scoffed just as Asa gushed, "Oh, absolutely, she can help anyone with *anything*."

Tommy took down the witch's e-mail address. Disgusted, I shook my head and dialed the Hudson Street Nursing Home. At least one of us was staying on track.

"Arturo," I said efficiently when the curt voice answered. "This is Zephyr Zuckerman, one of your volunteers. I wanted to stop by and check on Samantha Kimiko Hodges right now. Is she around?"

I heard papers rustle and something begin to beep. I wondered if he'd heard me.

"Extra-short? Japanese, sounds Jewish?" he said after a pause.

"Yes." I took a moment to be impressed that, despite his distracted appearance, Arturo really did know each of his elderly charges.

"Gone."

I was a little less impressed.

"Excuse me?"

"She left this morning. Packed up. Said she was headed north."

"How far north?" I asked, panicked. "A Hundred Twenty-fifth Street? Canada? What?"

"Poughkeepsie."

"*Poughkeepsie?* What's in Poughkeepsie?"

"Like I know. Okay, goodbye?"

"Wait!" I called out. I could hear the impatience in his silence. I needed him to stay on the line while I tried to think. "Spell Poughkeepsie?" I begged.

"I couldn't possibly," he said, and hung up.

I felt Pippa watching me.

"Two outta three ain't bad?" I suggested meekly.

"Yeah!" Tommy O. howled later that night at the White Horse Tavern. "Once you got the Father and the Son, who needs the fuckin' Holy Spirit?"

* * *

I tried to track her, I really did. I hobbled west on Waverly Place as fast as my mother's high heels and narrow skirt would allow. I headed straight to the nursing home to look for clues to where Samantha might have headed. I dreaded the thought of arresting an eighty-plus-year-old woman, but I was also unwilling to tolerate unfinished business. I had enough of that in my life as it was, without having to accept it as part of the conclusion of my first major case. There would be no loose threads, no strands trailing behind for Tommy and the peanut gallery to pull on whenever they encountered a dull moment.

I didn't even bother pretending to Arturo that I was an overeager volunteer concerned about the whereabouts of my newly adopted grandma. Dejected, I flashed my badge and asked to be let upstairs. I wasn't expecting him to be impressed and he wasn't. He still made me sign in.

On the way to Samantha's room—correction, former room—I scoured the hallway of the third floor, desperate for any kind of clue. The birthday decorations that had been disheartening to begin with were now completely shriveled, the limp balloons resembling scrota. What did I think I was going to find? Samantha had nothing left to lose except her freedom.

Outside the door to her own room, Alma Mae Martin was chatting easily with a man half her age. He wore a suit and carried a briefcase and stooped his shoulders deferentially before her. She was clearly delighted with the conversation, her laughter rolling down the hall in regular, tinkling intervals.

She waggled her fingers at me and continued talking to her . . . lawyer? Lover? Long-lost nephew? Whoever he was, I was certain I'd never get the true story. Still, I looked forward to letting her regale me with whatever tale she chose the next time I visited. And I *would* continue to visit, I vowed. My mother's proviso about childlessness crackled like static electricity along the back of my mind, but so, too, did the thought of my own old age. How many of these residents had no family to check in on them? How many, when they said farewell to their own lives, would be taking a chain saw to their branch of the family tree?

I opened the door to room 308 and surveyed its bareness. The walls were naked, the bed was stripped, the closet was empty. No surprise. I sat down on the mattress and allowed myself to stop, to really stop, for the first time in days. I kicked off my shoes and rubbed my aching toes. Below me, the trees in Abingdon Square Park looked dull, biding their time until they could embrace the oranges, reds, and yellows that were working their way south.

I would have fled, too, I thought, resisting the urge to lie down. Who wanted to experience autumn from this room? If you couldn't watch the leaves turn with someone you loved at your side—in which case the spot from which you viewed them didn't really matter—then you'd want your gazing location to be lovely, extravagant even, if you could afford it. A hot-air balloon. A cottage in the Catskills. The deck of a sloop in the middle of the Hudson.

Suddenly I was certain Samantha had not for a moment considered doing anything as uninspired as remaining in the tristate area. She would not retread old paths, nor would she forge new ones in familiar territory.

I jumped up and opened each of the three desk drawers. In the bottom drawer, almost invisible against the white background, was a folded piece of Greenwich Village Hotel stationery. I snatched it up.

"Dear Busybody Cop, Rest easy. This alter kocker promises not to <u>pretend</u> to try to you-know-what anybody else. I got what I need. Just let me finish out my days in peace. Don't take any wooden nickels." She'd signed it "Mrs. Kimiko Hodges." Samantha was on a plane by now to . . . anywhere. For a minute I was overcome with an envy so strong it left a bilious taste in my mouth.

Just as quickly, I chastised myself. What the hell did I have to be envious about? I was young, healthy, employed, loved, entertained, well fed, and had a warm bed to sleep in. Any gaps in my happiness were entirely of my own doing. I thought about Gregory's proposition, of his willingness to forgo offspring for me, if I would agree to have a conversation about it once a year. I was having a hard time remembering what about that plan had been so offensive to me only four days ago.

Infantilizing. I'd used the word "infantilizing." Infantile

was my reaction to him, I thought now as I watched a few overeager leaves float down from their branches, nudged along by a gentle breeze. In truth, like this case, it was the untidy conclusion in his proposal that bothered me. The "for now" of it. For now we would not arrest Samantha Kimiko Hodges. For now Gregory and I could be together in peace. I wanted big one-hundred-percent-forever yeses or nos in order to move forward. As I approached officially being in my early thirties (as opposed to the Big 3-0, which was all about the novelty of the odometer turning over), it seemed that I should be wrapping things up in order to move on to the next phase.

What next phase? This was it. I was living it, loose ends and all.

I shoved my feet back into the heels and tried to stand, but it hurt too much. Way too much. I freed them once more and padded out of room 308, down the hall to the elevator. It was a one-minute walk from the nursing home to my apartment, and I didn't plan to spend a second of it in those toe corsets.

Alma Mae's visitor was waiting for the elevator, peering up at the lighted numbers above the door. He nodded at me with a quick, shy smile and pretended not to notice I was shoeless. A true gentleman.

The elevator dinged open and we stepped in. I tried to ignore the various unsettling textures my stockinged soles encountered.

"Friend of Miss Martin's?" I inquired politely. I could pretend to myself that he was a potential witness to Samantha's escape, but I knew I was just being nosy.

He shook his head.

"Relative?"

He pursed his lips silently but pleasantly, the way I did when an unwelcome stranger made an unwanted overture.

"I'm a signature expert," he finally offered.

I glanced at him quickly to see if he was putting me on. I was the queen of donning cool-but-phony job titles for the duration of an elevator ride or a cocktail party. Was he telling the truth? Had Alma Mae been forging signatures for something? Was she in on this whole scam with Samantha? Was it even bigger than I thought? Were there even more loose threads? I couldn't hold back.

"Did Alma Mae forge a signature?"

"No," he said with alarm. "Not at all!"

"Did someone she know forge a signature?" I pressed.

He pushed his glasses up on his nose. "I'm on assignment from the John F. Kennedy Presidential Library and Museum. Miss Martin is in possession of some letters. Many letters."

"Ohhhh," I chuckled, relieved. "Yeah, from Jack, Bobby, and Robert."

"She's shown them to you, too?" he gushed earnestly, as if relieved someone else was in on a secret he was bursting to tell.

"Uh," I said, eyeing him cautiously. His face was bright and open, and he was finally looking at me instead of the door. "No, she's only told me about them."

"Oh, they're such lovely letters! Beautiful, astounding missives. Revelatory. The biographers are going to have a field day."

I opened and closed my mouth a couple of times before any sound came out.

"You've confirmed they're authentic?"

He nodded happily.

"Alma Mae actually had affairs with the Kennedy brothers and McNamara?"

"Well, now, that's Miss Martin's private business, isn't it? Though I suppose it won't be for much longer." He chuckled to himself and shook his head. The doors slid open on the first floor. He touched his fingertips to his temple in an old-fashioned salute, then disappeared.

I stared after him, a shoe hanging limply from either hand, and reevaluated everything I thought I knew about Alma Mae. Apparently you could be ladylike and have loose threads hanging out all over the place—it probably made it easier for a lover to undress you with his teeth.

Chapter 20

The Somali pirates survived Lenore, but just barely. They made her wash their dishes and scrub their floors and they berated her and even struck her once, but they were still no match for her. Before she would do the laundry they ordered her to do, she inspected the clothes they wore, and if she saw even a spot, she demanded they hand over the offending article immediately so that she could maximize efficiency. When they showed her their disgusting lavatories, she insisted she could not do a perfect job with the toothbrush they'd provided. They had only intended the task to be a form of punishment, not a productive act, but soon admitted to their stash of 409 and Dobie pads. Before long, the ship was gleaming. She reorganized the galley and the maps on the bridge and made suggestions to the head pirate for restructuring his chain of command. When a representative of the Seychelles government finally boarded the ship, bearing a suitcase full of cash (covertly provided by the U.S. government, which officially would not negotiate with terrorists), Lenore was sipping milky tea with the captain, chatting as easily as they could through the broken English of a crew member.

Lucy anticipated great changes in Lenore upon her return. She anticipated humility, the kind that comes after one has had a face-to-face with one's mortality. She anticipated a quieter, kinder, introspective mother-in-law. She anticipated that Lenore would at least stop changing her children's outfits when she came to babysit.

And Lenore did have an epiphany, but not the kind Lucy envisioned. Lenore simply realized how capable she was. She realized that many years had been wasted not being the CEO of something. She arrived home and promptly told her family that she had given them enough of herself for free and was going to business school. The moment the last members of the media departed her front yard, she enrolled in a GMAT course.

After Lucy got over her disappointment that Lenore's transformation would not include an apology for a host of insults and infractions, she began to take stock of her own life. She calculated how much of her recent unhappiness had been caused by Lenore, how much by Hillsville, how much by parenthood. With Lenore out of her hair, she figured that if she could get the hell out of Hillsville and find some part-time work, two luxuries she knew they could afford, the quality of life might improve markedly for everyone in her family. Leonard thanked her for trying Hillsville and then put in a bid on their old Perry Street apartment. He actually bought it back for less than they'd sold it, and so came out ahead in their otherwise failed suburban safari.

"Welcome!" Lucy shrieked at me as I stepped off the elevator and into a sunny space that looked nothing like the one she'd inhabited three years earlier, and not just because there was an enormous hand-painted *Welcome Back!* banner stretched across the foyer. (I wondered if I was the only one who thought it strange that Lucy had clearly painted it for herself.) Leonard's one condition for making the move back to New York had been that they acquire adult furniture and eighty-six the tatty brown couch. Lucy had happily agreed and, with Macy's help, found a decorator who operated on the same principles as No Divas. Lucy gave the woman a budget, handed her a pair of binoculars, and told her she wanted it to look just like Mercedes's place across the way. Mercedes couldn't have cared less about the copycat approach; she, like the rest of us, was relieved that Lucy was back in New York, her rightful title as the Princess of Perky restored.

"I'm sorry I'm late," I apologized as I stepped off the elevator, "and I'm sorry I have to leave early. I'm meeting—" But my host had darted off to check on the food for Housewarming Take II, which was already in full swing on this warm May afternoon.

I had hurried up from the Staten Island Ferry terminal after a conference with Pippa that had required two round trips to work out the details of my new assignment. On Monday morning, I was to register for a pedicab operator's license. It was the first step in a sting designed to catch licensing inspectors at the Department of Consumer Affairs who were allegedly extorting money from the rickshaw bikers. Even though my work would primarily consist of shuttling tourists from Madame Tussauds to the Nike store in the stultifying heat of midtown—Tommy and company had thoughtfully given me a bright-pink helmet, purple streamers, and a Barbie bell—I was looking forward to the opportunity to mount my own tourism campaign. Visitors who heard the siren call of the Olive Garden, American Girl store, or the Hard Rock Cafe would be strapped to their seats and given wax for their ears. It would be my mission to have them reach the Ithaca that lay beyond Times Square, otherwise known as bistros, galleries, and even underground theaters.

The gig would be my first as a fully licensed private investigator, a license that was now of less use to me since I'd been offered a contract to remain on at the SIC. I probably should have pretended to consider other options, but I accepted before Pippa had even finished laying out the terms ("junior" would be dropped from my title, and my paycheck would appear larger only under a microscope). I didn't care that the rest of my generation was hopping from job to job to avoid the appearance of stagnation. I aspired to stay as long as they'd have me, hopefully until I'd done the equivalent of accumulating a stash of Lucite handbags.

I pinched the top of my sundress and fanned some cool air down the front while I scanned the living room for familiar faces. There were shimmering *I ♥ New York* Mylar balloons bouncing near the ceiling, and it seemed that Lucy had bought out the entire stock of Fishs Eddy's skyline-patterned plates, mugs, and glasses. A framed print of *The New Yorker*'s "View of the World" was hanging prominently on the single non-glass wall of the living room—as if she was boasting about the myopia she planned to regain. She had brought in revolving displays of kitschy postcards, and more than a few guests were gamely sporting green foam Statue of Liberty headgear. It looked like Lucy had robbed a souvenir kiosk and kidnapped some tourists into the bargain. I stifled the thought that perhaps she could do with a quick visit to the eighteenth floor of Bellevue.

Even the guests were an homage to the city, including as they did people like Roxana ("Not a single one of my neighbors in Hillsville was a prostitute," Lucy said disdainfully), her favorite barista from Grounded, and one of the trainers from the local trapeze school. The menu was a mash of all her favorite comfort food from neighborhood joints and made no sense for a hot day: bacon burgers from BLT Burger, braised tofu from Gobo, lamb ouzi from Salam, mac and cheese from Chat 'N' Chew, and mint chicken noodles and fresh-squeezed watermelon juice from Republic. The aromas clashed horribly, but Lucy was unfazed.

I finally spotted Macy, who had kicked off her shoes and was curled up on the sage-green sofa, her fiery hair fanned out over the back cushions. At her feet was her new boy-friend, a pigeon-toed auctioneer named Kirk who had suf-fered nothing worse than a head cold after six dates with Macy (though, to be sure, a head cold was a serious profes-sional hazard for him). At her side was Asa, Macy's anointed savior, the man who had led her to Wendy the Wonder Wic-can of Fort Greene. Wendy, presiding over a ceremony that had included earthworms, down pillows, and sundry incan-tations, had, by all accounts (Macy's and Asa's), broken the curse. Indeed, as far as we knew, there had been no dead brides or suitors in Macy's wake for at least five months now.

Asa jumped up to give me his seat; he still regarded me with a strange kind of awe even though I had gone out of my way to show him my real life, to persuade him that I wasn't some Mata Hari with mystery spicing every gesture (much as I longed for that to be true). He was now fully insinuated into my friendships, sometimes a little too much so. I tried to hide my surprise that he'd been invited.

"C'mon, the suburbs aren't *that* bad," Kirk was saying. He adjusted the foam spikes atop his head.

"Oh, you just don't know what it was like for her," Macy said darkly, as if she had been sequestered upstate with Lucy.

"Of course I know. I grew up in the burbs," Kirk reminded Macy.

Lucy appeared out of nowhere and bounced onto the sofa. "Don't say that word at this party," she said lightly. "Are you guys having fun? Isn't this amazing? You can just walk over, Zephyr! No more Metro-North. Do you know, last night we were watching TV and we wanted ice cream, and I went out and got it before the commercials were over!"

"Don't you have TiVo?" Macy asked suspiciously.

"Seriously," Kirk persisted. "Lucy, there wasn't *anything*

you liked? Big supermarkets? The sounds of silence? Turning right on red?"

"I liked turning right on red," she conceded. "But the sounds of silence? More like tinnitus."

At that moment, matching shrieks pierced the air. Lucy shot off the sofa and in one deft move confiscated a salad spinner to which Amanda and Alan were each claiming sole ownership. In an act of astounding maternal mathematics, she grabbed two spatulas off the kitchen island—two spatulas apparently being equal to one Oxo salad spinner—and the battle ceased. She returned to us, beaming.

"I like them again, all of them," she confided. "Especially Leonard. I actually really think they're pretty terrific." Kirk and Asa looked startled, but Lucy didn't notice.

"Nothing to do with the fact that Lenore is out of your hair and you're going back to work?" Macy said this to Lucy but was looking at me. I avoided meeting her eyes, so I wouldn't begin to laugh. Lucy was at her most blissfully earnest and oblivious today.

"Oh, of course those help. Tremendously. But it's more that I don't feel so isolated. Neither does Leonard. He's a whole new person since we moved back."

We looked doubtfully at Leonard, who was hovering awkwardly over his offspring. He twitched a step backward as Roxana approached and asked him a question. He pointed to me.

"Ah, Zepheer!" she called as she strode over in a clingy wraparound dress, her blond knot of hair waggling at the back of her head. She kissed me on both cheeks and then greeted everyone else with equal enthusiasm. "Lucy, you are so luffly to invite me. I luuuf to see the beautiful real estate!"

I'm sure half the people there had come to see the inside of a Richard Meier apartment, but leave it to Roxana to admit outright that it was her primary incentive. I appreciated the honesty, and since Lucy had invited Roxana for her thrill value, I suspected she wasn't offended in the least.

"I'm so glad you came," Lucy told her, then lowered her voice. "I hope it won't be awkward if Gideon shows up."

Roxana looked genuinely perplexed. My brother's proposed documentary about her had died in its infancy, right about the time he made a pass at her and she gently laughed him off as "a leetle baby boy I could nut pussibly make luf to." It was the sort of rebuff she was no doubt obliged to make on a weekly basis to any number of men, but it had sent Gideon into paroxysms of indignation, humiliation, and scriptwriting. My parents, needless to say, had breathed a collective sigh of relief.

"Now, Lucy," Roxana said dramatically, waving away thoughts of my brother. "I hear your mother wus on layaway! Zees is so eggzyting, no?"

Everyone looked at me.

"She means Lenore," I interpreted. "It was Lucy's mother-in-*law*," I corrected Roxana, "and you mean stowaway, not layaway, but that's not really what you mean, either."

Luckily, I spotted my father striding in from the elevator and was able to excuse myself before I had to listen to the retelling of Lenore's maritime adventures as explained to Roxana.

"Darling daught!" my dad bellowed, unconcerned with the momentary halt in all conversation. I hugged him tightly, pressing my cheek to his necktie, extracting every last bit of parental approval.

"Where's Mom?"

"On her way," he said, and I couldn't help feeling a faint flash of relief that I would have a few moments alone with the parent who was not openly disappointed in me. "Wow! Look at this place!" He made a sweeping gesture that included the river, New Jersey, and beyond.

"Dad, you've seen this view a dozen times."

"Yes, but this is New Lucy's view. It's *Happy* Lucy's apartment! It looks vastly different," he gushed. Then he switched to a stage whisper, the lowest his voice was capable of dropping. "How is she, you know, *doing?*"

"Dad, don't," I murmured.

Under the assumption that it didn't count if I told my parents, I'd revealed Lucy's entanglement in the Summa–Recherché case and in doing so had exposed so much more than I ought to have. In part, I knew, I had told the secrets to my mother as a proxy for everything I couldn't confide to her about myself these days. Still, that one of my best friends had been directly and deeply affected by the crime, that I had helped her get hired by the city to offer counseling to the families involved, and that I had actually met the genetic mother of her children—it was all too much to keep to myself.

Zelda Herman's high forehead, square chin, and almond eyes worked beautifully on Alan and Amanda, but she had zero interest in viewing the results for herself, and so Lucy and Leonard considered themselves among the fortunate victims. None of the families whose children had been created out of what were supposed to be anonymous eggs had any desire for contact with the biological mothers. But many of the young donors—or, more often, their parents—had been shattered by the news that their eggs had been given life, and what followed had been a three-ring circus involving the courts, the professional counseling community, and, of course, the media. The only good that had come of it had been an extraordinary opportunity for Lucy to reenter the workforce.

My dad pointed out the window and across Perry Street to where Mercedes stood in her living room holding up a whiteboard. "What on earth is she doing?"

I grabbed the binoculars from the table behind us, kept there for just this purpose.

D just got home. Be over in a minute.

"Fantastic!" my dad said, watching as I scrawled a response on Lucy's whiteboard. "In an age of texting, this is pure poetry."

"I don't know if I'd call it poetry," I said, as I flashed the answer: *Hurry. I can't stay long.* "But it's fun. Like talking through tin cans."

We watched as Mercedes tried to bend over to retrieve her binoculars, then resorted to squatting. "Good thing she's not a cellist," my dad mused. "What *do* cellists do when they're pregnant?"

Mercedes and Dover had gone over to the drooly side. Mercedes was three months away from, as she put it, forever being mistaken for the nanny. But leave it to her, of course, to make pregnancy look downright sexy; no doubt she'd make parenthood look glamorous and romantic.

"Look at that beautiful silhouette," my dad said reverently, as Mercedes turned sideways to tuck the whiteboard away. I shifted uncomfortably. That was the kind of unsubtle nuance best left to my mother. He put his hands heavily on my shoulders.

"Oh, Zephy."

"What?" I asked, bracing myself.

He hesitated, which was so uncharacteristic that I looked up at him.

"When you're losing your friends, when your body is letting you down in new ways every day, when your memory is capricious at best, at least . . . at least you have your kids."

I nodded and put my hands over his, wishing I could vanquish the melancholy that he and my mom would always feel and that I was slowly—very slowly—learning to deflect.

"Well, but on the other hand," I said, as lightly as I could without sounding flip, "that means I have until I'm about seventy to enjoy having no dependents."

He squeezed my shoulders. "All you girls pride yourself on being so responsible, so on top of things, so *dependable*. What's the point of being dependable if you won't let anybody depend on you?"

I considered this. "I let lots of people depend on me," I reminded him. "You and mom. My friends. Gid, sometimes. My colleagues, my boss—"

"Me."

We turned to find Gregory standing behind us. The mere sight of him still made me feel as if my blood had dropped what it was doing and rushed back to my heart.

"My boy," my dad said, taking his hands off me to clap Gregory warmly on the shoulder. "Tell me, truly. Seeing that beautiful creature over there—" He pointed across the street to Mercedes.

"Da-ad!" I was shocked.

"She looks lovely," Gregory agreed easily. I searched him, as I constantly did these days, for any trace of resentment. As usual, I found none. "The Sterling Girls do everything in style," he added generously.

I took his hand and squeezed it. Gregory had moved back in with Hitchens and me on one condition: I had to agree to entertain the possibility of changing my mind. Not that I *would* change my mind, but I would no longer define myself as one hundred percent definitely certain that I was not having children. And so, for Gregory, I had done this. For his sake, I had bid farewell to the summer camp of certainty. In the annals of sacrifices, this was not a headliner, but it was a mental readjustment of major proportions for me.

To my surprise, rather than making me anxious or angry, a part of me that I hadn't even known was coiled unwound with this newly adopted outlook. Even my friendship with Macy became easier; whereas before I'd been suspicious of her morally commendable motives for passing on parenthood—afraid of intimacy!—I now understood that my suspicion was rooted in discomfort about my own decisions. The ability to make peace with uncertainty, to befriend open endings, had brought with it a clearer view of myself, an unanticipated freedom, and a hard-won sense of maturity.

"Is that a . . . marshmallow shooter?" Leonard asked, pointing with undisguised admiration to the small catapult at Gregory's feet. Leonard rarely initiated a conversation, and the fact that he had been magnetically drawn across the length of his living room to do so was notable.

"Technically, it's a mini-trebuchet," Gregory said, winking at me. The thought that I had come so close to driving him away forever made my stomach lurch.

"Are you two en route to a crusade?" my father inquired.

"I bet I know where you're going," Leonard said breathlessly. "You're going to the Marshmallow Civil War under the Brooklyn Bridge, aren't you?" His eyes shone, and it became clear to me that the return to the city had by no means been a sacrifice for him. "I *really* wanted to go to that," he said longingly. "You can't believe how many different kinds of launchers people design out of PVC. If it was me, I'd build a pneumatic cannon—"

"Maybe next year, Leonard," I comforted him.

"Shall we?" Gregory said to me, picking up the launcher and extending his arm. "We still need to buy ammunition."

"Are you going to get full-size or mini-marshmallows?" Leonard asked, frowning as he mentally weighed the pros and cons of each.

Gregory looked at me.

"We haven't decided," I told Leonard happily. "We're just going to see what we find."

Acknowledgments

I am so grateful to have been given the opportunity to continue Zephyr's adventures. Kerri Buckley, a young editor who possesses the talents, passion, and work ethic of an old one, made that possible, as did the enthusiasm of Jane von Mehren, Melissa Possick, Kathy Lord, Kelly Chian, Beck Stvan, Caroline Cunningham, Marisa Vigilante, Sonya Safro, Kate Miciak, and the rest of the Random House team. My heartfelt thanks again to my devoted, kind, capable agent, Tracy Brown.

I find it nearly impossible to write at home, where it is always tempting to take care of just a *few* little things before settling down to work. And so I thank the generous staff at Babycakes Café and Ken Kraft at The Crafted Kup, in Poughkeepsie, New York, for welcoming me into their establishments and selling me countless cups of coffee. I also thank my husband's colleagues for not thinking it (too) strange when I showed up, laptop in tow, to have a writing date with my beloved in his office.

I could not have written this book were it not for my children's babysitter, Jackie Ryan, a generous, thoughtful, funny young woman, and a superb storyteller in her own right. Knowing that my other creations were being loved, entertained, and cared for was the difference between writing and not writing.

Enormous thanks to Tom Comiskey, my former colleague at SCI (now part of New York City's DOI), who answered all my strange questions about Glocks and subpoenas and a dozen other minutiae thoroughly and quickly. I twisted many details to suit my purposes: Any factual inaccuracies are my own and usually deliberate.

As always, my boundless gratitude to my mother—whose prompt answers to my leftfield questions constitute the bulk of my legal "research"—and to my late father and to my in-laws, who make this writing life feasible. Once again, my friends have let me use (and twist) their stories: thanks especially to Jessica Orkin and Anna Gross for helping with details ranging from the fashionable to the medical, to Amanda Robinson for doing a thorough read way o'er yonder in Scotland, to Nava Atlas, Jenny Nelson, and Gail Upchurch for being my new writing buddies, and to Tracy Bagley White for making me feel at home away from our homes.

And of course, thanks to my truest love, Sacha Spector. I still can't believe my good fortune.

ABOUT THE AUTHOR

DAPHNE UVILLER is a third-generation Greenwich Villager who currently lives in the Hudson Valley with her husband and their two children. She is the author of *Super in the City* and co-editor of the anthology *Only Child: Writers on the Singular Joys and Solitary Sorrows of Growing Up Solo*. A former editor at *Time Out New York*, Daphne's reviews, profiles, and articles—ranging in topic from Jewish firefighters to breast reductions—have been published in the *Washington Post*, *The New York Times*, *Newsday*, *The Forward*, *New York* magazine, *Oxygen*, *Allure*, and *Self*, for which she used to write an ethics column. Daphne is a member of the SheWrites.com advisory board.